WARNING FROM A KILLER

A tiny smile twitched on Gabe's lips. "You're something else, Kelly Quinn. You've just received a threat and yet you're still trying to stick your nose into police business. My suggestion is that we focus on the matter at hand." He looked at the armless mannequin.

"This is serious, Kelly. The note is scary." Liv's hands covered her heart. "I'm scared."

Kelly hated seeing her friend worry. It made her angry and more determined to find out who was behind the break-in and creepy note.

"Liv mentioned a car followed you home. Did you get a look at the vehicle?" Gabe asked.

"I wish I had. They kept flashing their high beams and then cut the lights altogether. It could have just been teenagers," Kelly said.

"I doubt teenagers did this." Liv's hands made a sweeping motion toward the door and

mannequin.

"You're probably right." Kelly leaned against the counter and crossed her arms. From previous experience, she knew that when a killer lashed out at her somehow, it meant she was getting close to revealing their identity. Over the past couple of days, had she spoken to the killer?

Was she making him or her nervous? It seemed so.

Now, if she only knew who the killer was…

By Debra Sennefelder

Food Blogger Mysteries
THE UNINVITED CORPSE
THE HIDDEN CORPSE
THREE WIDOWS AND A CORPSE
THE CORPSE WHO KNEW TOO MUCH
THE CORPSE IN THE GAZEBO

Resale Boutique Mysteries
MURDER WEARS A LITTLE BLACK DRESS
SILENCED IN SEQUINS
WHAT NOT TO WEAR TO A GRAVEYARD
HOW TO FRAME A FASHIONISTA
BEAUTY AND THE DECEASED

Beauty and the Deceased

Debra Sennefelder

LYRICAL UNDERGROUND
Kensington Publishing Corp.
www.kensingtonbooks.com

LYRICAL UNDERGROUND BOOKS are published by
Kensington Publishing Corp.
119 West 40th Street
New York, NY 10018

All Kensington titles, imprints, and distributed lines are available at special quantity discounts for bulk purchases for sales promotion, premiums, fund-raising, educational, or institutional use.

Special book excerpts or customized printings can also be created to fit specific needs. For details, write or phone the office of the Kensington Sales Manager: Kensington Publishing Corp., 119 West 40th Street, New York, NY 10018. Attn. Sales Department. Phone: 1-800-221-2647.

Lyrical Underground and Lyrical Underground logo Reg. US Pat. & TM Off.

First Electronic Edition: December 2021
ISBN-13: 978-1-5161-1101-5 (ebook)

First Print Edition: December 2021
ISBN-13: 978-1-5161-1103-9

Printed in the United States of America

CHAPTER ONE

Kelly Quinn knew three things for sure her first full summer back home in Lucky Cove. One—summer people were good for business. Two—reconnecting with her cousin was just what she needed to help deal with…well, see number three. Three—getting over a breakup is hard when you see the guy practically every day.

She leaned closer to the mirror and applied a swipe of her new favorite lipstick, Beachy Nude by Define Beauty. The up-and-coming cosmetics company had been her cousin's brainchild. Becky Quinn's obsession with makeup in her teen years had paid off.

Kelly dropped the lipstick into her vintage Gucci clutch she used as a cosmetics bag. It had been a little treat to herself after the breakup from her boyfriend. Luckily the consignment website she purchased it from had a payment plan. She grappled around for her concealer and finally found the tube.

Dabbing on the Define Beauty's concealer, she knew something else for certain. And it made her belly quiver.

Family secrets that bubbled below the surface could suddenly erupt, swallowing everyone involved. Including someone like her who only knew merely about *the secret*.

Too bad her concealer didn't work on things like heartbreaks and secrets. She would have purchased a vat full.

A dramatic meow drew her attention from the dresser's mirror to the floor where her orange cat, Howard, sat staring up at her. He meowed again and ratcheted up the drama that time. She glanced at her watch and sighed. Right on time.

The furball had a schedule, and heaven forbid there was any deviation. After all, his first nap of the morning would be after breakfast.

"Okay, okay. I'm almost done." She stepped back from the dresser and gave a final look at her outfit. She nodded approvingly at her gray wide-leg linen blend pants topped with a black cotton shell and paired with block-heeled sandals. It was a fashionable yet comfortable outfit for the day ahead. Before she opened her shop, the Lucky Cove Resale Boutique, she had an appointment with a new consignor. According to the woman's sister-in-law, who worked with Kelly, Camille Donovan had a ton of clothes to sell.

Kelly's lips curled up into a smile. She loved clients like Camille. And she needed more of them.

Another meow, this time louder and more urgent, alerted Kelly to her cat's growing impatience with her dawdling. Over time, she'd learned to decipher his various sounds and body language. It would have been a whole lot easier if he'd come with a manual when she inherited him from her granny. Manuals would have helped with the boutique and her apartment too. Oh, and she couldn't forget relationships. A how-to guide on how to repair broken relationships would have been beneficial. Alas, there was no handbook on life. It looked like she, along with everyone else, was learning as she went along.

She zipped the cosmetics bag and carried it out of the bedroom with Howard right on her heels. When she stopped at the small table in the hall between the coat closet and the door, he gave her a questionable look.

Exactly who owned whom?

"I'm only dropping this into my tote," she reassured her feline.

Her cell phone chimed, and she slipped it out from its pocket in the bag. Another meow prompted her to walk and read the text simultaneously.

Wish you were here. Isn't this gorgeous?

Kelly smiled at the photo of the sunrise her cousin Becky had sent. Lucky Cove didn't have long stretches of beach that neighboring towns had, but it rivaled them in beauty and tranquilness. Her hometown wasn't a flashy summer village where people vacationed to be seen. Families and overstressed city-dwellers flocked to the town to recharge, not to be followed around by paparazzi.

She typed a reply as she entered the kitchen and nearly tripped over Howard. He was getting excited about his breakfast.

Can't wait to see the house.

To think, a year ago, she wouldn't have been navigating through her apartment and texting at this time of the day. No, she'd have been hustling from her brownstone walk-up to the Midtown offices of Bishop's department store. Life sure turned on a dime.

She set the phone down on the counter and got busy filling Howard's bowls with kibble and water. After setting them down on the mat, she eyed her coffee maker. Did she have enough time for a quick coffee? She checked her watch. No time if she didn't want to be late for her appointment. She'd grab a coffee on her way back to the boutique at Doug's Variety Store. Doug's was the central hub of town that caffeinated residents and sold newspapers and groceries. It was a hodgepodge of a store firmly rooted in Lucky Cove.

With Howard fed, Kelly grabbed her phone and then dashed out of the kitchen. At the door, she lifted her tote and slung it over her shoulder. Inside the bag were a notebook and her calculator. She liked to give a rough estimate on how much a client could expect to earn by selling her clothing. Out on the small hallway landing, which was bright and cheery thanks to a new paint job and decorative accessories, she pulled her door closed. Hurrying down the staircase, her thoughts shifted from her upcoming visit with Becky back to her business.

In-home estimates for consignees were something she scheduled for before the boutique opened. Even though she didn't do many of them, she found they were worth it because she often got more inventory. Plus, it was easy and convenient for the clients. And happy clients meant repeat business.

Kelly pushed open the door that led to the first floor of the two-story Colonial that housed the boutique. She closed it, making sure it locked, and then headed to the staff room.

Right before the unofficial start of summer, she had expanded the boutique's hours to include Sundays. Before the last holiday season, the boutique had been open seven days a week. After a review of sales data, it made sense to close on Sundays during the winter months. Once the weather turned warmer and foot traffic on Main Street picked up, it made financial sense to open on Sundays again. Adding an extra day to the work calendar meant she needed extra help, and she hired a new part-time sales associate.

It only took one day to fill the position. Yes, Kelly had acted on impulse. But when Terry Carlisle entered the boutique stylishly dressed in a bias-seamed flannel skirt topped with a cashmere tee sweater, Kelly instantly knew she was the one. The whole look was sleek in a casual way, signifying that Terry knew fashion.

And a big part of the sales job was knowing what was in fashion and what looked good on women.

Kelly passed through the multipurpose staff room on her way to the back door. Tucked in the corner was the dated kitchenette. In the center of the room was a round table used for meals and meetings. Off to the side was her desk. Next to an old filing cabinet was a clothing rack filled with items waiting to be put out on the sales floor.

She opened the back door and stepped outside. Tugging the door closed, she inhaled a deep breath of fresh, salt air. While fall was her favorite fashion season, summer had a special place in her heart. She'd spent her childhood sunbathing on the beach, roasting s'mores after nightfall, and traipsing around town with her friends in her flip-flops and cutoffs.

Her phone buzzed with a reminder. No time to dawdle. She had to get moving.

She slipped into her Jeep. Well, technically, it belonged to Pepper Donovan and was on loan to her indefinitely. Pepper and her husband had been more than generous to Kelly since she moved back to Lucky Cove. She had no idea how she'd ever repay them. She could start with making sure she did her best to sell every stitch of clothing Camille had to consign.

She backed the vehicle out of the space and headed off to Sand Dunes Lane. The cozy Cape Cod–style house was on a treelined street surrounded by similar homes. Some had additions; others, like the Donovans', were left untouched by a contractor.

Kelly pulled her Jeep into the short driveway and stepped out. She grabbed her tote from the front passenger seat and proceeded to the front door along a brick path worn and chipped with age. She was glad she was wearing block heels rather than stilettos because some serious damage could have been done.

When she reached the front door, she found a medium-sized box on the step. A quick look at the label told her it was a delivery from Petite Look. She frowned. According to Pepper, Camille was obsessed with clothing subscription services, hence the need for a cleanout of her wardrobe. Knowing this, Kelly had an idea of the merchandise she'd leave with— moderately priced, mass-market quality and an assortment of sizes.

Kelly picked up the box. The night before, she researched various style boxes, and Petite Look came up in the results. It catered to the 5′4″ and under crowd.

She reached for the lion head knocker to announce her arrival. She couldn't help but giggle when she lifted the handle and let it drop. It felt so formal. And then she wondered if it was heard inside.

Just as she scanned for a doorbell, the door opened, and Camille appeared, dressed in a turquoise romper.

"Kelly! I'm so glad you're here." Camille swung the door wider and reached out to grasp Kelly's hands but stopped when she saw the box. She flashed a sheepish look. "Busted, as my grandson says."

Kelly laughed as she handed the box to Camille. "It appears so."

"I'm trying to cut back; I really am. Please come in."

"No worries. I'm not here to judge. I'm here to help." Oh, gosh, that sounded so professional. Kelly made a note to use the line again.

She stepped into a small foyer that opened on both sides with a staircase directly in front of her. She peered into both rooms anchoring the foyer, and they were tidy and attractively decorated. Her gaze landed back on her client. Thinking of Camille as her client seemed odd since she'd known the woman her whole life. Kelly had spent countless hours out in the backyard playing with Camille's two children and Gabe, Pepper's son.

Camille was in her early sixties and slender now that she'd lost seventy pounds. The smile on her round face was hesitant. Her wide-set hazel eyes had a sweep of eyeshadow, and the golden highlights in Camille's wavy auburn hair had a gloss that made Kelly a tad jealous. Standing in front of her was a woman who, according to society, was supposed to be invisible. Yet she was rocking hair, makeup, and the cutest romper. Kelly couldn't help but wonder if Pepper's makeover last fall had something to do with Camille's reinvention. It had taken a while for Pepper to come around to the changes Kelly had made in the boutique, but when she did, she was all in, including a whole new look.

Camille hurried into the living room and set the box on the coffee table. She turned back to Kelly.

"I desperately need your help." Camille's smile had vanished, and in its place was a frown and two deep lines set between her thin brows.

"Pepper says you have clothing you'd like to sell. I'm happy to take care of that for you. Want to show me what you're going to consign? I can give you a quick estimate of how much you could make, and I also have a contract for you to sign."

"Oh, my, it sounds so official."

"The contract is to protect both of us." The agreement was professionally written and spelled out all the terms of the consignment, but over the years Kelly's grandmother, Martha Blake, had stopped using the document. According to Pepper, they both felt that the paperwork hadn't been necessary. Kelly disagreed and immediately began using the contract again once she took over the boutique's ownership.

Camille nodded. "Whatever I need to do, I'll do. I just have to clear out all the clothes. It's gotten out of hand. Come, I'll show you."

She led Kelly through the living room to the back of the house. A soft white paint unified the walls throughout, and area rugs covered the gleaming hardwood floors. When they arrived at a closed door, Camille pushed it open for Kelly to enter.

Inside what she guessed was a guest room was a massive amount of clothing. Kelly's mouth gaped. Piles of sweaters, tops, and jeans buried the double bed. On the floor were more piles of clothes. They looked like jackets, vests, and coats. She eyed the triple dresser and wondered if there were more clothes stuffed in there.

The momentary overwhelm of so much clothing subsided. Kelly approached the bed to inspect the clothes.

She picked up a snake-print blouse and unfolded it. The label was unfamiliar to her. Then again, many of the subscription services used brands that weren't available at retail.

"I loved that blouse. But it's too big for me now. I've been on a weight loss journey for two years now, so I have a large variety of sizes." Camille joined Kelly at the bed and fingered through a stack of striped sweaters.

Kelly was relieved that Camille had organized the clothing by category, color, and size. It would make her job a lot easier.

"I think I went overboard on all this stuff. But I like to look nice for my job, even though I'm an old lady."

Kelly looked up from the clothes. Camille worked as a secretary for Kelly's uncle, Ralph Blake. He owned a real estate development company in Lucky Cove and had projects up and down the island. He was also the cause of her ulcer in the making. She gave herself a mental shake. She was there for work and needed to focus on that.

"You're not an old lady. Besides, the love of fashion is ageless. This is a nice blouse." Before Kelly refolded the blouse, she inspected the seaming details. Not bad. Next, she checked the label. Machine wash. Perfect. Most of her customers preferred easy-to-care-for clothing.

"Luckily, I received another one, a size smaller, the following fall." Camille picked through a pile of jeans. "Do you really think I can sell all this?"

"I don't see why not? However, I have to say that you'll get the best prices for items that are in season. This blouse won't fetch the most money if I put it out for sale now."

"Right, no one is thinking about fall fashion right now."

Except for me.

Kelly's love for fall fashion had her watching all the videos from the fashion shows in London, Paris, Milan, and New York and taking notes.

Along with the new *it* hemline of the upcoming season she spotted her former boss, Serena Dawson, sitting front row. Serena was the vice president of merchandise at Bishop's. Only months ago she'd swooped back into Kelly's life and turned it upside down. Like she had when she fired Kelly in front of everyone at Bishop's.

"Well, there are some summer clothes in these piles and in that closet." Camille pointed. "And also upstairs."

Kelly snapped out of her thoughts about her former boss and the humiliating experience of being terminated from her dream job. "Upstairs? There's more?" Kelly couldn't remember the last time she'd met someone who had such an enormous wardrobe. Though, considering Camille had been shrinking for the past two years, it was understandable.

Camille's cheeks flushed. Even though she had a good reason for being a shopaholic, it looked like she felt some embarrassment about her excessive shopping.

"You have no idea."

Kelly stepped back from the bed and gestured toward the door. "Take me to your clothes. All of them."

"You're such a sweetheart." Camille laughed as she walked to the door and rested her hand on the knob. "You know, I'm wondering if you can help me with my wardrobe once I get everything sorted. I'm closing in on my goal weight. I just have no idea what I should wear to really flatter my figure. And, I'd like to have one of those minimalist wardrobes."

Kelly lifted her tote. "Like a wardrobe consultation?"

Camille nodded. "Exactly. As you see, I have tons of clothes, but I don't know if I'm dressing the right way for my body."

Kelly was familiar with dressing body types. She often advised customers when they were selecting items to try on in the boutique. Camille's body type was boy shaped. No curves, but all her weight settled in the middle around her abdomen.

"It's not something I've officially offered." She adjusted the tote's strap on her shoulder. Perhaps offering the service wasn't a bad idea. She'd been wanting to find ways to expand the boutique. Plus, the extra work would keep her mind occupied and off her latest breakup. "Why don't we focus on selling your clothes first? Then we can discuss a wardrobe consultation."

"Sounds like a plan." Camille smiled and then led Kelly up the staircase. She looked over her shoulder. "How is Terry working out? She's a lovely gal, don't you think?"

"You know her?" In retrospect, it was a silly question. Camille had lived her whole life in Lucky Cove, had raised her children there, and had been active in the community. She, like Pepper, knew practically everyone. Camille nodded. "Her mother and I are good friends. Have been for years. In fact, Lottie was over here yesterday. She's thrilled her daughter is working again."

Lottie sounded like a typical mom.

Kelly's own had worried when she lost her job last year. The firing had come unexpectedly and swiftly. One minute she was writing a purchase order for Calvin Klein sweaters, and the next she was piling her belongings into a cardboard box. Kelly's mom had been concerned how her daughter would pay the rent and buy food. Then came the inheritance with a job and an apartment, though Kelly wasn't sure how much inheriting the boutique had quelled her mom's worries. But she was doing fine. So no one needed to worry. However, she was a little concerned about her new employee. There had been a gap in Terry's résumé. When Kelly inquired about it, Terry explained she'd gotten burned out at her previous job, which was as a freelance social media coordinator for beauty brands. She claimed she needed time to recharge. It sounded reasonable to Kelly.

She knew firsthand that being self-employed meant that too often work crept into her personal life.

Yes, the hustle was real, and it could be exhausting.

"Terry is doing a superb job. She's a natural with customers." Working on a clothing sales floor wasn't an easy job. Long hours on your feet, low pay, and dealing with customers all day wasn't for the faint of heart. Yet, with all the downsides to the job, Terry seemed to flourish. Her suggestions for colors and clothing styles for customers were spot on. Kelly couldn't have asked for a better salesperson.

They reached the second-floor landing, which was a small square of hardwood. The bathroom's door was ajar, and sunlight streamed out to the hall. The two other doors had been closed. "Good to hear. As a mother, I empathize with Lottie's feelings. We want the best for our children. Bless you for giving Terry the chance she needs."

The chance she needs?

Before Kelly could ask what that meant, Camille opened the bedroom door and stepped aside to allow Kelly to enter.

Kelly's eyes widened at the sight of a room bursting with clothes.

"Holy Manolos."

"I know. It's a bit much." Camille ushered Kelly into the room. She stepped around Kelly and walked toward the armoire. "There's clothing in here too. Would you like something to drink? A cup of tea perhaps?" Tea? Kelly would have preferred water to keep her hydrated while sorting through all these clothes. Still, she declined the offer. The clock was ticking, and she needed to get back to the boutique. For the next hour, Kelly assessed the items Camille wanted to consign. Her calculator was on fire as she tallied an estimate of how much she could sell the clothes for. It took four trips to her Jeep to remove the garments that would go on sale this week. On her last trip to her vehicle, she promised Camille she'd be back for the rest. Now she just had to figure out where to store the windfall of merchandise in her small shop.

* * * *

Because she was at Camille's house longer than she expected, she only had a few minutes to make a quick stop at Doug's Variety Store. While she loved the seasonal coffees Doug's offered, she settled for a plain large coffee with a dash of cream. On her way out of the shop, she passed two women about her age eyeing some Lucky Cove memorabilia.

"So kitschy, isn't it?" The slim brunette lifted an ale mug from the display and laughed. "Maybe we should get Whit this? Surely we can find something naughty to put in it and give it to her tonight."

The petite blonde with a glacier vibe to her snatched the mug out of her friend's hand.

"Not even close to being an appropriate bridal shower gift."

"Sorry to interrupt." Kelly stopped. "If you're looking for gifts, you should visit Courtney's Treasures. I'm sure you'll find something. She has a great selection." One of the most important things Kelly had done after inheriting the boutique was to become involved with the local chamber of commerce. The best way to build her business was to support the other businesses on Main Street.

The blonde rolled her eyes. It appeared she wasn't interested in Kelly's support of Lucky Cove businesses. "Thanks, but we already purchased our gifts in the city." Her emphasis on *in the city* made it clear their shopping wasn't done in just any part of Manhattan but rather on that stretch of prized real estate—Fifth Avenue.

The brunette shrugged. She seemed used to her friend's pretentious behavior. "Let's just get our coffees and get back to the inn."

With their designer straw bags slung over their shoulders, they breezed past Kelly and headed to the counter. Kelly sighed and reminded herself that for the most part, the summer people were pleasant and friendly. She continued out of the shop, determined to forget about the snobbish city girls.

* * * *

Kelly arrived back at the boutique a few minutes after opening. Shoot. She'd wanted to be the one to open, even though both Breena and Terry were working. It was vital for her as the owner and boss to set an example to her staff. Though, she had been working, not out dillydallying like her granny used to say.

She gathered her tote, coffee, and an armful of clothing from the Jeep's cargo area. That armful barely made a dent in what was stashed in the space. She'd have to make a few trips to get everything inside.

With some maneuvering and juggling of everything in her arms, she twisted the back door's knob. With her foot, she kicked it open wider and entered the staff room. The air conditioner's cooling was a welcome relief as she made a beeline for the round table.

Breena Collins looked up from pouring coffee into her mug. Her hair color had changed again. She was now a strawberry blonde. Her shoulder-length hair was set in soft waves, and a wisp of bangs brushed her eyebrows. Last spring, she began a workout routine and had stuck to it, leaving her hourglass figure lean.

"Look at that haul! Pepper wasn't exaggerating about Camille's shopping obsession."

Kelly let go of the clothing. The garments fell onto the tabletop, and she let out a whoosh of relief.

Breena returned the carafe to the coffee maker. She worked part-time as a sales associate while juggling college courses, working another job, and raising her daughter. Like Kelly, Breena had left Lucky Cove for New York City. There she pursued an acting career but learned she wasn't the only star of high school plays looking to make it big on Broadway. "I now see why you're late getting back. But no worries, we got everything covered."

"Good to hear. And thank you." Kelly dropped her tote on her desk chair. "By the way, this is only part of the clothes I have to bring in. The Jeep is packed."

"Seriously? She has that many clothes?"

Kelly nodded as she reached into her tote and pulled out a hair tie. She gathered her shoulder-length blond hair into a ponytail. The back of her neck was clammy, and sweat beaded on her temples. She reached back into the bag and pulled out Camille's contract.

"There's a Lilly Pulitzer–inspired maxi dress still in the Jeep. It'll look amazing in the window."

"Oooh, do you think it could be used for your spot on *Long Island View Point*?"

"It's not my spot...yet. But, yes, I think it would be perfect to showcase during the segment." Kelly had been contacted by the producer of the sixty-minute lifestyle show that covered community organizations, local businesses, and cultural events. They planned a feature on sustainability and wanted to interview a consignment shop for the segment. Kelly had jumped at the chance to promote her boutique and was waiting for the confirmation.

"Don't fret. You'll be on the show. I feel it in my bones." Breena smiled as she lifted her electronic tablet from the countertop and tapped on the device. "Want to hear your horoscope for today?"

Kelly shook her head no. She didn't believe in that stuff, and Breena knew it.

Nevertheless, Breena ignored Kelly's objection and read from her device. "There are a lot of things up in the air right now in your life, but you don't need to feel nervous."

She looked up from the tablet.

Kelly blew out a breath. She hated to admit it, but the horoscope was right on point.

The door from the hall swung open, and Terry Carlisle breezed in. Wearing cropped trousers and a cap-sleeved blouse, she looked chic and comfortable.

"Good morning, Kelly." Terry's gaze landed on the table. "Look at all those clothes. Camille's closet must be huge."

"She has several closets." Kelly gazed at her laptop. It was a reminder she had bookkeeping to do and an article to edit. Several months ago, she landed a regular column on a fashion website. Budget Chic appealed to financially savvy women who wanted to look good but not spend a fortune. The pay wasn't great, but every little bit helped, and it also boosted her presence online.

"I was just reading Kelly's horoscope. Let's see what yours says. You're a Pisces, right?" Breena asked. When Terry nodded, she groaned.

"What's wrong?" Terry asked.

Breena's forehead crinkled as she read out loud. "A visitor from your past will challenge your day. Do your best not to engage."

Terry frowned at the forecast of her day. She looked to Kelly with wide eyes suddenly clouded with concern. Kelly didn't need half of her staff depressed all day waiting for doom and gloom to happen thanks to a couple sentences written by some woo-woo charlatan.

"Hey, don't look so worried. Those things aren't accurate. No one can predict how your day will turn out." Kelly walked back to the table. "There are a bunch more clothes out in the Jeep. Would you mind bringing them in? Then we can get them ready for sale."

Terry didn't look comforted by Kelly's words. She shrugged her shoulders and uttered, "Sure" as she made her way to the back door. When she was gone, Kelly turned her attention to Breena.

"Look what you did." Kelly pointed toward the door. "Now she'll be worried all day."

Breena pressed her lips together. "Maybe she should be. Contrary to what you think, these horoscopes are correct. I wonder who the visitor from her past will be."

CHAPTER TWO

When all the clothing was unloaded from the Jeep, Kelly asked Terry to prep the newly consigned merchandise for sale. The garments would be added into the inventory system and tagged with their prices. The task would keep Terry occupied, and hopefully, she'd feel better. As much as Kelly wanted to give her new employee her privacy, she was dying to know, like Breena, who the visitor from the past could be. Who had jarred Terry so much?

As the boss, Kelly knew she shouldn't pry, so she busied herself at the sales counter to keep her mind off Terry, but it wasn't working. Her curiosity was growing by the minute. Plus, she wanted to inquire about the comment Camille had made about Terry deserving a second chance. But considering the state Terry was in, that inquiry would have to wait. Kelly returned her attention to the task at hand—reviewing the past week's sales.

A quick glance revealed sundresses and shorts were still the biggest sellers in the clothing category. At the same time, canvas totes and straw handbags were the tops in accessories. Her thoughts flitted back to Doug's Variety Store and the expensive bags those two city women carried. Kelly would have loved to get her hands on one of those bags for consignment. It would be an easy three-figure sale. She shifted her attention back to the spreadsheet. Every pair of wedge sandals had sold out.

She made a mental note to check with Camille to see if she had any in good condition for sale. Then she continued scanning the report.

The bell over the front door jingled, alerting Kelly to a customer. Since the day her granny opened the boutique, there had been a bell. When Kelly was a little girl, she loved spending the day in the boutique and always raced to greet customers when they entered. She had no idea back then she'd own the business one day. She set aside the papers and lifted her head, ready to greet her customers. But neither woman was a customer, and Kelly wasn't disappointed at all.

"Oh. My. Goodness!" Kelly dashed out from behind the counter. "I didn't expect to see you today."

Becky Quinn threw open her arms. "We're all settled. I just had to get off those conference calls and out of the house."

Kelly hurried to her cousin, and they hugged.

"It's so good to see you." Kelly pulled back but still held on to Becky's arms. She stared at her cousin. They hadn't seen each other in person in over three years, though they video called each other at least once a month.

Becky was two years older than Kelly, and in the looks department, she was striking. Shorter by a couple of inches, she had straight black hair that had a lustrous sheen, and her porcelain skin tone was a couple of shades lighter than Kelly's. She looked casual and cool in a sleeveless cotton top tucked into a pair of linen drawstring shorts in a lovely shade of terra-cotta and a pair of espadrilles. She held a designer canvas bag. Kelly recognized the logo and was almost drooling. Chanel had started the whole trend with a four-digit canvas bag Kelly would never consider taking to the beach.

"I've been dying to see the shop in person." Becky shifted as she looked around. "Your granny would be so proud of you. This place looks amazing. And the window! Very eye catching."

Kelly smiled at the compliment. She'd hoped her granny would have been proud of the changes she made in the boutique.

"I even love the new name." Becky slipped the tote off her shoulder, and it rested on the crook of her arm.

When the boutique opened decades ago, it was named the Lucky Cove Consignment Shop, which was ho-hum and uninspiring. Kelly's first choice as a new name was met by a lukewarm reception from Pepper, who had worked at the boutique for over twenty years. So, Kelly decided on a compromise and surprised Pepper at the grand reopening with the new signage. That gesture had made Pepper happy, and in turn, Kelly was delighted.

"I normally don't shop in consignment shops, but this place is really nice. And those maxi dresses in the window really piqued my interest." The woman who had entered with Becky stepped forward and extended her hand to Kelly. "Hello, I'm Jessica Barron."

"Oh, where are my manners? Forgive me." Becky blushed. "Kell, this is Jessica. Finally, you two get to meet."

BEAUTY AND THE DECEASED   19

"It's nice to meet you. My cousin has told me so much about you." Kelly did feel like she knew Jessica from everything Becky had shared. Before Becky left New York to move out to California, the two of them met online. At the time, Jessica had been a beauty influencer with a large following. When they finally met in real life, they hit it off and became fast friends. Within months, they became roommates and now were business partners in Define Beauty. Becky had told Kelly it had been a no-brainer to go into business with Jessica since they shared the same vision for the company.

"Well, I already feel like I know you." Jessica took back her hand. "And this shop. And, Lucky Cove."

Becky laughed. "I've always loved being here. Even though I lived minutes from the beach in California, nothing compares to Lucky Cove."

"I'm so glad you've decided to spend the summer here. It'll be like old times," Kelly said.

Becky laughed again. "That could be a problem. You remember how much trouble we got into, right?"

"Do I? At least now we won't get in trouble for breaking curfew." Kelly's tone was lighthearted, but a late-night party she went to when she should have been home had resulted in a tragic accident. Having a friend's life changed forever was worse than being grounded until she was thirty, as her dad always threatened.

"We can't forget you're here on a working vacation." Jessica's comment earned her a sharp look from Becky, which quickly vanished. If Kelly hadn't been watching her cousin, she would have missed it. The subtle interaction between them made Kelly wonder about the power dynamics between them. Who had the upper hand?

"Well, I'm free this afternoon. There isn't one task on my to-do list. How about lunch, Kell?" Becky smiled hopefully.

Kelly considered the invitation. Breena and Terry were scheduled to work until closing, so she could have a proper lunch break. Usually, she made a salad and ate it at her desk while working. It would be nice not to scarf down her meal over a keyboard.

"I'd love to." Kelly suggested a restaurant just up the street, and they agreed upon a time. With one more hug, she escorted her cousin and Jessica to the front door. "It's going to be so great having you here all summer."

Before Becky could reply, a loud gasp drew their attention to the doorway that led to the small hall where the changing rooms were located. Terry stood there frozen. Her face was as white as the cotton shirt she held.

Kelly then looked back at Becky and Jessica. Their expressions had changed. Now they looked surprised and not in a good way. In a flash, Kelly felt the tension ratchet up in the room.

"What's going on?" she asked, her gaze darting between the three women. She wished one of them would answer her.

"What on earth is *she* doing here?" Jessica pointed at Terry as she stepped protectively in front of Becky.

"She works here. Will someone please tell me what's going on?" Kelly locked her gaze on her cousin, since they were family. "How do you three know each other?"

"Through social media," Becky said.

"She used to be a beauty influencer but had a breakdown and was hospitalized. Isn't that right, Terry?" Jessica's tone was scathing, and it irked Kelly to hear her talk to her employee like that.

Terry's face all about crumbled, and she swallowed hard.

Kelly willed Terry to defend herself because she had a sinking feeling Jessica was just getting started.

"You've constantly been messaging Becky." Jessica propped her hands on her hips. "It's been nothing short of harassment."

Yep, Kelly was right about Jessica.

"I…I needed to talk to Becky. That's all." Terry's pleading eyes focused on Kelly. "She's making it sound like I'm stalking Becky. I'm not."

"How many times do you need to hear she doesn't want to talk to you? Come on, Becky. Let's get out of here." Jessica opened the door and gestured for Becky to exit.

Becky looked torn and then gave a half shrug to Kelly before turning and following her business partner out the door.

Kelly blew out a breath. "What on earth just happened?" She swung around to ask Terry for an explanation, but her employee ditched the armful of clothes on the counter and darted out of the room.

Kelly pursued, determined to get answers.

She reached the staff room, and its door had just swung closed. She pushed it open and entered the room.

Terry was at the coat tree, lifting her purse off the peg.

Kelly crossed the room. "Terry, we should talk about what just happened."

Terry shook her head as she dug into her purse for her car keys.

"Is what Jessica said true?" Kelly's curiosity was piqued. Had Terry been hospitalized? If so, now Camille's comments made sense. Had Terry harassed Becky? If true, that wasn't cool, and Kelly couldn't keep her on if she had done it.

"No. No. I can't talk about it. I won't talk about it. I have to go." Terry spun around and rushed out the back door.

"What's going on?" Breena entered the room with a confused look on her face. "Where's Terry going?"

"I wish I knew." Kelly walked to the coffee maker. She needed another coffee. And a moment to sort out what happened. "Somehow, Terry knows my cousin and her business partner."

"You mean like they're from her past?"

Kelly groaned. She knew where this was going.

"Yes, it appears that way."

Breena grinned. "Looks like her horoscope was right."

Kelly didn't respond. There wasn't any need to encourage Breena's silly obsession with horoscopes. She returned the carafe to the coffee maker and sipped her coffee before turning to leave the staff room. With Terry gone and Breena gloating about the horoscope being right, someone had to work the sales floor. As she approached the counter, the bell over the door jingled, and Mrs. Daley, a regular, entered with a cheerful greeting.

Kelly set her mug down and returned the greeting. She knew Mrs. Daley liked to browse the entire store before selecting items to try on. This would give her time to regroup from the scene that just went down between her cousin and her employee. Her cell phone chimed, and she pulled it from her pocket. It was a text from Becky.

Sorry about what happened. Still on for lunch?

Kelly didn't hesitate to reply.

Of course we are.

She started typing but stopped mid keystroke, her fingers paused over the keyboard as she realized that any questions about what happened earlier weren't for a text conversation. Since they were meeting soon, she'd broach the subject over lunch. Kelly deleted what she'd started texting. Before continuing with her message, she reviewed the day's schedule in her mind. Aside from administrative work to tackle and a review of the boutique's social media calendar, she also had to cover Breena's break time. She sent off a time suggestion to her cousin.

Mrs. Daley approached the counter with a bunch of dresses in hand.

"Would you be a dear and keep these while I continue to browse?" The plump, fluffy gray-haired bargain hunter smiled and turned swiftly to head into the accessories department.

Kelly checked her phone and found a thumbs-up emoji from Becky.

Good. They were all set to meet later. A ripple of anxiety worked its way through her body. Not only did she want to catch up with her cousin, but she also wanted to determine if her new employee was indeed a stalker.

The bell over the door jingled again, announcing a mother-and-daughter duo entering. They were the start of a steady stream of customers for the day.

When Breena returned from her lunch break, she took over assisting two best friends from New Jersey vacationing in Lucky Cove for the week.

"They have a pile of clothes set aside on the counter," Kelly said as she handed off the energetic women to Breena. She breathed a sigh of relief when she walked out of the accessories department. The once bland and overstocked square room had been an addition constructed with little thought. Her granny had wanted to expand her business and decided to sell home goods.

What happened instead was she ended up with a room full of uninspired inventory that hadn't sold. Not wanting to keep merchandise that didn't turn a profit, Kelly had emptied the room and gave it a makeover. A fresh coat of paint to the walls and a polishing of the hardwood floor gave the room a freshness it had been lacking. Next, she'd added petite chandeliers, framed mirrors, and tufted ottomans. When she was done, she had a space that was inviting to shop.

On her way through the staff room, Kelly grabbed her purse and left for the Gull Café. It was a short walk to the charming restaurant. Every time she entered, she remembered how her mom would treat her and her sister, Caroline, to lunch there. She smiled at the memory.

A server swept by with a packed tray and nodded toward the dining room. Kelly caught a glimpse of Becky at one of the linen-draped tables, looking relaxed and reading on her phone. As she threaded through the dining room, she passed several familiar faces. She nodded and smiled at each one until she reached Becky's table.

"Hey," she said as she pulled out a chair and sat.

Becky looked up from her phone. Her cheekbones were subtly highlighted, and her lips were the perfect shade of red. If Kelly remembered correctly, the color was called Marilyn—an old-school Hollywood red that worked on all skin complexions. Becky was a natural when it came to applying makeup, much to the chagrin of her parents when she was a preteen. As soon as she could get her hands on lip gloss and mascara, she began testing the boundaries with how much makeup she could wear. Now, look at her. She was the president of her own cosmetics company.

Kelly wanted to pick her cousin's brain about business. While her granny had been content running a small consignment shop, Kelly had bigger dreams. Perhaps another store or maybe e-commerce or a shift into fashion styling. Her thoughts were all over the place, and she figured her cousin could help steer her in the right direction. But first, she wanted to find out the deal with Terry.

"I'm starving." Becky set her phone down and picked up the menu.

"Same here. It's been nonstop at the boutique." Kelly didn't need her menu. She knew what she was going to order. The grilled chicken salad with the dressing on the side. It was summer, and whenever she could get away to the beach, she did, and that meant putting on a bikini. Not only was her dressing on the side these days, but her morning runs were a lot more consistent.

"Everything looks so good. I think I'm going to have the cobb salad." Becky set the menu down and reached for her water glass.

"There's so much I want to talk to you about. But I have to start with Terry. She ran out of the boutique after you and Jessica left."

Becky shrugged as she set the glass down. "I really don't know much about her. I started receiving DMs from her. She wanted to meet with me. When I received the third one, I mentioned it to Jessica. She knew who Terry was because they were both beauty influencers."

"I had no idea. On Terry's résumé, she said she worked in social media." It looked like Kelly should have asked more questions. She lowered her gaze. Her cousin must have thought she was an amateur. And she'd be right. Before inheriting the boutique, she had no experience in hiring staff. Pepper had come with the business. Breena was an old high school friend who needed a job after quitting her waitress job at the Thirsty Turtle, a bar with a questionable clientele.

"You probably need to vet your employment candidates better. Just something to consider."

Their waitress approached for their orders.

When she walked away, Becky continued. "According to Jessica, Terry had been a successful online beauty vlogger with a decent following. Then one day, she had a meltdown on a live video. Could you imagine?"

Kelly paused her sip of water. Meltdown? That didn't sound good. And no, she couldn't imagine.

"She accused other influencers of bullying her and encouraging their followers to troll her."

Kelly set her glass down. Social media had its good points, but it could also be a cesspool of jealousy and meanness. She knew from friends that the influencer crowd could turn from supportive to destructive at the bat of a false eyelash. Even so, Kelly found it hard to believe the claims against Terry, but she had fled the boutique.

"Was it true? Was she being bullied by other influencers? By Jessica?"

"I don't know if her claims are true. However, I doubt Jessica bullied her. Jess had been doing great as an influencer. She's far too professional to behave in such a heinous manner. I don't doubt that something happened to Terry. After she made her farewell video, she was gone from the internet. Then out of nowhere, she messaged me." Becky unfolded her napkin and placed it on her lap. "Look, Kell, I think Terry may have problems, but I don't feel threatened by her even though Jessica thinks she could be dangerous. Something about being obsessive and blaming others for her own failures."

"Does Jessica know how you feel? She seemed..."

"Intense? Protective?" Becky nodded. "It's her way. I'm lucky to have her in my corner."

Kelly made a mental note to stay on Jessica's good side.

"That's good to hear. You are family, and I'm worried about you. I'll have a talk with Terry."

"We've talked enough about her and Jessica."

"I hope she's not upset she wasn't invited to join us."

"No worries. I knew she had back-to-back calls when I suggested lunch. Besides, she usually works through lunch. So, let's enjoy it. Okay? This is our time and I want us to enjoy it. And let's talk about us!" Becky smiled.

"Okay." Kelly returned the smile. Within moments, they eased into conversations ranging from work to the upcoming fall trends to relationships as they ate. Both had their hearts put through the wringer too.

Kelly's breakup with local attorney Mark Lambert still stung. Even though Becky claimed she was over her ex, Kelly wasn't buying it. After falling head over heels for the guy, Becky found out he had a fiancée. Kelly never got the chance to meet the guy, but she was furious with him on her cousin's behalf.

When lunch was served, they continued talking and soon found themselves reminiscing about their childhoods and teen years. Which meant, they'd lost all track of time.

Becky glanced at her phone. "Look at the time! I have to get going. I might be renting a house on the beach, but these two months are a working vacation for me."

"I know I've said it before, but I'll say it again. I'm so happy you came out here for the summer." Kelly reached for the check that the waitress had set on the table a moment earlier.

"What was that all about?" Kelly silently acknowledged she really was nosy by nature. Maybe that's why she'd been so good at being an amateur sleuth in the past. A few times since moving back to Lucky Cove, she'd gotten caught up in some murder investigations. Her natural curiosity had turned out to be a benefit to solving the crimes, but it also had been a hindrance since she found herself face-to-face with killers. "How do you know her?" She stopped herself from asking what her cousin had done to cross Whitney, who had a reputation for being spiteful. Well, at least, that was the word on the street.

Becky gave a dismissive wave.

"Nothing. Really. It's ancient history. In typical Whitney fashion, she's overly dramatic."

"She was dramatic, all right."

Becky busied herself by looking through her purse for something. "You know, this has been quite a day. Not exactly how I pictured our first in-person visit. I have an idea. Why don't you come to the beach house for dinner tonight? We can grill and make s'mores like when we were kids."

"Sounds like fun. I'd love to!"

"Oh, we should invite Frankie and Caroline." Becky smiled at the waitress who picked up the credit card and bill on her way past their table.

Kelly tilted her head sideways. "Caroline is away for a few days. She's on vacation with her fiancé." While she was disappointed Caroline was away, she realized that once her sister returned from her spontaneous getaway, she'd have most of her family in Lucky Cove. And they'd be talking, visiting, and having meals together. Her heart warmed. It'd been a long time since her fractured family enjoyed time together. Especially her and her sister. Kelly swallowed the hard lump that formed in her throat. Even to this day, thinking about what happened ten years ago and how it had divided her family still got to her, although they were all rebuilding their relationships.

Becky frowned. "Bummer."

"I know. But I'm sure Frankie will want to come. I'll call him."

Frankie was the son of her uncle Ralph and his first wife. He was also a French-trained chef. After internships and apprenticeships, he had made the bold and unexpected move to walk away from his promising career in New York City. He followed his passion and opened his own restaurant, Frankie's Seafood Shack. It was a seasonal eatery, so he worked as a personal chef in the winter months and for his restauranteur friends when they needed help. She hoped he'd be off tonight.

"Great. I'll text later with a time." Becky's cell phone chimed, and she flashed an apologetic look. "Sorry, I have to take this."

"No problem. I have to get back to the boutique." Kelly stood, slung her purse over her shoulder. She hugged her cousin goodbye and walked out of the café.

The glass door closed behind her as she stepped out onto the sidewalk, and she spotted Whitney standing beside a dark SUV, talking on her phone. Maybe she could get an explanation from her about why she was so upset with Becky.

"Whitney," Kelly called out.

The PR guru turned her head in Kelly's direction and rolled her eyes. Now, Kelly was even more determined to find out what Whitney's problem was with her cousin. Kelly marched toward the vehicle, parked at the curb a few spaces down from the restaurant.

But it appeared the lunch crasher had no desire to talk with Kelly. She pulled open the passenger side door and scooted into the vehicle. A moment later, the SUV pulled out of the space and drove off.

Kelly stopped, propped her hands on her hips, and stared at the fleeing vehicle.

"How rude." Then again, it probably wasn't a smart idea to get on the wrong side of someone who was influential in the PR scene. One too many times, the boutique and Kelly had been on the receiving end of negative publicity, which had affected her business. She couldn't risk that again. In the spring, she'd had a new roof put on her building, and she had to pay back the money she borrowed for the project. Nope. It wasn't smart to tick off Whitney Mulhern. She dropped her hands and turned around. Not expecting anyone to be there, she gasped in surprise.

"Who's rude?"

Kelly sucked in a relieved breath and slapped her cousin, Frankie Blake, on the chest. "Don't sneak up on people."

"I didn't. You're standing in the middle of the sidewalk."

Kelly couldn't argue his point. She was standing outside of Gregorio's Specialty Shop. The store offered a host of delicacies from around the world and the freshest ingredients for home-cooked meals. By the looks of the overstuffed bag he held, Frankie was planning on cooking up a storm.

"Who were you griping about?" he asked.

"Whitney Mulhern."

Frankie smiled. Tiny lines feathered out around his brown eyes. His sandy-blond hair had a slight wave, and a wayward curl grazed his brow. "How do you know Whitney Mulhern?"

"I don't know. I guess it doesn't matter." Kelly pursed her lips. No. It did matter. The PR world's darling had upset Becky, and she wanted to know why. "She interrupted lunch with Becky. She said Becky would regret her decision to come to Lucky Cove."

"Wow." Frankie dragged his fingers through his hair, repositioning the wayward curl. "What did Becky say about it?"

"Nothing. She didn't want to talk about Whitney."

"So, you saw her and chased after her?"

"Well, when you put it that way, it sounds like I had a terrible idea."

"From what I hear about Whitney, she knows everyone, and if you end up on her naughty list, you can kiss your career goodbye. So, I suggest you don't pursue her anymore."

An older man passed by them on his way into Gregorio's. Frankie stepped back and opened the door for him to enter. He'd always done good deeds like that out of the kindness of his heart. Unlike his father, he wasn't looking for anything in return. Ralph always seemed to have an agenda when dealing with people. He could learn a thing or two from his son.

"What's in the bag? What are you going to make?" Kelly asked, intentionally changing the subject from Whitney.

"Testing a few recipes. Look, I gotta get back to the restaurant." Frankie smiled and then walked past her.

"Oh, wait." Kelly grabbed Frankie's arm. "Becky is having a little dinner at her house. She'd love for you to come. And bring a dessert."

"All you want me for is my food."

Kelly giggled. "Guilty. So, can you come tonight?"

Frankie paused for a moment. "Sure. It'll be fun. Too bad Caroline is away. Text me the time, okay? I really have to go."

"Don't forget dessert," she called out as Frankie walked away. While he had to get back to his restaurant, she needed to get back to the boutique.

* * * *

The rest of the day passed by quickly. The steady stream of customers they had in the morning continued through closing time, which kept Kelly and Breena hopping between the changing rooms and the cash register. It was this kind of day she'd been hoping for since inheriting the boutique.

She'd managed to step away from the sales floor to text Terry but hadn't received a reply yet. She had no idea if Terry would show up for work tomorrow. Or, if she'd quit.

By closing time, Breena looked exhausted and was changing out of her sandals and into sneakers. At the same time, Kelly felt a second wind coming on. She was excited for a relaxing night on the beach with her cousins. Frankie had replied to her text earlier with a string of exciting emojis followed by a confirmation he'd be at the beach house right after he finished work.

Upstairs in her apartment, Kelly fed Howard and then got ready for dinner. She glanced out the window of her bedroom. It was promising to be a beautiful evening, and she couldn't wait to watch the sunset while sitting on the beach. She pulled out a lilac-colored dress to wear along with a big beach hat. Standing in front of the full-length mirror, she adjusted the floppy hat. On her way out of the bedroom, she grabbed her rattan tote.

At the door, she gave Howard a pat before he trotted into the living room to snooze on the sofa. After dinner, naps were a big part of his evening routine. She quickly transferred all the items from her purse into her tote and was out the door.

Ten minutes later, Kelly pulled her Jeep into the driveway of the multilevel cedar-shingled house. Outside lighting illuminated the paths to the front door and around to the back deck. She grabbed her tote and stepped out of her vehicle. At the front door, Becky ushered her inside. Becky wore a pair of gauzy wide-leg pants and a matching tank top. Her hair was swept up into a loose bun with fallen tendrils framing her face.

Inside, she introduced Jessica's boyfriend, Smith Henshaw. He greeted Kelly with a toothy smile and a firm handshake. His sleek, golden-blond hair suited him and reminded Kelly of a Ken doll. He made small talk about the weather and the long drive from the city as he swirled his drink, which looked like scotch on the rocks.

"Would you like a drink?" he asked before taking a sip.

"Not right now. Thank you." Hard liquor wasn't Kelly's preferred drink. She'd rather have a glass of wine or a spritzer.

"Come on, let me give you the tour." Becky led Kelly through the spacious home. The tour of the first floor was pretty quick since the layout was an open concept. The rental must have been costing her cousin a fortune for the season. But it looked like it was worth it. Becky looked relaxed and happy. Launching a business and continually releasing new products was daunting, no matter how much passion you had for the business.

Kelly followed Becky upstairs. The first stop was Becky's bedroom, which was as neat as a pin except for the top of the triple dresser. From end to end, there was a stash of cosmetics and skincare products. Some had simple white labels, which meant they were in a testing phase. A large makeup brush bag was open and displayed the vast collection of brushes Becky had accumulated. Kelly was impressed and a little jealous. They all looked so lush and soft.

"I really do need all of them." Becky must have seen the look on Kelly's face. "Besides, I've acquired them over the years. One of my plans is for Define Beauty to have its own makeup brushes. It's not as easy as it looks."

"I wouldn't think so. The right brushes are the foundation for a great makeup application."

Becky nodded as she smiled. "Impressive. And very accurate. Come on, want to see the closet?"

"Like you have to ask." Kelly laughed and followed her cousin toward the double doors. When Becky pulled the doors open, Kelly looked into the cavernous space. Custom built-ins and a center island with a chandelier hung above had her sighing. "Wow. I'd kill for a closet like this."

"I just wish I had more clothes. It seems like a waste." Becky stepped back and closed the doors. "Frankie should be here soon, right?"

"You know him. He always runs a little late." Kelly followed Becky out of the bedroom. Before they returned downstairs, Kelly got a glimpse of the three other guest rooms. As they approached the staircase, there was another room whose door was shut. She guessed it was Jessica's bedroom, and she didn't expect to see inside.

Back in the foyer, there was a knock at the door. Becky swung the door open and let out a squeal of excitement. She pulled Frankie into a hug, jostling the thermal tote he carried. Kelly lunged for the tote. She wasn't going to let anything happen to their dessert.

She loved everything he cooked, but his desserts were ridiculously delicious.

For the casual dinner party, he wore a pair of madras plaid shorts and a polo shirt. He slid off his Ray-Bans and gave her a kiss on the cheek.

"This place is sweet," he said.

"Glad you like it. Let me take the dessert, and you two go out on the deck." Becky took the dessert and carried it to the high-end kitchen.

"Drink?" Smith had approached and gestured with his glass.

"Oh, Frankie, this is Smith Henshaw. He's Jessica's boyfriend," Kelly said.

"Nice to meet you. I'll pass for now. Thanks."

Smith shrugged and walked away, sipping his drink. He disappeared upstairs.

Frankie gave Kelly a *what's with him* look and then slid on his sunglasses. He linked arms with her as they walked across the glossy hardwood floor to the slider and stepped out onto the expansive deck.

"This place must be costing her a fortune," he said, taking in the view of the beach and water.

"I'm sure it is." Kelly joined Frankie in taking in the breathtaking view. It never got old even to her, who was born and raised in Lucky Cove. Watching the waves crash and the salty water lap up onto the pristine beach was one thing she missed most when she lived in the city.

"Too bad Caroline is away. When she gets back, we all have to go out to dinner. Sans the business partner and her boy toy. Speaking of the business partner, where is she?"

"I don't know. Guess she's not too far since Smith is here. Hey, I have an idea."

Frankie arched a brow.

"Let's go down to the beach." The sun's rays were still strong, and Kelly wanted to enjoy a short walk before dinner. She popped up and slipped off her flip-flops; carrying them, she walked to the staircase. She was ready to get some sand between her toes.

"Hey, where are you two going?" Becky called from the railing.

"For a walk. Come join us!" Kelly waved, and Becky nodded. She dashed down the stairs to catch up with them. The three cousins linked arms and walked along the beach. On their short walk, they easily fell into conversation like the old days.

Dusk was setting and the air was cooler by the time the three of them returned to the house. They hadn't realized how long they'd walked. When they reached the deck, Jessica opened a bottle of wine, and Smith was adding the steaks to the grill. Kelly and Frankie set the table while Becky slipped on a cardigan.

"There's extra sweaters inside if you need one, Kell." Becky topped off her wineglass.

"Thanks." Kelly wasn't chilly yet; though, once nightfall happened, the temperatures dropped by the water. Maybe she should have brought a wrap.

Smith plated the steaks and told everyone to come to the table. They all sat to enjoy the meal.

"So, how did you two meet?" Kelly looked across the table at Jessica and Smith, who from observation didn't seem like a couple. There was no display of affection, not even a modest display like holding hands, throughout the evening. It had seemed Smith was more interested in his drink than his girlfriend.

Smith and Jessica looked at each other and then turned their gazes on Kelly. "At a cocktail party at an art gallery opening," Jessica said.

"We both reached for the last stuffed mushroom," Smith added before he ate his last bite of steak, and he washed it down with a gulp of his scotch.

"We just hit it off, didn't we?" Jessica looked adoringly at Smith, but Kelly wasn't buying it. Something was off.

"Dinner was simply delicious." Becky pushed her plate away. "I ate way too much."

"We're not done. We have s'mores to make and Frankie's dessert." Kelly sipped her water. Because she was driving home, she'd passed on the wine. She'd seen the effects of drinking and driving firsthand ten years ago. A chill zipped through her body at the thought of a friend's life-changing accident.

"I don't think I have any room left to eat another bite." Jessica stood and lifted her plate and utensils. "But I'm going to do my best and make room."

"Here, let me help." Kelly stood and lifted her plate and utensils too. She followed Jessica inside to the kitchen. "This is a lovely house."

"We got lucky in renting it, since Becky decided at the last minute she wanted to spend the summer out on the island." Jessica opened the dishwasher and set the dishes and utensils in it. Her auburn hair was cut in a severely angled bob above her shoulders. It was a sharp contrast to the boho maxi dress she wore with a sensible pair of Birkenstocks. "Your uncle Ralph helped us get this place. I hear he's a big deal out here."

Well, if you listened to Ralph Blake talk about himself, then yes, he was a big deal. Kelly supposed he was a mover and a shaker in their corner of the world, given he had grown his real estate development business over thirty years.

"You could say that," Kelly said.

A commotion out on the deck drew Kelly's attention away from the conversation. She hurried to the slider with Jessica behind her. A loud, garbled voice boomed in the darkness, and it was coming from the deck's staircase.

The top of a head appeared before the whole person came into view as Kelly and Jessica stepped out onto the deck. The man unlatched the gate, and as his foot raised to step onto the decking, it dropped, and he stumbled forward, landing on his hands. Becky and Frankie rushed to his aid and helped him stand up.

Kelly recognized him. He was Todd Wilson, a friend of Becky's.

"What on earth are you doing here?" Becky wrapped an arm around his side and led him from the stairs. Smart move considering he appeared drunk and clumsy.

"I'm here to get what I'm owed." Todd's words slurred. "You owe me, Becky. Owe me big-time."

"This isn't the time for this. You need to leave." Jessica had pushed past Kelly and inserted herself between Todd and Becky. While he appeared shaky, she was 100 percent steady on her feet. "Now!"

Todd stretched his neck forward so his face was closer to hers and blinked several times. "I don't work for you." He swung around, nearly striking Jessica, pointing at Becky.

She pulled back and hissed, "You're making a fool out of yourself."

Todd ignored Jessica. "You, Becky, you stole Define Beauty from me and gave it to her. How could you?"

Becky's mouth fell open, and her fingers touched her lips. "Todd, please don't do this." Her voice was soft and pleading.

Smith stepped forward with his hand extended. "You heard Jessica; it's time to leave."

Todd pulled back and nearly lost his balance again. "I'm not done. I...I demand to be paid...when you sell to Chantelle. Do you understand, Becky?"

Kelly's head cocked sideways. What was Todd talking about? Chantelle? Her mind raced to place the name. It was a vast global beauty company that owned many of the biggest brands in the industry. Was Becky selling to them? If so, why hadn't she mentioned it before? Like during their lunch date?

"That's it, you're out of here." Smith reached for Todd again and gripped his arm.

Todd resisted, but he was no match for Smith, who towered over him and looked like he worked out regularly. Their scuffle prompted some colorful language from both men, but Smith got Todd down the stairs, handling him a bit roughly.

"Don't hurt him," Becky cried from the railing.

"If he gets hurt, it's his own fault." Jessica had come up behind Becky and rested her hands on her shoulders.

"I hate seeing him like this." Becky pulled away from Jessica's hold. "It's all my fault, isn't it?"

"No. You never promised him anything. Look how he's behaving. Can you imagine being in a partnership with him?" Jessica moved to Becky's side and leaned on the railing. "He's weak."

"It sounds like he feels betrayed," Kelly said, earning her a glare from Jessica.

"Beck, this is another reason you should sell. Todd will always have his hand out." Jessica walked away from Becky, and on her way past Kelly, she shook her head. Kelly recognized the move. It was one of disgust. But Kelly wasn't sure if Jessica was disgusted with her or with Todd.

"Hey, let's finish cleaning up." Frankie moved back to the table and gathered the remaining plates.

"Good idea." Clearing the table gave Kelly something to do while she digested everything that had gone down, not only at dinner but throughout the day. Who would have thought her cousin arriving in Lucky Cove would stir up so much drama?

As she set the glasses in the dishwasher, she had so many questions for Becky but kept them to herself. At least for now.

Frankie wiped the counter and then disposed of the towel. "I should get going. How about you?"

"What about dessert and the s'mores?" Kelly rested her palms on the counter and looked out to the deck where Becky sat on a lounge chair, checking her phone.

Frankie shrugged. "Not tonight. The vibe has gotten weird."

Kelly nodded. "I guess you're right. I'm going to stay a little longer, though."

"Stay out of it," Frankie said as he grabbed his thermal bag.

"I don't know what you're talking about." She hated that her cousin knew her so well. He knew she would stick her nose in Becky's business the moment they were alone.

Frankie gave an exaggerated nod. "Ah-ha."

"You don't know me as well as you think."

Frankie leaned in and kissed her on the cheek. "Yes, I do." He turned and stepped out onto the deck to say good night and then left. A few minutes later, Jessica disappeared with Smith, leaving Kelly and Becky alone in the living room. Becky had come inside and relaxed on the sofa with her third glass of wine. Kelly settled next to her, ready for a heart-to-heart.

Darn Frankie for being right.

Kelly couldn't help but ask about Todd's claim. Was her cousin selling her company?

"It's true. I've had an offer from Chantelle. They're offering a lot of money. A lot." She dipped her head and sipped her wine.

"Do you want to sell?"

Becky shrugged. "I don't know. It's an incredible offer. They can do things for Define that will take me years to achieve." She took another drink of her wine. "Jessica is encouraging me to sign the contract. It's one reason I came out here for the summer. I needed to unwind, recharge, and get some perspective. Selling is a huge decision."

"I understand. Tell me, why does Todd claim you owe him money?"

"When we worked together..."

"He was a makeup artist trainer, right?"

"Yes. We were close. Really close. Like best friends close. There were a lot of late nights eating Thai and thinking about our futures. We brainstormed what the ideal cosmetics company would be like over too many glasses of"—she lifted her glass, indicating those conversations happened while drinking. Well, that helped Kelly understand why Todd thought he was rightfully part owner of the business. "Though, we signed no papers or even had a verbal agreement. We were just batting around ideas."

"I'm sure it will all work out. If he continues to pursue his claim, I'm sure you have attorneys to handle the matter." Kelly didn't have an attorney on retainer as she expected her cousin did. What Kelly had was her sister, and more than once she'd asked her for legal advice. There was that time she was accused of murder, that other time when a customer sued her for emotional distress, and then there was that freak-out moment when she thought she would lose her inheritance. Yes, she knew lawyers came in handy. Well, except the one she broke up with. No, she would not go there. "It's getting late. I should go."

"Despite how the evening ended, I'm so happy you and Frankie came for dinner. It was like old times." Becky stood, setting her glass on the coffee table. Her hand swept by the pocket of her cardigan, and she then reached into the pocket. "Huh." She pulled out a folded piece of paper. As she read it, her brows furrowed and she bit down on her lower lip. Without saying a word, she slipped the note back into the pocket.

Kelly lingered for a moment, hoping Becky would share what was on the note. But she didn't. "How about we have coffee tomorrow before the boutique opens?"

Becky looked distracted. It took a second for Kelly's question to register. "Sure. Doug's?"

"Perfect." Kelly turned and walked to the entry, where she grabbed her tote. She glanced back at Becky, who had swiped up her glass and padded into the kitchen.

At lunch earlier in the day, Kelly had told Becky that she was worried about her and that concern had been primarily about Terry. But having spent several hours with the other people in her cousin's life, she was now more concerned. Why was Becky being so secretive? Something wasn't right.

CHAPTER FOUR

The next morning, Kelly woke an hour earlier to get her run in before meeting Becky for coffee. She'd planned it so she'd stop at Doug's Variety Store on her way back to her apartment. Inside the shop, she ordered a large iced coffee and an egg white sandwich.

"There you go." Breena handed Kelly her order. Working at Doug's was her other part-time job. This morning she looked tired, and she wasn't her usual perky self. "Anything else?"

"No. This should do it." Kelly snatched a napkin from the dispenser.

"Have you heard from Terry?"

Kelly shook her head.

"I read her horoscope for today. Do you want to know what it said?"

Kelly shook her head again. She knew the horoscope hadn't caused yesterday's problem, but having the unpleasant prediction hadn't helped either. Kelly didn't want to think of what today's horoscope said.

Breena pouted.

"See you later." Kelly turned and walked past the long line of caffeine-depleted early risers. She made her way to a table and sat. Settled, she checked her messages first before devouring her breakfast. Her run had been intense thanks to a new playlist. Staring at her phone, she frowned. No new messages. It seemed as if Terry had ghosted her. She unwrapped her sandwich and took a bite. Then she washed it down with a drink of her iced coffee. By the time she was half-done with the sandwich, she had checked her phone again. Becky was ten minutes late. Kelly sent off a text. She tapped her finger on the table while the rest of her sandwich went cold. Becky had always been punctual. Something wasn't right. Kelly had been having that feeling a lot since yesterday.

She reached for her phone and checked her texts again. She scrolled. Nothing new.

Not knowing who would open the boutique, Kelly couldn't wait any longer for Becky to show, so she decided to drive out to the beach house and check on her.

A commotion drew Kelly's attention to the door. Two middle-aged women huffed loudly as a man stumbled into the shop. He removed his mirrored sunglasses and bowed, apologizing for bumping into them. Kelly immediately recognized Todd.

He looked as if he had a hangover and desperately needed a strong black coffee. He straightened and held the door open for the women, who passed by him muttering something unintelligible. He gave a sharp wave and then continued into the shop. His steps were unsteady as he approached the counter. He'd looked right at Kelly but didn't acknowledge her. Her guess was he didn't remember much of last night. He was served quickly by Breena, and on his way to the exit, Kelly called out to him.

Todd looked confused, disoriented, and in need of a couple of aspirins. "Do I know you?"

"Not really. I'm Becky Quinn's cousin, Kelly. We kind of met last night." Kelly pushed aside her cup and sandwich. She hoped he'd sit, and she could ask him about the claims he made after barging into the dinner party.

"Huh. Last night, you said?" He squinted. "Right. Right. I went to Becky's house. You were there?"

Kelly nodded.

"Don't remember. Huh. Was there anyone else there?" He took a long drink of his coffee.

"Oh, yes. Our cousin, Frankie. Smith and Jessica."

Todd grimaced.

"You don't like Jessica, do you?"

"There's not much to like about the Prada-wearing snake." He slid on his sunglasses. "I warned Becky about her. You should be careful around her, too." Before Kelly could ask why, Todd walked away and exited the shop, bumping into another customer on his way out.

She grabbed her coffee, tossed what was left of her sandwich, and hurried out of the shop. It seemed the beauty business was as cutthroat as the fashion industry. From her days at Bishop's department store, she knew a few designer-clad snakes herself. She hoped Todd's assessment of Becky's friend and business partner was wrong.

* * * *

Minutes later, she arrived at the rental house and parked in the driveway. Unlike last night, the place looked quiet. There were no lights on, no sign of anyone home. But Kelly noticed two vehicles parked in the driveway.

She went to the front door and knocked. When there was no answer, she headed around to the back deck and climbed the stairs. Perhaps Becky was sunning on the deck and had lost track of time.

When she reached the top of the steps, she found the deck empty. She started for the slider door. But the sounds of the water lapping onto the beach and the seagulls flying above pulled her toward the railing.

The view was more breathtaking in the early morning hours. There was something special about this time of the day on the beach. She shook her head. Who was she kidding?

Being on the beach was special all the time. How had she gone ten years without this?

As she scanned the beach, she noticed someone already out on the sand. It looked like that person wasn't wasting any time enjoying a lazy day at the shore. Then what she was looking at finally clicked in her brain.

The woman wasn't sunbathing.

She was fully dressed and even wearing a cardigan. Her hair was the same color as Becky's.

Kelly's heart slammed against her chest and her mouth went dry when she realized she wasn't looking at someone who looked like her cousin.

It was Becky!

CHAPTER FIVE

She rushed to the stairs and descended the steps so fast she almost tripped—twice. Her eyesight blurred with tears as she raced toward the log where they'd planned on making s'mores last night.

Kelly came to a hard stop at the sight of Becky sprawled out. Becky's usually sparkling blue eyes seemed to stare off to the ocean, and a look of horror was pasted on her face.

"Becky!"

Kelly's stomach lurched. Oh, goodness, she was going to be sick. But she couldn't. She had to help her cousin.

She dropped to her knees beside her cousin and checked for a pulse. There was none.

No, no, no. You can't be dead. You can't be.

Kelly's mind raced to recall the CPR training she took a lifetime ago. Open airway. Begin chest compressions. Bring her cousin back to life.

She tilted Becky's head backward slightly to raise her chin and then positioned her hands on top of each other on Becky's chest.

With each compression and rescue breath, Kelly willed her cousin to open her eyes. Yet Becky remained lifeless and when checked, still not breathing.

Adrenaline pumped through Kelly's body, but the surge was depleting, making each press of Becky's chest harder. She needed help to continue CPR. Jessica could help her. Why wasn't she there trying to help Becky?

Kelly's gaze shifted from the house to her cousin back to the house. Why wasn't anyone there helping them? She sniffled and raised a hand from Becky's chest to wipe away the tears streaming down her face as reality hit—Becky was dead.

No! She had to continue.

She repositioned her hands and began compressions again.

"Hey! What's going on?" someone called out.

Kelly looked up into the direction of the voice. It was a man who looked like he was out for a morning jog on the beach.

"Yes! Call 9-1-1. My cousin isn't breathing and she has no pulse," Kelly said between rescue breaths.

The man jogged over to Kelly and dropped to his knees.

"What are you doing? Call for help!" She returned to chest compressions.

The man checked Becky's pulse and then placed a hand on Kelly's shoulder. "I'm sorry, your cousin is gone."

"What? No. She's not. I'm doing CPR. I can bring her back."

"I'm sorry, you can't."

"How do you know? Who are you?"

"Dr. Arnold Linden. I'm an ER doctor. Believe me, your cousin is gone." He stood, retrieved a phone from his pocket.

"We have to save her!" Kelly wasn't ready to give up like the stranger. She had to help her cousin. Like when they were kids and Kelly had helped Becky after she'd fallen from her bike. Becky had bruised her knee and twisted her ankle. Not too far from home, Kelly settled Becky by a tree and then biked home to get her mom. What she wouldn't give to have her mother there by her side. She did a few more chest compressions with breaths, and yet there was no change. The stranger was right—Becky was gone.

"I'll call 9-1-1 for you. What's your name?"

"Kelly Quinn," she said as she removed her hands from Becky's chest. She leaned back on her heels and sucked in ragged breaths as she stared at Becky's body. She shivered. Maybe it was the cool salt air or shock settling in. She wasn't sure. Her gaze fixed on Becky's face. What was Becky doing on the beach wearing the same clothes she wore last night? How long had she been lying there?

She blew out a deep breath, hoping it would steady her breathing and her mind. In the smallest fragment of clarity, a thought pushed through her muddled mind—where was Jessica? She glanced at the beach house. Was Jessica inside? Asleep, perhaps? Or...Kelly's gaze darted back to her cousin and then back to the house. Had something happened to Jessica? She scrambled to her feet.

As she stood, she noticed a piece of paper by Becky's body.

Meet me at midnight on the beach. We need to talk.

"Is there someone I can call for you?" Dr. Linden asked with his phone still in his hand.

Kelly looked up from the note. Staring at the doctor, she realized she'd have to call her family and tell them about Becky. Her chin trembled as a wave of sadness slammed her. "I...I really don't know. I...I have to find Jessica. She should be in the house." As she stepped away from her cousin's body, something shiny caught her eye. It was a necklace beside Becky's hand.

"I'll stay with your cousin." Dr. Linden put his phone away. "Let me know if you need any help."

Kelly pulled her attention from the necklace and nodded. She attempted to say thank you, but the words caught in her throat. She worried she'd dissolve into a sobbing mess if she tried to speak. Turning, she headed toward the staircase.

On the deck, she hurried to the slider but stopped. Could she even get into the house? Was Jessica inside? Was she alive? Hurt? There was only one way to find out. She grabbed the handle and tugged. The door slid open easily, and she poked her head inside.

"Hello! Jessica!"

She waited for a response. There was none.

Darn!

She scanned the first floor. The open concept gave her a clear sight line to the front of the house, and she didn't see Jessica. Then she looked to the staircase. She had to check the upper floor. Careful not to touch anything, she entered the house and made her way to the stairs.

When she reached the landing, she looked down the hall in both directions. Becky's bedroom door was open, and she peered in. The bed appeared not to have been slept in. A sudden wave of grief hit her hard, and she shook it off. She couldn't succumb to the heaviness of sadness she felt. Back out in the hall, she walked to the next door—Jessica's bedroom. Or, at least she thought so.

She grasped the knob of the closed door and then hesitated. *Smith.* She'd forgotten about him. The last time she saw him, he was going upstairs. What if Smith was in there with Jessica? What if they weren't sleeping? What if she—no, she couldn't worry about any potential awkwardness.

Her cousin was dead. If there was a momentary embarrassment for them, so be it.

She twisted the knob and opened the door. Her gaze landed on the queen-sized bed, and Jessica was asleep. Alone. Kelly pressed her palm to her heart. *What a relief.*

Before she moved from the doorway, she glanced around the room. It appeared Jessica wasn't a neat freak like her business partner. Instead, she appeared to be living out of her suitcases. Three of them were open and scattered throughout the room.

Jessica twisted in the bed, startling Kelly.

"Jessica. Jessica, wake up." Kelly hurried to the bed. "Come on, you have to get up. Something terrible has happened."

Jessica moaned and tugged at her covers.

Kelly leaned forward and shook Jessica's shoulders. "Wake up!"

Jessica moaned again, and her eyes fluttered open. It took a few seconds before they were fully open, and she registered someone was in her bedroom shaking her. Her neck corded, and her eyes went from sleepy to panicked.

"It's me, Kelly."

"What the devil are you doing in my room?" Jessica pulled herself from Kelly's hold and struggled to sit up.

"It's Becky. She's dead." Saying the words out loud triggered another wave of grief, and it threatened to undo Kelly completely. She dropped down to the mattress and ran her fingers through her hair.

"What did you say? Dead? How? Where?"

The rapid fire of questions overwhelmed Kelly, who was sinking into a state of shock. The surge of adrenaline from finding Becky's body had vanished, leaving her to deal with the horror of her discovery, and it was devastating.

She wanted to answer Jessica, but she couldn't. Her throat constricted with sorrow. Any attempt to speak would result in gibberish.

"No! You have to be mistaken!"

Jessica flung the covers off and swung her legs over the side of the bed. The motion was swift, and she suddenly stopped, grabbing her head with her hand.

Oh, dear goodness. She was having a stroke or something. Kelly reached out to help steady her. "Are...are you okay?"

"I'm not sure." Jessica stood and reached for her short terrycloth robe. "It doesn't matter. I have to see Becky."

"It's probably not a good idea." Kelly was speaking from firsthand experience. She would have loved nothing more than to erase the image of seeing her cousin's lifeless body on the beach.

Jessica slipped the robe on over her graphic T-shirt and pajama shorts. "I have to help her."

"I'm so sorry, but it's too late." Kelly pressed her lips into a thin line. "Believe me, I tried."

"Where is she?" Jessica's tone was demanding and impatient. "Where?"

Before Kelly could answer, Jessica blew out a disgusted breath and was out the door.

"We should wait for the police." Kelly popped up and chased after Jessica. She caught up with her downstairs. "The police are on their way."

Jessica spun around. "I have to see her. Where is she?"

"On the beach. By a log."

Jessica whirled around and ran to the slider. She stepped out onto the deck.

"Jessica! Stop!" Kelly followed, and when she reached Jessica on the deck, she grabbed her arm. "You shouldn't go down there. The police need to investigate. We don't want to disturb the scene." At least not any more than Kelly had when she rushed to her cousin and attempted to revive her.

"You can't stop me," Jessica snapped as she yanked her arm back.

"Do you seriously want to compromise the scene?" Kelly placed her hands on her hips. She was projecting a firm stance to Jessica, but the reality was that she feared the anguish rippling through her would swallow her up if she didn't ground herself.

"Scene? You think she was murdered?"

"I don't know."

Jessica looked down at the beach. "Who's that man?"

"Dr. Linden. He's an ER doctor who was jogging by and stopped to help."

Jessica turned and faced Kelly. "He couldn't save her?"

Kelly shook her head as Jessica moved to the sectional and dropped to a cushion.

"What happened after I left last night?"

"I don't know. After the dishes were cleared, Smith and I went to my bedroom." Jessica stared off into the distance. Her gaze fixed on the water. "The last time I saw Becky was when we said good night."

"When did Smith leave?"

Jessica shrugged. "I don't know. Much of last night is foggy. I'm not sure why. I didn't have that much to drink."

"You didn't hear Becky go out at midnight?"

Jessica shook her head. "No. No. Wait"—she raised her forefinger and pointed—"why are you asking all these questions? Have you been deputized between last night and now?"

Kelly didn't miss the snarkiness in Jessica's tone. "I'm trying to figure out what happened to my cousin. You were here last night. You should know something."

Jessica jumped up. "Wait, are you accusing me of harming her? How dare you? Becky was my friend."

"Lucky Cove Police," a male voice called from the bottom of the staircase.

Kelly recognized the voice and was grateful that her childhood friend Gabe Donovan was the responding officer. Though her stomach knotted at the thought of who the detective assigned to the case could be.

"Kelly?" Gabe arrived on the deck. Finding her cousin's body had put all of Kelly's senses on high alert, so she heard the subtle tone in his voice that finished the sentence for him. *Kelly, you found another dead body?*

"It's Becky. She's down there." Kelly pointed over the railing, but she couldn't look. She'd seen enough.

"Your cousin?" Gabe's brows pinched, and he moved toward the railing. Leaning forward, he looked down at the beach. "I'm so sorry, Kell."

Kelly only nodded; if she spoke, she'd start sobbing again, and that wouldn't help anyone.

Gabe turned back to Kelly and gave a remorseful look, his baby blue eyes clouded with sadness and his lips set in a grim line. He stroked her arm to comfort her. When she gave a weak smile, signaling she was doing okay, he pulled back and shifted into his official mode.

"And you are?" he asked Jessica.

"Jessica Barron." She composed herself, squaring her shoulders and lifting her chin. "I'm Becky's business partner and friend."

"We're going to need statements from both of you," Gabe said.

"Of course. Should we go inside and wait?" Kelly knew the drill because she'd been at one too many crime scenes since moving back to Lucky Cove.

Another officer who had walked out to the beach to secure the scene called up to Gabe, requesting him to come down.

Gabe acknowledged the request, and before he left, he said, "Yes. Please wait inside. And don't discuss the incident."

Well, he was a little late with that warning. But Kelly kept mum. She turned and gestured for Jessica to enter the house with her. Jessica heaved an enormous sigh, as if it were a big inconvenience to go indoors while the police investigated her friend's death.

"I can't believe she's dead." Jessica broke from Kelly and walked to the kitchen. At the peninsula, she rested her palms on the countertop. "You saw her. What happened?" Clearly, she was ignoring Gabe's instructions, and it didn't bother Kelly at all. She wanted to gather as much information as she could to figure out what happened to Becky.

"I really don't know." Kelly sat on a stool at the peninsula. "She may have hit her head on the log. Though there wasn't a lot of blood. Has she been feeling well?"

"As far as I know." Jessica pushed off the peninsula and moved to the coffee station. "I need coffee." She inserted a pod into the single-serve machine, slid a cup on the drip tray, and pressed the power button. While the machine brewed the coffee, she turned to face Kelly. "She's been tired, but it's because she's been working so much. Coming here was supposed to give her a break. Not kill her."

Kelly lowered her gaze to the granite counter. The flecks of color mesmerized her and allowed her mind to stop thinking. It was a welcome reprieve from the nightmare she was currently living. Sure, she had found other people dead—murdered, in fact—but this time, it was a family member.

Her cell phone chimed. The ringtone was Pepper's. Kelly pulled the phone from her leggings' side pocket and tapped on it to accept the call.

"Hey, Pepper." Kelly didn't even attempt to sound upbeat.

"What's going on? Did Terry quit? Clive just called. He went to Doug's for coffee and saw that the boutique isn't open. Where are you?"

The rapid fire of questions overwhelmed Kelly. Her shoulders sagged. The weight of the day was already too much to bear. All she wanted to do was to crawl into bed and pull the covers over her head.

"I don't know if she quit. She hasn't returned my calls. Look, Pepper, something's happened." She inhaled a deep breath and then broke the news of Becky's death. Oh, gosh. She had to call Frankie and Caroline with the news.

"How awful! I'm so sorry. Sweetie, don't worry about the boutique."

Sweetie.

The simple little word had Kelly undone. Her granny used to call her sweetie. She dropped her head in her hand and cried. She missed her granny, but maybe it was for the best Martha wasn't around anymore. Even though Becky hadn't been her grandchild, she loved Becky and treated her as one of her own. The loss would have devastated her.

"I'm getting dressed as we speak. I'll open the boutique and call Breena to see if she can come in for a few hours. You don't have to worry about anything."

Kelly swallowed and then lifted her head. "Thank you."

"I know you're grieving right now and in shock, which means you're probably not thinking clearly."

Kelly knew where the conversation was going. A gentle reminder was about to be given to her.

"Let the police do their job. Please stay out of the investigation. Okay, sweetie?"

"I'll do my best," Kelly promised and then disconnected the call. She set the phone on the counter and wiped her eyes dry with the back of her hands.

Jessica was leaning against the counter, sipping her coffee. She looked calm and collected while Kelly was dissolving into a puddle of tears at the mere mention of a nickname. Had Jessica moved on from the shock of finding her business partner dead to calculating the options available to her? Would she inherit Becky's half of the business? Would she sell Define Beauty like Becky said she wanted to?

Kelly blew out a breath. "I think I need another coffee."

"Help yourself." Jessica nodded to the basket of pods.

"Thanks." She stood and walked around the counter to the coffee maker. She selected a pod and dropped it in the machine. "Thank goodness for these things, right? Though, maybe caffeine isn't a good idea right now. My mind is racing with so many things. Like, I have to call my family and break the news. I guess you'll be calling Smith. Just curious, what time did he leave last night?" She pulled a mug off the cup tree and set it on the drip tray.

"I'm not sure…wait, you already asked me that."

"You didn't hear Becky leave the house to go out to the beach?"

"I told you I didn't. You really think I had something to do with what happened to her?" Jessica set her mug on the countertop with a thump. "Perhaps you should ask your employee, Terry Carlisle, and find out where she was last night."

"You really think she's dangerous enough to have harmed Becky?"

"I don't know! What I do know is that I'd like for you to leave." Jessica's head cocked sideways, and her lips tightened into a severe line.

"I can't." Kelly pressed the power button, and the coffee maker hummed to life.

"Then I'm going to my room. I don't have to answer any of your questions."

"But you have to answer mine." Another familiar voice to Kelly had her and Jessica looking to the deck's slider door. There stood Detective Marcy Wolman. "And my first one is to Kelly. Why are you asking questions?"

CHAPTER SIX

Of all the detectives on the Lucky Cove Police Department, it had to be Marcy Wolman who was on duty that morning. Didn't the woman ever take a day off?

"I'm asking questions because I found my cousin dead this morning." Kelly usually would have regretted speaking to the detective in such a harsh tone, but not that day. If anyone thought she would sit by and not ask questions, turn over every rock, and pursue the truth about Becky's death, they were delusional. She realized the cause of death could very well be accidental. If so, then that's what happened, and she'd accept it. If not, she would make sure the person responsible was caught and put away for a very long time.

"I'm sorry for your loss, Kelly." Wolman's tone softened as she entered the house. Dressed in khaki pants and a lightweight denim blazer over a V-neck shirt, she looked professional and competent as always. Her dark hair was pulled back into a sleek bun, and she wore simple stud earrings. The detective had worked the murder cases Kelly had found herself entwined in, so maybe she never took a day off, and then there was the whole thing of her being Kelly's ex-boyfriend's sister.

"Thank you." Kelly's gaze flicked away because tears welled in her eyes, and she didn't want to break down in front of the detective.

Wolman gave Kelly a moment to compose herself by turning her attention to Jessica. "Is there a place where I can speak to each of you privately?"

"There's a room downstairs. It's an office." Jessica pointed to the staircase. "You can use it."

Wolman nodded. "Kelly, let's go downstairs."

Kelly composed herself and then walked away from the coffee maker. On her way past the peninsula, she grabbed her phone and walked to the staircase with Wolman. They reached the lower level, which was as sleek as the upper floors. Definitely not a typical basement by any means. The room straight ahead had its door open, and it appeared to be the office Jessica referred to. Inside the room, a glass-top desk dominated the space. Along one wall were minimally decorated bookshelves, and a slider led out to a paved patio.

Wolman took the seat at the desk and pulled out a notepad and pen from her jacket pocket. Kelly settled on the white sofa.

Wolman asked for details that led up to finding Becky's body. Kelly began at the beginning—from the time she left Doug's when Becky was a no-show.

The detective listened and jotted notes. She was still writing when Kelly wrapped up her statement. "I couldn't help but notice the note that was by Beck…Becky's body. Someone had wanted to meet her at midnight."

Wolman looked up from her notepad, and her brows were raised.

"Also, I saw a necklace by her hand. She wasn't wearing that yesterday. Besides, she preferred silver jewelry. The necklace must belong to the person she met last night."

"I appreciate your insight, Kelly. I also appreciate the fact that you will stay out of my investigation."

Kelly inched to the edge of the cushion, ready to object. But Wolman raised her palm.

"I assure you I will do everything within my power to find out what happened to Ms. Quinn." Wolman lowered her hand. "Please trust me."

Kelly chewed on her lower lip. Wolman looked sincere. Besides, what choice did she have?

"I do trust you. It's so hard to believe I'll never see her again." She raised her hand and waved it at her face, hoping to stave off another round of tears. She would need an ice pack for her face and a miracle cream to get rid of the eye puffiness. With the tears at bay, she cleared her throat. Breaking down wouldn't help the situation. "Yesterday, Whitney Mulhern rudely interrupted our lunch. She was furious with Becky."

"What about?" Wolman jotted something on her pad.

"Becky wouldn't tell me. Then last night, her, I guess now-former friend, Todd Wilson, showed up drunk and demanding Becky compensate him for his part in creating Define Beauty."

"Isn't Ms. Barron the business partner?" Wolman asked.

"She is. From what Becky told me last night, she and Todd hung out a lot when they were coworkers and brainstormed ideas for a business.

I guess he took that as being a part of the company. Smith had to escort him off the property. This morning I saw him at Doug's, and he barely remembered last night." She wished she could get so lucky and forget the moment of finding Becky's body on the beach.

"He's still in town?"

"I guess so. I don't know where he went after he left Doug's. There's something else you probably should know." Kelly hesitated. "Yesterday, when Becky and Jessica came into the boutique, Terry Carlisle was working. Turns out, the three of them know each other. Well, at least online." Kelly described the incident, which led Wolman to write more notes.

Kelly leaned back and formed her own theories about what happened on the beach last night. The more she thought about what she'd shared, the more she realized that several people had a motive to harm her cousin. That meant it was more than likely that Becky was murdered.

"Kelly...Kelly," Wolman said.

Kelly snapped out of her thoughts and locked her gaze on Wolman. "My cousin was murdered last night, wasn't she?"

Wolman closed her notepad and clasped her hands together. "At this point in the investigation, I am unable to label Ms. Quinn's death as a homicide. It could have been an accident. Perhaps Becky had too much to drink and fell, striking her head on the log."

"Becky wasn't the type of person to drink so much she couldn't stand up." Kelly heard the defensiveness in her voice but didn't care. Though she did remember that Becky had had three glasses of wine before Kelly left.

"When was the last time you saw your cousin?"

"Before yesterday? A couple of years ago in person. We video chatted at least once a month."

"People can change. Was she under an unusual amount of stress?"

Kelly pressed her lips together to keep herself from lashing out at the detective. The truth was, she wasn't really angry with Wolman. She was mad at herself for letting so much time go between visits with Becky.

"She was stressed. There had been a nasty breakup recently. Last night she told me a huge company, Chantelle, wants to buy Define Beauty, but she was hesitant. Though Jessica was in favor of it. You know, she says she doesn't remember much from last night, and she was in a deep sleep when I found her. Yet she hadn't had a lot to drink at dinner. Could she have been drugged?"

"Kelly, I appreciate your insight and all the information you've given me. However, let me reiterate: I don't want you to interfere in my investigation like you've done in the past. Am I clear?"

Before Kelly could say anything, Wolman dismissed her and went back to her notepad to review her notes. Perhaps it was for the best because Kelly couldn't promise anything. After all, Becky was family.

An officer escorted Kelly back upstairs and directed her to sit and wait on the sofa. He then requested Jessica follow him downstairs. Kelly tried to get comfortable like she had the night before when she and Becky talked there on the sofa, but it wasn't happening. Instead, a numbness settled over her body. It allowed her to view what was happening around her with a detachment she hadn't thought possible.

The Crime Scene Unit was out on the beach doing their job of collecting and documenting evidence. Like the note and necklace she'd seen beside Becky. Then Becky would be taken away and examined to determine the cause of her death. Would they find any evidence of a struggle that indicated her death wasn't an accident? Or, could Wolman had been right about Becky drinking too much and falling?

The officer returned upstairs and informed Kelly she could leave. Relieved, she stood and left the house as quickly as she could. A sob caught in her throat as she approached her Jeep. She shook her head. Becky couldn't be dead. She couldn't be. Even though she saw the body and gave her statement, she hoped it had all been a mistake. Any moment Becky would appear, saying she was just taking a nap.

So, when she heard her name called out from the side of the house, her heart skipped a beat, and she was about to scold her cousin for scaring her. When she turned, her hope faded. It was Gabe and not Becky.

She swore she'd heard Becky's voice.

She swallowed hard and did her best to hide her disappointment. Gabe jogged toward her and offered to drive her home. It was a sweet gesture and one she probably should have accepted, but instead, she declined.

Kelly wanted to be alone. She needed the time to collect herself before making the dreaded phone calls to her family. Her stomach ached at the thought. She drove straight back to the boutique, parked her Jeep, and stalled. Going inside, she'd have to face Pepper and Breena. She couldn't handle their sympathy. She'd undoubtedly dissolve into a puddle of tears. And she didn't want to in front of them. She grabbed her purse off the passenger seat and considered what to do. She really wanted to locate Todd and find out if he returned to the beach house after being tossed out by Smith. While Jessica was shining a spotlight on Terry, Kelly's gut told her Todd could be more dangerous. Not only had he felt betrayed by Becky, but there was also a lot of money at stake if Define Beauty was sold. Money he seemed to believe he was entitled to.

She pushed open the door and stepped out and headed around the building toward Main Street. A gentle breeze swept by, and she inhaled a deep breath. Too bad her mood was too dark to enjoy the mild July day.

Since Todd had been in Doug's early in the morning, she suspected he'd stayed overnight in town. There were several inns along Main Street with a dozen motels closer to the beach.

Where to begin?

Since she was on Main Street, she might as well start there. Hoofing it from inn to inn wasn't appealing, though. Neither was finding Becky's body. So, she headed in the direction of the Captain's Inn. The tidy little Victorian had a quirky charm to it and was always booked in season.

Not halfway to the inn, she saw the last person she wanted to run into approaching her.

Mark Lambert, aka Smokin' McHottie, Esq. Not his official title, but it's what popped into her head when they'd first met. It was kind of like a meet-cute from the dozens of romantic comedies she enjoyed. He had represented one of her customers who sued her. The elderly woman believed an item she purchased from the boutique was haunted. She claimed there was emotional distress and wanted to be compensated. Truth be told, it was Kelly who suffered pain during that whole ordeal. She was facing a lawsuit she couldn't afford, and the whole haunted thing had risked the boutique's future.

Kelly had gone to Mark's office with walnut muffins to ask for his help in ending the lawsuit. She found out as she was handing him the pastry box that he was allergic to nuts. It wasn't the best introduction. However, he had managed to work out a settlement that kept all parties out of court; it also led to their first date.

However, it hadn't taken long for the hot lawyer to turn lukewarm. Kelly put a hold on those thoughts. She had more important things to focus on than another failed relationship. Like finding Todd.

"Hey, Kelly." Mark halted in front of the Captain's Inn. "Everything okay? You look upset."

Kelly shook her head, and her chin trembled. She wanted to remain stoic, especially in front of Mark, but she couldn't help blurt out what happened. "My cousin Becky is dead. I found her body this morning."

"Oh, my goodness. That's terrible." He closed the space between them, pulling her into an embrace. "I'm so sorry. Finding her must have been awful."

Kelly welcomed the security of Mark's strong hold. She rested her head on his shoulder and squeezed her eyes shut. Would the vision of Becky's body on the beach ever go away? Based on previous experiences with finding dead people, the answer was a firm no. The scene would always be there, tucked away in her mind's eye, and would surface at any moment.

"We were supposed to have coffee this morning."

"What happened?"

Kelly shrugged. "I found her on the beach. It looked like she hit her head on a log."

Mark caressed her back, and her body tingled at the soothing touch. Even though her mind was muddled with grief and anger, she had the wherewithal to recognize she was in a gray area with him at the moment. She removed herself from his hold and put some space between them.

"I'm sorry. This isn't your problem. I'm okay. Really."

"Are you sure? Even though we're not a couple anymore, I still care about you. And I'm always here for you."

She expected he thought his words were comforting. While they were nice and thoughtful, they hadn't erased the things he'd said to her before she broke up with him.

He was there for her until he had to go solo to a luncheon with a bigwig legal firm's senior partner. What he'd really meant was that she embarrassed him and therefore she needed to stay home. *Solo.* The word still irked her. But she knew she couldn't go there again. It wasn't healthy and would only delay her being able to move on. Move on? She wasn't sure when she'd be ready to dip her toes back into the dating pool. At the moment, she couldn't even think about a new relationship. What would she say to the guy? *Hi, my name is Kelly, and I just found my dead cousin's body on the beach. Want to get a drink?* Yeah, that wouldn't send the guy running to the Long Island Expressway.

"Thanks." Kelly nodded, and they stood in awkward silence. *Say something, Kell.* "Don't let me keep you."

"Oh, I'm not in any rush. Are you going into the inn?" He pointed to the house.

"Yes. I'm looking for someone."

"Who?"

"Todd Wilson. He was a friend of my cousin."

Mark lowered his gaze for a moment. "Would you like me to come with you while you break the news to him?"

"Oh...oh... I'm sure he won't be upset."

"Why not?" His brows furrowed as he gave her a puzzled look.

"He had a falling out with her. Last night, he barged into her house demanding he be paid because he supposedly helped create her company."

Mark tilted his chin. Gone was the puzzled look, and in its place was an all too familiar look. It was like his sister's when she suspected Kelly's curiosity was ratcheting up. "What are you up to?"

"I told you. I'm looking for someone."

"The police must be investigating."

Kelly didn't confirm or deny.

"My sister?"

Kelly didn't confirm or deny.

"You know how she feels about you interfering in her cases."

"How your sister feels isn't my concern. My cousin is dead, and I'm going to find out where exactly Todd was last night around midnight."

"Midnight? How do you know she died then?"

Kelly blew out a breath. She'd already said too much to him. He probably would call his sister and tell her what Kelly was doing. "I really have to go, Mark." She sidestepped around him.

"Kelly, wait. I know there's nothing I can say that will change your mind about tracking this guy down, but is it something you really want to do now? Shouldn't you be with your family at a time like this? Just take a moment to think this out clearly. Take care." He gave a small smile and dotted a kiss on her cheek before walking away.

She looked at the inn and then back at Mark, who disappeared into the building where his office was located. She hated when he was right. She wasn't in the best frame of mind to confront Todd. Maybe she should stop putting off the calls to her sister and her parents. They needed to hear the news from her. She winced. Her stomachache intensified. Tracking down Todd wasn't the most important thing she needed to do. She needed to hear the voices of her family.

CHAPTER SEVEN

The next morning when Kelly woke, she went through the motions of starting a new day. Everything seemed to take twice as long—getting out of bed, dressing, feeding Howard. Her shoulders sagged, her thoughts muddled and her heart heavy with anguish as she stood in the kitchen watching her cat gobble down his breakfast. She glanced at her watch. Normally she'd be eagerly heading out the door for her daily run. She'd dressed for it—even chose her pricey Lululemon leggings as an extra motivator to get going. On her way out of the kitchen, she caught her reflection in the microwave's glass door.

What she saw wasn't pretty. Moping wouldn't get her any answers, and it was far too early in the day for any updates from the police. It was settled. She'd go on her usual three-mile run. Maybe it would clear her head and keep her from crying.

Halfway through the run, she realized she'd been wrong. She'd have to run a marathon to feel even a little better. But she was better than the day before.

When she'd returned to the boutique yesterday after finding Becky's body, Pepper had swooped over her and gone into full-on mothering mode. She made a cup of tea and fixed a sandwich despite Kelly's claim she wasn't hungry. Then Pepper sat beside her while she made the calls to her sister, her parents, and Frankie. A few times when Kelly felt as if she couldn't go on, a gentle squeeze on the arm from Pepper reminded her she was strong and could continue. When the calls were done, Pepper insisted she take the rest of the day off.

The thought of being alone in her apartment with nothing to think about but Becky had seemed to be the worst thing to do, but it turned out Pepper had been right. Like always.

Upstairs, changed into a pair of cutoffs and a tank, she'd curled up on the sofa with a glass of iced tea and an old photo album from her teen years. For hours she stared at the photographs of her, Caroline, Frankie, and Becky. Even her best friend, Liv Moretti, was in some pictures. Taking the trip down memory lane had her smiling and laughing at memories long forgotten. Now they were the most treasured.

After hours of looking through the photo album, she'd had more phone calls to make. The first was to Becky's parents and her siblings. Kelly's father had offered to call his brother, so Kelly didn't have to break the news. She was relieved she didn't have to be the one to tell her aunt and uncle their daughter was dead. Instead, she'd shared with them how much fun Becky and she had catching up over lunch and then dinner on the beach. But by the end of the call, she was exhausted, and they were sobbing.

The whole day had wiped her out emotionally, and since she had no appetite, she'd headed to bed without dinner. But Howard had an appetite thanks to his bottomless pit of a stomach, so she made a pit stop in the kitchen to fill his bowl. Finally, in bed, she cried herself to sleep. Howard must have sensed her despair and felt sorry for her because he'd curled up next to her all night. He hadn't even woken her up with his early morning craziness, which usually included laps through the apartment and knocking things off surfaces. He'd given her the tremendous gift of sleep. Sleep she'd desperately needed.

The rest hadn't helped her run at all, though. She ended up walking most of it because, even though she'd had enough shut-eye, she was still tired and in need of a strong coffee. Her home brewer couldn't make the strength she needed, so, wrapping up her pitiful workout, she popped into Doug's for a latte with not one but two shots of espresso. That should give her the jolt she needed to get through the day.

She walked along Main Street on her way back to the boutique with her latte in hand and her sunglasses on to hide her swollen eyes.

The quaint street was waking up like the rest of Lucky Cove. Beauty Wave and Curl, the hair salon, had its lights on, and the florist a few doors down was setting out her displays and signs to draw in customers.

Kelly glanced at her watch. She had enough time to get back to her apartment, shower, and make herself presentable for work. Even so, all she wanted to do was to crawl back under her bedcovers.

"Kelly!" Liv Moretti called out from her family's bakery doorway. Tall and lanky with a dark pixie haircut, Liv had an Audrey Hepburn vibe about her. She was the type of woman who could confidently wear leggings without a tunic, something Kelly could never pull off. She rushed to Kelly and pulled her into a big hug. "I'm so, so, so sorry."

Kelly hugged her back, keeping her latte from being sloshed too much. "Thank you, Liv."

"I can't believe she's dead. It's terrible." Liv squeezed tighter. For someone who was so slim, she was enviably strong.

"Liv, you're squeezing too tight," Kelly said.

"Oh, sorry." Liv released Kelly but kept hold of her hand. "You know if there's anything you need, all you have to do is tell me. Anything."

Liv had been a good friend to Kelly through thick and thin. Through their awkward and complicated high school years, through the accident that paralyzed Ariel and left Kelly at odds with family and friends, and now through their twenties as they navigated life.

"Thanks, and I will let you know." Kelly sniffled and then pulled a tissue from her waist pack. "Why can't I stop crying?"

The bakery door swung open, and Liv's aunt Mia bustled out, holding a pastry box. She had Liv's slender frame and dark hair, though there was a touch of gray at her root line. Over her jeans and black shirt, she wore an apron with the bakery's logo—a cupcake topped with blue icing.

"Oh, Kelly. We couldn't believe it when we heard about Becky. So tragic. She was a beautiful, kind, smart young woman." Aunt Mia looked upward. "She's with the angels now."

"Is there any word yet on what...how she..." Liv fumbled for words to ask the question that had been ruminating around Kelly's brain since she found her cousin on the beach.

"No. No word yet on what caused her death." Even though she had strong suspicions her cousin was murdered, she kept an open mind that the death could have been accidental, as Wolman had suggested.

"I can't imagine what her parents are going through. They are good people. It's a shame." Aunt Mia handed the pastry box to Kelly. "This is for you."

"Thank you," Kelly said. She looked through the box's window and saw two rows of cannoli. In the Moretti family, they believed cannoli made everything better. She wished it were true. But the reality was, it would only make her waistline larger.

"You take care, dear. Be sure to let us know if you need anything." Aunt Mia gave Kelly a kiss on the cheek and then returned inside the bakery.

"I have to get back inside too. Call me later." Liv gave Kelly another hug—this time, it wasn't a smothering embrace—before she turned and entered the bakery.

With her latte and box of cannoli, Kelly continued to the boutique. When she reached the back door, she entered the staff room and set the pastry box on the table and then took a sip of her latte. Yowza! It was strong enough to curl her lashes.

A knock at the back door had her glancing at her watch. She didn't know who would visit so early. Then a spark of hope ignited. Maybe it was Wolman with an update. She set her latte down and hurried to open the door. Her spark was gone when she realized it wasn't the detective. Instead, she was surprised to see Jessica standing on the welcome mat.

"What brings you by so early?"

Jessica's gaze cast downward, and she sighed.

Kelly realized she hadn't sounded very welcoming. She reminded herself she wasn't the only person who had suffered a loss yesterday.

"I need to talk to someone. I know it's early, but I've been awake for hours. I couldn't sleep." Jessica's messy hair and dark circles beneath her eyes proved her claim. As did her denim overalls and navy shirt—while the outfit could look fun and casual, it looked rumpled on her.

"Of course. Come on in." Kelly stepped aside so Jessica could enter. She led her to the table and gestured to a chair as she sat.

Jessica dropped hard onto the chair and rubbed her face, pushing back her hair. "This is a nightmare. I still can't believe Becky is dead." She leaned forward, resting her forearms on the table, and her words came faster. "None of this makes any sense. Why did she go out to the beach after everyone left? Then while I was being interviewed by the detective, I got the impression she thinks Becky's death wasn't an accident. From the questions she asked, I think Becky was murdered. And I think she suspects me."

"Whoa. Slow down, Jessica. Breathe." Kelly worried that the woman would hyperventilate if she didn't take a breath. Then she opened the pastry box and offered her a cannoli. If it was good enough for the Moretti family, then the Quinn family should try it too.

Jessica hesitated.

"Have you eaten anything since…our dinner?"

"Not really. I had some fruit yesterday. I haven't been hungry."

Kelly understood the feeling. She also knew Jessica needed to eat, just like she'd had to yesterday. Thankfully, she had Pepper to make sure she had some nutrition. Looking at the pastry box, she realized there wasn't much nutrition in the cannoli, but as Liv's mom and aunts would say, they were made with love. Wasn't that worth something?

She nudged the box closer to Jessica. "Try one."

Jessica plucked a cannoli out of the box along with a napkin. "These look delicious."

"Trust me, they are."

Jessica took a bite of the pastry and rolled her eyes in a good way.

"How about some coffee?" Kelly stood and walked to the kitchenette and started a pot brewing. "Why do you think the police consider you a suspect?"

"Isn't it obvious? I was alone in the house with Becky."

Kelly couldn't argue with that logic. She pulled a mug from an upper cabinet. As she set it on the countertop, she had second thoughts about plying Jessica with sugar and caffeine first thing in the morning when she was already on edge.

"Did you do it?" Kelly kept her tone neutral and cast a glance at Jessica as she poured the coffee.

"No!" Jessica practically threw down what was left of her cannoli.

"Then you have nothing to worry about. Detective Wolman wouldn't be doing her job if she didn't ask you or me those tough questions. What she's doing is ruling us out."

Jessica shook her head. "From her tone and those questions, she's looking for an easy way to close this case. Well, I won't be a scapegoat." She stabbed her finger on the table to make her point.

"You still don't remember when Smith left that night?" Kelly set the mug in front of Jessica.

"Why do you keep asking me that?" Jessica reached for the mug and took a sip.

"Because it's important to know where he was that night. Was he there before Becky went down to the beach? Wait, do you really not remember, or are you just saying that?"

"You're accusing me again," Jessica said.

"What I'm doing is asking questions. It happens when there's been a suspicious death. What usually doesn't happen is the supposed friend of the victim being intentionally vague."

"I'm doing no such thing."

Kelly disagreed, but she'd get nowhere with Jessica if she said so. "Besides being home with Becky, is there another reason why Wolman would suspect you?" Kelly sipped her latte. She remained silent, giving Jessica time to answer. It was a technique she'd learned from watching *Law & Order* marathons.

Jessica wrapped her fingers around her mug. "There isn't. We were friends and business partners. We had a good relationship."

"So there were no issues between you two? Differences about the company? Or personal problems?" Every friendship had its ups and downs at some point. Even she and Liv had bickered over the years.

"No. We shared the same vision for Define Beauty. And our friendship was solid." Jessica lifted the mug and sipped.

Now there was a lie. According to Becky the other night, there had been a difference in how the two women saw Define Beauty's future. Had the disagreement pushed Jessica to kill her partner so she could control the company 100 percent? Was she seated across from a murderer? Kelly attempted to quell the uneasiness in her belly.

"The police should investigate Terry Carlisle. She's capable of anything given her unstable personality."

"Becky told me what you said about Terry. How she had a meltdown online and accused other influencers of bullying her. She blamed them for her own failures. You also warned Becky that Terry could be dangerous."

"All of it true. She had the nerve to blame me for destroying her career. I barely knew she existed. Trust me, her presence wasn't very impactful on the community." Jessica glanced at her chunky watch. "I should be going. I have a conference call with our department heads. We have to plan a memorial for Becky."

"Have you been in contact with her parents yet? They're planning her funeral."

"We spoke briefly last night. Of course, we'll coordinate with them."

Jessica's words were unemotional. *Coordinate with them.* As if she was planning a conference. Perhaps it was for the best she was composed. After all, she had a company to run and employees relying on her.

"I'm glad you came by, and if you need to talk again, don't hesitate to reach out to me." Kelly leaned back.

"You'll keep me updated on the funeral arrangements?"

Kelly nodded, and Jessica stood to leave out the back door.

When the door closed, Kelly pulled her phone out of her waist pack. Even though she felt some loyalty to her employee, she had to do what she hadn't done so far, and that was to check for herself.

She typed Terry's name into the search field along with the words "beauty influencer."

A short list of results came back.

She tapped on the links to each blog post and quickly scanned the articles that recounted Terry's very public crash and burn. It looked like what Jessica had said was true.

A text from her friend, Ariel Barnes, stopped her cyber-research. She wanted to meet for a quick breakfast and refused to take no for an answer. Kelly knew if she tried to decline the invite, Ariel wouldn't give up. She'd show up on the doorstep looking cross and drag Kelly by the arm out of the boutique. Her motorized wheelchair could do warp speed, so Kelly would be unsuccessful in resisting. It was better to just say yes to breakfast, even though she had no appetite.

She replied she could meet in an hour. It gave her enough time to shower and change out of her running clothes. As she stood, her phone dinged and she opened the new message. There was a smiley face emoji. For the first time in what seemed like days, she smiled. Maybe having breakfast, or another coffee, with her friend, would be a good thing. She'd at least have a distraction. Before heading upstairs, she wanted to review her to-do list. She swiped up her latte and moved over to the desk.

She opened her planner and scanned the day's schedule. It was pretty light. Her article for Budget Chic had already been submitted, and there were no consignment appointments. However, there was social media posting to do later in the day. If she were inclined, she could ask Breena to do the task. She closed the agenda and pushed it off to the side. When she did, she noticed a piece of paper.

She'd forgotten about Mrs. Engle's sweaters. The persnickety customer had given Terry a hard time when she was in the boutique last. Unlike Camille Donovan, Mrs. Engle hadn't understood she'd earn more money if she sold her seasonal clothing when customers wanted them. Now, Kelly had to smooth things over with the customer and not lose the merchandise.

Before slipping the paper into her agenda, she paused for a moment and stared at the handwriting.

Her mind's eye flashed back to the scene on the beach and the note beside Becky's body that read—*Meet me at midnight on the beach. We need to talk.*

At the time, she hadn't given it much thought. Now, studying the handwriting of Terry's note, she couldn't help recognizing some similarity to the one on the beach.

Had Terry written the note found with Becky? If so, she might have been the last person to see Becky alive. She could also have been the... Kelly hated suspecting her employee of murder, but she couldn't dismiss the possibility.

Another memory flashed in her mind. The necklace. She recalled the pendant had an intricate design of two curved lines connected with a centerline, like a fancy H. Her first thought about the piece of jewelry was that it wasn't her cousin's because Becky preferred silver to gold. If she had worn it, Kelly would have noticed. The necklace had to belong to the person who met Becky on the beach.

Why hadn't she paid more attention to those things yesterday? She should have told Wolman about them.

Kelly went to the kitchen drawer to grab a plastic zip baggie. When she returned to the desk, she carefully placed the note into the baggie and then zipped it shut.

To feel less guilty for suspecting Terry, she decided to hold off giving Wolman the note until she talked to Terry. She wanted to get her side of the story first. Or her confession.

CHAPTER EIGHT

Kelly breezed into the Lucky Cove Inn barely on time for her breakfast date with Ariel. A bout of indecisiveness on what top to wear had her running late. After she'd showered, she reached for a flowy red skirt that grazed her knee. Next, she grabbed a pair of two-tone slides. Comfortable and chic with a Chanel vibe, they were perfect for walking to the inn and standing on her feet all day in the boutique. All was going well until she had to choose her top. Three options kept her gaze bouncing between the hangers—a delicate eyelet top, a cap-sleeved silky blouse, or her favorite graphic T-shirt with the word "Vogue" scrawled in gold on it.

She looked to Howard for assistance, but he was too busy washing his face to be concerned with her wardrobe dilemma.

"You're no help," she muttered to her feline, and it had earned her a peeved look. He stopped rubbing his eye with his paw and held her gaze for a beat and then returned to his grooming.

It was definitely going to be one of those days.

After minutes of staring at her reflection, Kelly chose the graphic T-shirt and then dashed out of her bedroom. Finally dressed, she traded her purse for her rattan tote to complete the summery look. With a forecast of close to ninety degrees for the day, a light and airy outfit was an absolute must.

Kelly passed through the lobby where guests milled around, preparing for their day to relax on the beaches, visit nearby wineries, or shop in the towns and villages Lucky Cove was tucked among. She arrived in the dining room and spotted Ariel. She wended her way toward her table, passing families who were finishing their quick breakfasts and locals who were savoring the inn's famous waffles. Well, at least famous in their neck of the woods.

"Good morning." Ariel beamed as she reached out her arms from her wheelchair for a hug. She looked relaxed and refreshed, two things Kelly envied at the moment. Her bangs experiment was finally growing out, and she wore a lightweight cotton sweater over white slacks.

"Thank you for getting me out of my apartment." Kelly sat across from Ariel, setting her tote on the extra chair that they didn't need. "I probably wouldn't have eaten anything."

"Understandable considering what happened yesterday. To make sure you ate something, I ordered two plates of waffles!" Ariel's smile broadened. She was obsessed with them. She'd even dated the innkeeper's son in hopes of learning the secret recipe. He confessed that his mom never shared it with him, and then Ariel moved on. Admittedly, it wasn't her finest moment. But in her defense, she was a teenager at the time, and the waffles were freaking amazing. "How are you doing?"

Kelly unfolded the napkin and set it on her lap. She reminded herself to be careful of what she said. Becky's death had allowed Kelly to do something she hadn't been able to do for months—forget her uncle's deep, dark secret. He'd blurted it out in a moment of frustration, leaving Kelly with information she had no desire to know.

Information that could destroy her newly rebuilt friendship with Ariel.

For years, Kelly had believed her uncle's disappointment in her was because she'd bailed on Ariel at a late-night summer party ten years ago. After all, her parents and sister were disappointed in her, so why shouldn't her uncle have been also?

Kelly and Ariel had gone to a party, and, rather than stay with Ariel, she snuck off with a boy. It was getting late, and Ariel wanted to go home. Unable to find Kelly, she got a ride from Melanie Grover, who was drunk. Not ten minutes away from the party, Melanie lost control of the vehicle and it crashed. The accident left Ariel paralyzed.

Everybody, including Kelly's family, blamed her for what happened to Ariel, and she blamed herself.

How could she not?

If she had stayed with Ariel… No, she wouldn't go down that road again. Melanie was the one driving while impaired, and Ariel made the decision to get into the car. There was plenty of blame to go around, and it shouldn't all have been shouldered by her.

When Kelly's granny died, her uncle had been adamant she sell the boutique and leave Lucky Cove. At the time, she thought he was bitter that his mother had cut him out of her will. Turned out she was wrong.

He'd been more than disappointed in Kelly all those years ago—he blamed her for the car accident that ruined his daughter's life. Once he uttered the secret during their argument a few months ago, Kelly froze, hoping she misheard her uncle. She hadn't. The news shocked Kelly, but finally the way he treated her made sense.

He confessed he'd had an affair with Ariel's mom when she was briefly separated from her husband. After the couple reconciled, she found out she was pregnant with Ariel—Ralph's child. They'd kept the secret all those years. Well, until he blurted it out to Kelly. Which happened to be at the same time Ariel decided to take a DNA test. So far, Ariel hadn't pursued the relative matching part of the test.

Now looking across the table at her friend, she saw the similarities between Ariel and Frankie. She also worried every time she talked with Ariel that she would blab the secret. Finding out her mother had lied to her all these years would crush Ariel. And Kelly hadn't wanted to be the person to do that to her friend.

"Hey, earth to Kell." Ariel snapped her fingers.

"Sorry. Where were we? Oh, I'm looking forward to those waffles." As if on cue, their waitress appeared with their plates. The cinnamon and vanilla mingled together and delighted Kelly, lifting her mood instantly.

She picked up the syrup pitcher and drizzled the fresh maple syrup over the hearty serving. She couldn't wait to cut into the thick, fluffy waffles.

"I knew this would make you feel better." Ariel took the pitcher and drizzled syrup on her waffles. "I have some good news."

Kelly looked up from her plate. Good news would be a welcome change of pace. "Tell me."

"I'm going on a vacation with my family up to Cape Cod. We've been talking about it for a few weeks and finally decided we should go. I have some time off at the library, and I have no open assignments, so I can go and relax."

Ariel worked part-time at the Lucky Cove Library and was a ninja researcher. She even helped Kelly solve the murder cases she'd been involved with. When she wasn't at the library, she worked as a freelance writer.

"How exciting. The whole Barnes clan together under the same roof. Sounds like you're going to have a wonderful time." Kelly took another bite of her waffle. Ariel's parents were a lot of fun to be around. They loved to travel and explore new places. Despite the hand their daughter and family had been dealt, they remained optimistic and hopeful for the future. It was what Kelly believed helped the most in dealing with her paralysis.

"It's going to be fun. My aunt and uncle from New Hampshire are going to join us for a few days. I haven't seen them in a couple years. Their son is also coming."

As Kelly chewed her forkful of waffle, envy pricked at her. She would have loved to go on a vacation. Somewhere secluded with no Detective Wolman or crime scene tape. Alas, that wasn't in the cards for her now. After swallowing her bite, she reached for her water glass and took a sip.

"I've also decided when I get back from the trip, I'm going to pursue discovering my family tree through the DNA database," Ariel said. "Maybe find some cousins I don't know about."

Kelly choked on her drink, her water spilling over the rim of the glass. Coughing, she set the glass down and tried to sop up the water with her napkin.

"Are you okay?" Ariel threw her napkin down on the table too.

Kelly gave herself a mental shake. *Keep calm. Play it cool— no need to panic.*

"Yeah, I'm okay. Ah…the water just went down wrong." Kelly hated lying. She lifted her fork and tried her best to act like there was nothing wrong. Even though warning screams were going off in her head.

It's only a matter of time before she learns Frankie is her brother.

That Ralph is her father.

That I'm her cousin.

That I lied.

As if she didn't have enough on her plate, now she had to figure out a way to make the blow that was about to hit Ariel less hurtful.

Darn Uncle Ralph.

He had to be the one to tell his daughter the truth. He'd been evading Kelly for months. Somehow, he magically disappeared when Kelly dropped by his house to visit with his third wife, Summer, and their baby daughter, Juniper. He also managed to arrive late or leave early at any family events to make sure he missed Kelly.

But not any longer.

She was going to corner him and make him take charge of the mess he'd created.

Kelly practically wolfed down the rest of her waffles so she could leave and run over to her uncle's office. She paid her part of the check and said goodbye to Ariel, who stopped to talk to a library patron as they were exiting the dining room.

On her way toward the inn's impressive wooden front doors, arched and embellished with stained glass panels, she spotted Todd at the registration desk flirting with the pretty brunette clerk, who was far too young for him.

So, this is where he's staying.

She took a sharp turn and approached the desk with two intentions. First, to shift his attention from the high school junior and second, to find out where he went after Smith escorted him off the beach house's deck two nights ago.

"Good morning, Todd." She wasn't sure if he'd remember her from Doug's Variety Store yesterday.

And her guess was correct. He eyed her curiously as he shifted from the clerk. Then a sly grin tugged on his lips as he rested an arm on the desk. Sobered up, he looked like a scoundrel.

Kelly hated players. They were nothing but trouble and heartbreakers.

"Good morning indeed." His grin broadened into a smile, flashing perfectly straight and white teeth.

"You don't remember me from the other night or yesterday morning, do you?"

"Night and morning?" His brow arched. "How could any man forget a beautiful woman like yourself?" He chuckled. "But I do admit to having way too much to drink a couple of nights ago, so everything is kind of fuzzy right now. Why don't we go back to my room and we can get reacquainted? It'll be fun," he said in a low, deep voice as he pushed off from the desk and reached for Kelly.

"Ewww." She pulled her arm back. "We didn't meet like *that*. We met at Becky's beach house when you stumbled up the stairs two nights ago. You were demanding money from her."

Todd gave her a blank stare.

"You still don't remember? How much did you drink?"

He shrugged sheepishly.

She wasn't too surprised, though she wondered how he got back to the inn that night. "Have you heard what happened to Becky?"

"Honey, I've been recovering from a massive hangover." He pointed to his temple and grimaced. He was hurting, she was sure. "This is the first time I've been out of my room since I went to Becky's house. I do remember that. Vaguely."

Kelly squinted. "No, actually, this isn't the first time you've been out of your room. You got a coffee at Doug's Variety Store yesterday morning. We ran into each other."

"Seriously?" He gave her a doubtful look as he walked past her toward the lobby's seating area.

"Seriously." She swiveled and followed him.

He dropped down onto one of the deep-cushioned sofas that offered respite to guests after a long day of sightseeing or a comfortable place to sip morning coffee and plan the day.

"I've never hurt so much in my life." He leaned back and crossed his legs.

Kelly didn't doubt that statement. It must have been some bender for him to lose not one but two days. She sat at the end of the sofa, making sure there was enough space between them if he decided to reach for her again. Too bad she wasn't carrying her pepper spray.

"Becky is dead," she said.

Those three words snapped Todd to attention. His pale blue eyes grew serious, and his jaw tensed.

"What? No. You have to be mistaken."

"Sadly, I'm not. I found her body yesterday morning on the beach. You didn't know?"

Todd scrubbed his face with his hand. His eyes watered, and he exhaled a deep breath. He looked genuinely shocked by the news. "How? What happened?" He combed his fingers through his jet-black hair, lifting wayward strands that had fallen down his forehead.

Kelly told him how she found Becky but left out the details of the note and necklace. She shared her suspicion the death might have been a homicide.

Todd threw his hands up in the air as he straightened. "Isn't it obvious to the police? Jessica did it."

Kelly cocked her head. "Why do you think she did it?"

Todd rolled his eyes. "You clearly don't know her well. She's a conniving woman who wormed her way into Becky's life."

"In doing so, she forced you out, didn't she?"

"Becky and I were close. Best friends, until she connected with Jessica. I never trusted her." He slumped. "I can't believe Becks is gone."

Becks. Kelly hadn't heard that nickname in years. *No. I won't start crying again.*

"Todd, where did you go after you left the beach house?"

"Back here to my room. I think I got a rideshare."

"You're not sure?"

He shrugged. "Like I said, I was a bit drunk."

"Wouldn't you have a confirmation? How about checking the app?"

He shook his head. "I have nothing to prove to you."

"You'll have to prove to the police that you left the beach house and didn't return." Why they hadn't already been in contact with him was a mystery to her. Unless they'd already ruled Becky's death was from natural causes or accidental. It was a possibility. Okay, maybe she needed to shelve the alibi questions for now. There was another question she was curious about.

"When you were at the house, did you slip Becky a note?"

Todd's gaze assessed her, making Kelly wonder what was rolling around in his mind. Was his memory coming back? Or, was he planning his next lie?

"What are you talking about? Who are you? Look, never mind. I have no idea what you're talking about or what you're up to."

"Up to? I'm not up to anything." She inched to the edge of her seat, tamping down her irritation. How dare he accuse her of being up to something when he was the one claiming a memory loss…just like Jessica. Were they in on it together? A chill skimmed along her spine. Pretending to be enemies while all along they'd been plotting to take Becky's company from her. She had to tell Wolman. Like now!

"Oh, you told me…yeah, yesterday is starting to come back…you're her cousin." His gaze softened. "I'm sorry for your loss."

Kelly stared at him, not sure if she believed him.

"Since you're looking for the truth, here it is. Your cousin swindled me out of my share of the company we created. I'm sorry she's dead, but to be honest, I'm not feeling very mournful. If you change your mind, I'm in room twenty-two." He stood and then walked away toward the elevator. When the door slid open, he disappeared inside.

"Good morning, Kelly." Renata McPherson, an employee at the inn and a customer at the boutique, approached. She wore a smart taupe pantsuit, and her auburn hair was swept up into a French twist. She held a platter of giant chocolate chip cookies, another legendary treat the inn offered. "You look like you could use a cookie."

Kelly couldn't resist the aroma of the buttery, chocolatey cookies. No one could. She reached for one and took a bite.

"Delicious, as always," she said after swallowing.

Renata leaned in and lowered her voice. "I couldn't help but see you with Mr. Charming."

Kelly nearly choked on her next bite. "Mr. Who?"

"The guest in room twenty-two. That's what we're calling him. He thinks he's all that and a gift to every female he meets." Renata shook her head. "Can you believe he even hit on me?"

"Why wouldn't he?" Kelly hated seeing Renata doubt her attractiveness. When helping her friend pick out clothes, she saw how much Renata struggled with her body image. Each time, Kelly reminded her that style wasn't a size; it was an attitude. Case in point, Renata's pantsuit. Tailoring had helped it fit Renata's curves perfectly, but it was her confidence that made her striking in it.

"For starters, I'm married." She raised her left hand and wiggled her fingers, flashing her wedding set. "Guess he plays the odds. Flirts with X number of women, and he's bound to find one who doesn't think he's a jerk. Like the gal he met a couple nights ago."

"You saw him two nights ago? What time?"

"Let's see…it was late." Renata shifted her attention for a moment, offering cookies to a senior couple who had entered the lobby. They each happily took one and continued to the registration desk. "Sorry. Where was I? Oh, right, I was upstairs because there was a plumbing emergency in one of the rooms. I saw him get off the elevator with the woman, and they went into his room."

"Do you know who she was?"

Renata shrugged. "Sorry. I never saw her before." She glanced at the wall clock. "Oh, I have a meeting in ten minutes. Have a nice day."

Kelly finished her cookie as Renata hurried off to the back office. The cookie served as a boost for Kelly's next stop—her uncle's office.

Outside on Main Street, the day's heat had ratcheted up, as had the humidity. She put on her sunglasses and set her sights on the Blake Real Estate Development office just up the street just as a familiar person came into view.

She slid her sunglasses down her nose to make sure it was him. Yep, it was Smith. And he was with a woman who wasn't Jessica. They were walking arm in arm and chatting.

Since Jessica couldn't recall what time he'd left the beach house, he certainly should be able to. She picked up her pace, and when she reached him and his companion, unlike Todd, he remembered her.

"Kelly, I'm sorry for your loss. Becky was a wonderful, smart person." Smith's voice was somber, and his expression was sympathetic.

"Thank you." Kelly waited a moment for an introduction to the woman hanging on to Smith, but none was forthcoming. However, she looked familiar to Kelly. "I don't want to keep the two of you—"

"Good. Because we really must be going." Smith glanced at the tall, tanned woman beside him. So much for being sympathetic.

Kelly pressed her lips together. She wouldn't lecture him on how interrupting people was rude, yet she wasn't about to be deterred. "As I was saying. I don't want to keep you, so I'll get right to the point. What time did you leave after we finished dinner? Jessica can't seem to recall."

"I thought you owned a clothing store?" Smith asked.

"I do. The Lucky Cove Resale Boutique. It's just up the street." She pointed.

"Good for you." He pulled out his cell phone from his pants pocket and checked the screen. Without looking up, he continued. "I don't understand why you're asking me questions about my whereabouts."

"Haven't you already spoken to the police?" his companion asked as she leaned over to view the cell phone.

"I have." He looked up at Kelly. "As far as I'm aware, I'm under no obligation to answer your questions. Now, if you'll excuse us." He returned the phone to his pocket and led his companion to the curb.

When there was a lull in traffic, they jogged across the street and stepped up to the curb. Kelly had a hunch and pulled out her phone to snap a photo of the woman. She didn't think she knew the woman from Lucky Cove, perhaps from the city. And she had a good friend back in Manhattan who knew everything about everybody. Julie was obsessed with Page Six and the *Social Register*. Maybe she could identify the woman.

After sending off the text and photo, Kelly continued to her uncle's office. But a honk caused her to divert and approach the police vehicle parked at the corner.

Gabe was behind the wheel. He slipped off his sunglasses and lowered the passenger window.

"I have to talk to Wolman." Kelly leaned into the window. "I think Becky was murdered, and I have a theory."

CHAPTER NINE

"Why am I not surprised?" Gabe rested his arm on the steering wheel, and his expression said he'd expected as much from Kelly. "You know how much she really dislikes you interfering in her work."

"I know. I know. But I can't help it if things come to me, like a theory. Isn't that what detective work is all about? Identifying theories, motives?"

"It's about working the case and collecting evidence. Which, you're not supposed to be doing."

Kelly caught her lip between her teeth. She did have Terry's note about Mrs. Engle's sweaters safely tucked away in the boutique. That probably was considered evidence. Once she heard Terry's side of the story, she'd turn it over to the police.

"You're doing it, aren't you?" Gabe asked.

Kelly tilted her head and pressed her lips together. He was onto her. Then again, they'd been friends since childhood, and he was like a brother to her, which meant he knew her all too well.

"Gosh, Kell, you're going to make Detective Wolman very angry."

"Well, it wouldn't be the first time. You know, I wouldn't have to come up with theories if I knew what was going on with the case. Are there any updates?"

"You know if there were, I couldn't tell you."

"Officially, you mean, you couldn't tell me. However, unofficially you can tell me anything."

Gabe shook his head firmly. "No, I can't."

She hesitated a moment before speaking. Gabe had such kind and honest eyes. It spoke to the type of guy he was, and she hated herself for saying what she was about to say, but it was the only way to get the information she needed.

"Your ten-year high school reunion is coming up, isn't it?" She tilted her head, and the corner of her mouth tugged upward. She knew he knew exactly where she was going with the question.

"You wouldn't."

She shrugged and blinked. "Maybe. Maybe not. There's one way to guarantee that photo never sees the light of day."

"You're blackmailing me?"

"I like to think of it as giving you an incentive to share information you know."

"Blackmail."

"Whatever. What do you know?"

"Fine. But I want that photo."

"Deal." Since she and Gabe grew up together practically as siblings, she had plenty of dirt on him, so giving up the photo of him dressed as the back end of a donkey wasn't a big deal. While she couldn't remember the exact details of how he ended up in the costume with Bernie Jones, she did vividly remember the razzing he took because of it.

"Should I be worried that was too easy?"

She sighed, growing impatient with Gabe.

"Okay. It's not official, but I've heard that the case is now considered a homicide."

"I was right," Kelly muttered.

"Oh, boy. Kell, don't go and get yourself any more involved. Remember what happened last time?"

"Yes, I do. I helped your department solve a murder."

"You also almost got yourself killed."

She hadn't forgotten about the near-death experience and had no intention of putting herself in danger again. "Don't worry. The only thing I want is for the person responsible to be arrested and sent away for a very, very long time." She glanced at her watch. She had to get a move on if she was going to make it back to the boutique in time to open after her next stop. She said goodbye to Gabe and walked away from the vehicle.

With her pace picked up, she arrived at Ralph's office within minutes and was greeted by Camille. Shoot! With all the distractions, she'd gotten none of her clothing ready for sale.

Camille offered a kind smile as she came around her desk. She wore a sleeveless white blouse with a ruffled neckline and a pair of cropped turquoise trousers.

"Good morning, Kelly. It's good to see you. Please accept my condolences for the loss of your cousin."

"Thank you. It's much appreciated. I promise to get your clothes up for sale today so you can start earning some money."

"I'm not in a hurry. You have a lot going on. So whenever you can get over to my house, that would be great. I'm hoping for a fresh start this summer with less clutter and a more minimal wardrobe."

"Actually, I think working is the distraction I need. I'll be back to your house to get everything else."

Where Kelly would store the merchandise was undecided. "Have you canceled any more subscription boxes?"

Camille tipped her head to the side. "Two more canceled this week."

"Good job." Even though Kelly was disappointed to hear only two subscriptions had been canceled, it was better than none. What was important was that Camille was making a solid effort to take control of her wardrobe, finances, and life.

Kelly's gaze drifted over Camille's shoulder, and she saw her uncle emerge from an inner office. In his late fifties, he was out of shape, balding, and relentlessly ambitious. He was also a bear to deal with on good days. Today wouldn't be one of them, not with what Kelly wanted to talk to him about.

"I guess you're here to see Ralph. Go on back to his office." Camille hitched a thumb in the direction of the interior offices for management.

"Thanks." Kelly didn't want to waste any time getting back there. If her uncle had seen her, he'd be planning his getaway. An image of him shimmying out his office window flashed in her mind. It was quickly followed by another one of him getting stuck. Actually, that wouldn't be a bad idea because he'd probably be stuck and then be forced to listen to her.

She arrived at his office, and the door was open. He was walking around his desk to his luxurious leather chair.

"Hi, Uncle Ralph."

He looked in her direction and frowned. "Kelly, I'm sorry to hear about your cousin. I always liked her." His collared shirt was unbuttoned, and his cuffs were rolled up, revealing thick, hairy arms. When he wasn't trying to impress investors or buyers with his expensive car, tailored suits, and country club membership, he looked like your average middle-aged man.

She appreciated the sentiment and wished she wasn't there for the reason she was. Maybe she should have accepted his condolences and left. Not worry about the fallout sure to come once Ariel got her family tree information with Kelly as a branch on it.

He sat on the chair and pulled himself close to the desktop, which was neatly organized. A pair of trays for incoming and outgoing documents were placed in one corner. A tidy penholder was set on the massive blotter that protected the glossy wood, and off to the side was his laptop computer. He clasped his hands together and looked at her expectantly.

Right, he's waiting for me to say something.

"We need to talk about Ariel." She stepped into the office, closing the door behind her. "She's planning on finding relatives through the DNA database. You need to get out ahead of the situation by telling her the truth."

Ralph's dark eyes seemed to drill into her. "I told you, I'm not telling her."

She wouldn't let him rattle her. He was accustomed to acting like a bull trampling over people to get his way. Well, not this time.

"Are you forgetting Frankie also took a DNA test from the same company? They're going to be matched as half siblings."

Ralph slammed a fist down on his desk, and Kelly flinched.

"Why on earth did he have his DNA tested? There wasn't any reason. He knows where he came from."

Kelly didn't have time to debate the pros and cons of DNA testing. The clock was ticking. Ariel was on the cusp of finding out the truth. She had to somehow get her uncle to change his mind. "Please, I'm begging you."

Ralph remained stone faced.

"If she finds out from a report that Frankie is her half brother and that you're her biological father, it's going to be far worse than if you take her aside privately and break the news to her."

Ralph shook his head sharply.

Kelly pushed down her urge to scream. Dealing with her uncle was like dealing with a toddler.

"Why are you so stubborn when you know you're running out of time?"

"This isn't your business, Kelly."

She marched to the desk and leaned her hands on its surface, extending her neck and looking her uncle right in the eyes. "You made it my business when you dumped your secret in my lap. Own up to what happened and deal with the repercussions."

"Back off."

"Or what? Tell me. What's your game plan? How do you see this playing out, Uncle Ralph?"

"You need to leave."

"*You* need to deal with this situation."

Ralph sprang up and pointed to the door. "Out! Now!"

Kelly pulled back, startled by his outburst. They stared each other down for a long moment.

"Fine. I'll go. Good luck dealing with your daughter." She spun around and marched to the door. When she pulled it open, she was met by a cluster of stunned employees gathered in the hall. It appeared they'd heard Ralph's angry outburst, and their curiosity had drawn them closer to the action. Had they heard the last thing she said to her uncle? Gosh, she hoped not. She did her best not to let the awkward moment affect her as she walked past them and out of the building.

* * * *

Kelly arrived at the boutique with minutes to spare, but it appeared she hadn't needed to rush. Either Pepper or Breena had shown up for an early shift and opened. She had the best employees.

Well, the jury was still out on Terry.

She reached the front door and stopped for a moment to check out the window display. At the end of last week, she'd changed it for a more beachy vibe. She dressed one mannequin in a tropical-print swimsuit and the other in a pair of denim cutoffs and white T-shirt. For props, Kelly added beach balls and a beach umbrella. The space she had to work with was small, so she tried to make the display visually attractive but not too cluttered.

"Nice window display." The husky male voice sent a surprise spark through Kelly, and she pressed her lips together to keep from smiling. Now wasn't the time for sparks of any kind, especially ones caused by Nate Barber.

"Thank you," she said, spinning around to face him. She'd met the no-nonsense, yet handsome, police detective in the spring when he was investigating a murder she'd gotten caught up in. Was he involved in Becky's case? Was he there for an update?

"What brings you by? Something's happened with my cousin's case?"

"Sorry. It's not my case."

"Oh, I see." She broke eye contact and wondered when it would be over, when she'd have the answers she needed, and when her cousin could be laid to rest in peace. If her granny were alive, she'd be encouraging her granddaughter to have patience. Kelly would argue she wouldn't need to be patient if the police did their job faster.

"I'm actually here to see you." He closed the space between them, and Kelly caught a whiff of his spicy cologne. "How are you holding up?"

She shrugged. "It changes every hour."

"Understandable." He reached out and squeezed her shoulder, sending another spark zipping through Kelly. Not only was there the spark, but now she felt secure and comforted. The urge to burrow into his broad chest and hide away from the world was overwhelming and highly improper. He was a police detective, not her boyfriend.

Speaking of boyfriends, she saw her ex was walking toward them. Oh, the perks of small-town life. When she made eye contact with Mark, a weird mix of embarrassment, bitterness, and sadness whirled inside her. She homed in on the first emotion—embarrassment. Why had she felt it? Because she was in what could be considered an intimate moment with Nate? So what? Mark wasn't her boyfriend anymore. She could be in as many intimate moments with Nate as she wanted. Whoa. Even thinking that to herself hadn't sounded good. Though with a guy like Nate, who wanted to be good? She gave herself a mental shake. It was time to step off the ex-girlfriend's crazy brain train and put the brakes on any improper thoughts about the detective.

Nate followed her gaze. "Your ex, right?"

"Let's go inside." She stepped to the door and opened it. They could finish their conversation in private. Before she walked inside the boutique, she glanced at Mark. Even from a distance, she could see on his face he was jealous. It served him right for how he'd treated her. It had taken a few months, but she finally realized he viewed her as an accessory, not as a partner in their relationship. She knew as well as anybody that accessories had a way of going out of fashion. She had no doubt it wouldn't be long before she'd be traded in for a newer, younger, and prettier accessory. Even though it had hurt and still did, it was better to get out before her heart got in too deep.

"Hi, Kelly," Breena called out from a four-way rack. She was adding newly consigned items, including a bunch of Camille's tops. "I got all of Camille's clothes in the system and tagged. Have you heard anything from Terry?"

Kelly shook her head. "I don't think she works here anymore." Another thing Kelly had to deal with—hiring a new salesperson. Maybe she'd let Pepper take the lead on the project since she'd failed at adequately screening Terry.

"Good morning, Detective Barber." Breena gave him a big smile and then gave Kelly a thumbs-up before dashing out of the room.

"Terry Carlisle works here?" Nate asked.

"She did until she took off the other day." Kelly dropped her tote on the counter and then moved to a circular rack to straighten the blouses.

"What happened?"

"It was the day Becky and Jessica came into the boutique. Things got weird, and Terry took off." Kelly spotted Mark lingering out in front of the boutique's window. She had to force herself not to smile with satisfaction at the fact that she had made him jealous. Boy, did she want to gloat.

"I hear Marcy wants to talk with her. Do you have any idea where she is?" Nate asked.

Kelly dragged her attention from the window and looked at Nate. He filled out the space nicely. Tall and solid, he'd probably played high school football, Kelly guessed. Probably had been a quarterback. His dark hair was cut short, and his green eyes were the brightest she'd ever seen.

"Do you know where she is?" Nate asked again.

Kelly blinked, pulling her gaze from his eyes, and focused on the question. "I wish I did. I want to talk to her myself and find out what happened with her and Jessica."

"It sounds like you're planning on poking around Marcy's case."

"You got that right." Kelly marched away from the window. Suddenly, Hot Cop wasn't all that hot looking. He had the official cop mode look on his face, and the last thing she wanted was a lecture. She'd already dumped one guy who thought he could control her.

Her cell phone chimed, and she pulled it from her tote. It was her uncle's wife, Summer. She raised the phone to her ear. "Hi, what's up?"

"It's Ralphie," Summer cried. "He's being taken to the hospital. Camille thinks he had a heart attack."

"A heart attack? Oh, my goodness. I'm on my way." She disconnected the call, and a lump caught in her throat. What had she done? She had gotten him so upset; surely that had raised his blood pressure. She shouldn't have pushed him so hard, made him yell and lose his temper.

"Who had a heart attack?" Nate crossed the floor, his stride long, and stood in front of her within a second.

"My uncle. Summer, his wife, said he's on the way to the hospital. I have to go."

"I'll drive, and don't argue."

"Okay, I won't. I can't believe this." Kelly dashed into the staff room to tell Breena what happened, and then she was out the front door with Nate. She tried not to let her thoughts get out of control with worst-case scenarios. In doing so, the only thing she could think of was that she caused the heart attack.

CHAPTER TEN

The drive to the hospital seemed to take an eternity. Kelly kept her gaze glued to her phone just in case there was an update on her uncle's condition. Nate didn't attempt small talk. He focused on his driving and zipping through the occasional yellow light. Bless him. When they finally arrived at the medical center, Kelly jumped out of Nate's sedan.

She ran to the emergency room's automatic doors, and they whooshed open. Inside, the vast space was bright with harsh overhead lighting, and her nose wriggled at the antiseptic odor hanging in the air. She scanned the area, looking for Summer or Frankie.

The throbbing in her temples buffered out the snippets of conversations from all directions—the registration desk, the patient waiting area, the corridors branching out to other parts of the hospital.

The throbbing intensified, and her vision blurred. She squeezed her eyes shut. For a long moment, she was transported back ten years to the night of Ariel's accident.

She and her parents had rushed to the emergency room once they heard about the incident. Her stomach had knotted, and her head had grown foggy from despair when she listened to the details of how Melanie Grover lost control of her Camaro. When the news came that Ariel had been paralyzed, Kelly broke down not too far from where she now stood.

Her legs quaked at the memory, but when she saw Summer seated by the door labeled Authorized Personnel Only, the feeling disappeared. She had to pull herself together and be strong for her family.

She walked past the seating area, chairs arranged in a large square with a row placed in front of a bank of windows.

Summer looked up and offered a weak smile. The model turned Pilates studio owner looked scared. Kelly couldn't recall her looking so vulnerable or worried before. Not even when she was the target of a killer and an attempt was made on her own life. Summer's arms were crossed over her slender body, her brows low and her mascara smudged. But it was the depth of worry in her usually sharp eyes that was a punch in the gut to Kelly. Had she caused this?

Summer stood and held out her arms to embrace Kelly.

Kelly felt Summer's body shake, and her heart ached for the woman, who wasn't much older than herself. Yet they weren't close. She had been hard pressed to say they were friends. However, they shared an interest in fashion, they both loved Juniper, and they were family. Indeed, there should have been enough common ground to build a friendship. So, why hadn't they?

One reason could have been that Summer looked down on the boutique. There were also her opinions on Kelly's knack for stumbling into murder investigations. Though, thanks to Kelly's sleuthing, Summer had escaped a cold-blooded killer not too long ago. Kelly let go of those thoughts. Now wasn't the time for ridiculous opinions about selling used clothing or for trivial grievances. While Kelly wished Summer would see her as a smart businesswoman, now was the time to let all that fall by the wayside.

"How are you holding up?" Kelly asked. Squeezing Summer, she made a promise to herself that once they knew Ralph would be okay, she would start building the friendship with her…aunt. It had seemed weird thinking of Summer as her aunt since they were only a few years apart in age.

Summer pulled back and returned to her seat with a heavy sigh. She wore a lightweight tie-dyed bomber jacket over her workout tank and leggings. She must have been at her studio when she got the call. After she retired from modeling, she became a Pilates instructor and opened her studio with the encouragement of her husband. Her hair was gathered in a ponytail, and nearly blinding diamond stud earrings, along with her equally blinding wedding ring, were the only jewelry she wore.

"He had a heart attack at his office?" Kelly sat on the chair next to Summer.

"Camille said he suddenly started not feeling well and complained of a crushing feeling in his chest. Then he turned deathly white, she said." Her chin trembled, and she dragged in a breath. "He collapsed onto a chair, and she called for help."

"Good thing she did." Kelly patted Summer's knee. Despite the fact they hadn't been the closest of family members, she wanted to support her uncle's wife.

"I'm so worried about him. He never listens to me about his diet or about exercising. Now look what happened." Her slender hand pointed to the closed door for authorized personnel.

"He's going to be okay. Uncle Ralph is strong and a fighter." *And stubborn.*

"The staff here is excellent, so he's in good hands." Nate had held back at first when Kelly rushed to Summer; now he stood in front of them.

Summer gave him a curious look. "And you are?"

Nate extended his hand to Summer. "Detective Nate Barber."

Summer shook his hand; all the while the questioning look on her face grew more concerned. "Has something else happened?"

"No, ma'am," Nate assured.

Ouch. Summer just got a ma'am, and Kelly silently counted…one…two…three…

There it was—the confused look on her face morphed into a scowl. She was nowhere near ready to be called ma'am.

"I was with Kelly at the boutique when you called about your husband." Nate wisely took back his hand. He may have been used to dealing with criminals, but calling a former model who was barely in her thirties the M word was possibly more dangerous. If Summer hadn't been so worried about her husband, he probably would have needed backup.

"What have you gotten yourself mixed up in this time?" Summer swiveled her head toward Kelly.

"Nothing. I swear. Nate came by to see how I'm doing with Becky's death," Kelly said.

"Oh, what a tragedy. She was so young and smart. Her cosmetics line was poised for greatness. I heard from my former agent that Define Beauty was in talks with Helena Montfort for next spring's ad campaign."

"Who's Helena Montfort?" Nate asked.

"Only the biggest supermodel in the world right now." Summer's tone revealed she wanted to add—*Have you been living under a rock?*

Kelly wondered how her cousin's company afforded to pay Helena, who had once claimed she wouldn't get out of bed for less than ten thousand dollars a day. Then it hit Kelly. Define Beauty couldn't pay supermodel wages, but Chantelle could.

"Mrs. Blake," a woman called out from the Authorized Personnel Only door. "Mrs. Blake."

"I'm here." Summer raised her hand and waved. "I hope this means I can see him."

"We'll wait here," Kelly said.

"Oh, you don't have to. My sister is on her way, and she's going to stay with me. I doubt they will allow Ralphie any visitors besides myself today."

Kelly hated to admit it, but she was relieved. She wasn't up to seeing her uncle a second time that day. "Then how about I go and stay with Juniper until you get home?" She loved spending time with the baby and couldn't believe she turned a year old a few months ago. Where had the time gone?

"She'd love to see you, and I would appreciate it. Thank you, Kelly."

And just like that, their new friendship was taking shape.

"It was nice to meet you, Detective." Summer scooped up her Fendi Peekaboo purse. Every time it was in Kelly's presence, she almost drooled. The classic bag was one of her lust-after items and way out of her budget. Way, way out.

"My best to your husband." Nate shifted to the side to allow Summer to pass by.

Summer strode toward the door as if she was walking along a runway. Perfectly paced, shoulders squared, head held high, and her hips swayed like she was walking in four-inch heels, not designer sneakers.

Kelly guessed her aunt lived by the motto of the whole world is your runway.

"She seems to be holding up well," Nate commented as he moved closer to Kelly.

"It's what models do." When Nate gave her a quizzical look, she filled him in on Summer's background. "She also takes being Mrs. Ralph Blake very seriously. According to her, there's a standard for all of us Blakes to live up to."

"I'm sensing you sometimes fall short of that standard?"

"No wonder you're a detective. I sell secondhand clothes. Oh, well. It's not important now." None of the petty stuff mattered. She looked around the waiting room. Was there anyone else waiting for news if a loved one would make it through the day? Life was unpredictable, and the recent events in her life proved it. Less than an hour ago, she was yelling at her uncle, and then he had a heart attack. If she could, she'd go back and handle their discussion differently.

"You're right. We shouldn't waste time sweating the small, insignificant stuff." Soberness came over his face, and his lips twitched as if he remembered something. He shook it off as quickly as it appeared. "Come on, I'll give you a lift to your uncle's house."

"Thanks, but I need to go back to the boutique to make sure Breena can work the rest of the day. If not, I have to call Pepper."

She stood and walked through the waiting room, heading for the exit, with Nate behind her. Before she reached the automatic doors, she stopped.

"I need to use the restroom. Where is it?"

Nate pointed, and she pivoted. She listened to his direction. After nodding her thanks, she walked through the waiting area again and then entered a long corridor. The hum of machines and the murmured voices of medical staff were mixed with soft instrumental music floating from the outpatient unit. It was all muted to her because her mind was busy turning over the events that led up to her uncle landing in the emergency room. It appeared it would be a long time before her guilt subsided. Why had she confronted Ralph like she had? Whether or not he told Ariel, it was his decision to make. She had no right to force him to reveal the secret.

A headache stretched across her forehead, temple to temple. Stress headaches were the worst. No amount of aspirin would dull the pain. All she could do was suffer until it went away.

The sign for the public restrooms came into view, directing her to make a slight turn off the main corridor.

When she was done, she exited the bathroom feeling a smidge better. The quick splash of cold water to her face helped improve her mood. Stepping out into the main corridor to head back to Nate, she stopped abruptly, doing a double take at a person who'd just passed by.

What was she doing in the hospital?

"Terry." Kelly's call went ignored.

Terry kept walking, and her speed kicked up, forcing Kelly to dash after her. She couldn't believe she had to chase her employee in a hospital. "Terry. Stop, please. We need to talk."

Terry's pace increased.

From behind, Kelly heard heavy footsteps. When she looked over her shoulder, she saw Nate closing in on her.

"Hey, hold up. What's going on?" He caught up with her, touching her shoulder to stop her.

"I need to talk to Terry." When she turned back, the automatic door was sliding shut. Terry had exited the hospital already. "I have to catch up with her. If you have to leave, go. I'll get a ride back to the boutique."

"Wait. No, I don't have to leave. Tell me why you need to catch up with her. What do you know or think you know?"

Darn. His cop instinct was right on the money.

"First, I need to know if she's planning on coming back to work. Second, I learned she had a breakdown and was hospitalized after a bad incident online, which she blamed Jessica for. She'd been trying to meet with Becky. Then—"

"Then what?"

"I found a note Terry wrote, and the handwriting looks similar to the handwriting on the note found by Becky's body."

"When did you find it?"

"This morning."

"Where's the note now?"

"At the boutique. Look, I really need to talk to her." She went to turn, but Nate grabbed her arm. Her eyes widened, and she glared at him as she yanked her arm back.

"I'm sorry. But I don't think confronting her is a good idea."

"Thank you for your opinion." She propped her hands on her hips and toned down her glare, but not by much.

"Look, I saw where she came out from."

"What does it matter where she came from? I need to talk to her." Kelly dropped her hands and stepped forward, but Nate blocked her. She sighed.

"She came from the outpatient psychiatric unit."

"The what?" She whipped her head around and stared down the corridor, looking for the sign. "I guess what Becky and Jessica said about her was true."

"And it's a very good reason for you not to confront her. Let us, the police, do that, okay? Come on, let's get out of here so you can visit Juniper. By the way, that's a unique name," he said as he guided Kelly toward the emergency room so they could use the exit closest to where he'd parked his sedan.

"It is, and she's a very special little girl. She's always so happy." The distraction of thinking about her youngest cousin was a nice reprieve from all the sadness and worry of the past few days.

They stepped out into the heat of the day. The clingy air was a shock to her system from the chilled, antiseptic cocoon Kelly had been in. It took a moment for her body to adjust to the soaring temperature. She walked beside Nate, taking his cue when to zig to another row of cars. In the panic state she was in when they arrived at the hospital, she had no clue where he'd parked.

When they reached his car, he walked around to the driver's side. Before getting in, he leaned one arm on the roof while the other rested on the door. "I strongly suggest you stay away from Terry. We don't know what her condition is or what, if any, role she played in your cousin's death."

Kelly jerked open the passenger door. A lot of people were telling her what to do, and it was becoming tiresome.

"I'll keep your suggestion in mind." She slid into the passenger seat and buckled up. Despite Nate's warning, she was determined to find out if she had hired a killer.

CHAPTER ELEVEN

The drive back to the boutique was quiet. Incredibly quiet. Kelly hadn't wanted to rehash the conversation about wanting to talk to Terry. What would be the point? Nate wouldn't change his point of view on the subject, and neither would she. Her mind was made up. One way or another, she and Terry would have a conversation.

Nate pulled up in front of the boutique. Kelly thanked him for the ride and for staying with her in the emergency room. She got out of the car, and before he could give her another warning to stay out of the investigation, she spun around and hurried to the boutique.

Inside, Pepper rushed to her and pulled her into a warm hug that Kelly needed. She breathed in the jasmine and orange blossom fragrance Pepper had spritzed on liberally. The bright scent lifted her mood, slightly.

"How's Ralph? Was it a heart attack?" Pepper asked.

"Kelly!" Breena appeared in the doorway from the back hall and bustled forward. "How's your uncle?"

Kelly pulled herself from Pepper's hold and walked past Breena toward the sales counter.

"When I left, Summer was allowed to see him. I'm going to their house to stay with Juniper until she gets home." Kelly glanced at a pile of T-shirts on the counter.

"Oh, Renata stopped in a little while ago to consign those." Breena walked to the counter and scooped them up. "I already put them in the inventory system. Pepper said she'd steam them and put them out on the sales floor. I do have to run; my shift at Doug's starts in like fifteen minutes. See you tomorrow." She flashed a smile and then left the room with the shirts.

Pepper joined Kelly and squeezed Kelly's arm. Kelly smiled, grateful she had the older woman in her life. Though, looking at Pepper, she hardly looked like an old woman. Last fall, she'd updated her hairdo and wardrobe. Now, her color-treated blond hair fell in soft waves to her shoulders, and she wore a short-sleeved shirtdress cinched in at the waist by a snake-print belt. The look was a far cry from the supposed age-appropriate, sensible wardrobe she'd been fond of.

"Breena told me that the nice detective drove you to the hospital. Did he drive you back here?"

Kelly's smile grew wider, and she tried to hide it from Pepper. "Yes, he did. Though I'm not too sure about him being so nice."

"What happened?" Pepper walked around the counter and pulled out a container of wipes and plucked one out. She glided it over the counter, carefully moving around the collection of miniature American flags. Each season, she changed out the decorations. To her, they were festive and fun, to Kelly they were dust collectors and always in the way. But they were Pepper's tradition, which meant Kelly kept her opinion to herself.

Kelly wandered to the cascading rack of blouses and tidied them. "When we were leaving the hospital, I saw Terry. I called out to her, but she ignored me."

"Why would she do that?" Pepper disposed of the wipe and set the mini flags in a straight row in front of the cash register.

"It may have to do with the fact she came from the outpatient psychiatric unit." Kelly looked up from the blouses and saw Pepper's mouth pinch. Shoot. "Nate said I should stay away from her."

Pepper gave Kelly a pointed look over the rim of her glasses. Ouch. The Pepper glare was laser sharp, leaving no doubt in Kelly's mind what she thought. But just to make sure Kelly knew, Pepper shared.

"He sounds like a smart man."

"He sounds like he's telling me what to do," Kelly huffed. "I need to know if Terry is involved in Becky's death. If not, then I'd like to know how to help her."

"You have a good heart. Though sometimes it gets you into trouble." She wagged a finger at Kelly.

"How could wanting to help Terry, if she's not a murderer, be a bad thing?"

Pepper raised a palm. "Hear me out. You have to accept that Terry may not want your help. Either she's involved in Becky's death or she's embarrassed you found out about her problems. Let's, for argument's sake, say she had nothing to do with Becky dying. If she's still having issues, she might not be thinking clearly and she could be dangerous."

"Do you really think so?" Kelly moved over to a rack of shirts and flipped through the hangers.

Pepper returned the container of wipes to their cubby and rested her hands on the counter's edge. "I have no idea. The only thing I know is that I don't want you to get hurt. Leave Terry alone and let the police do their job."

"I wish they'd do it faster." Kelly pulled a cap-sleeved white shirt from the back of the rack. She marched over to the circular rack of pants and pulled off a pair of red capris. Holding the items together, she thought they'd look perfect on a mannequin.

"I know you do. Unfortunately, these types of things take time. Now, can we talk about something other than death?"

Kelly gave a half shrug. "I guess it would be nice to discuss a different topic. What do you have in mind?"

"I'm glad you asked." Pepper's face lit up. "Tonight, I'm going to my pottery class."

"Pottery? Really? Since when?"

Pepper stepped out from behind the counter. She moved over to the table where a selection of sunglasses and scarves were displayed and straightened the items.

"Last week was my first class. And it's a good thing I signed up for it because according to Breena, today's horoscope said I have a need to enjoy and express myself. So tonight, I'm going to make something amazing." She wiggled her fingers and smiled.

Kelly sighed. "Not you too?"

"What? Don't be a Debbie Downer."

"Who, me?"

"There's nothing wrong with reading horoscopes. Let me take those." Pepper gestured to the clothes in Kelly's hands. "You want them on a form?"

Kelly nodded and handed the clothing to Pepper. "Thanks. I have to get going. Where's my tote?"

"I set it under the counter," Pepper said.

"I'm going to stay with Juniper until Summer gets home." Kelly grabbed her tote beneath the counter and headed for the door.

"Remember what I said about staying out of police business. You know Gabe will tell me," Pepper called out as Kelly left.

Kelly heard Pepper's warning loud and clear. Gabe would no doubt rat her out in a heartbeat. Of course, when he did, he'd claim it was for her own good and safety. What they failed to accept was that she'd helped solve a few other murders and survived. Sure, there were scary times, and she'd prefer not to relive them. Still, honestly, she wouldn't have done anything differently because killers had been caught.

She reached the driveway to the communal parking lot that ran behind the businesses on Main Street to get her Jeep. She paused for a nanosecond and made a quick change to her plan. She was in the mood for something decadent. She scrunched her face when an image of Nate popped into her head. *No. No. No.* He was off limits. What she wanted and could have was a to-go iced caramel coffee from Doug's.

She made the detour to the store and found a long line at the counter. Did she really need the coffee? After all, there was coffee at her uncle's house. And ice cubes. But she really wanted a caramel coffee, so she got in line. She spotted Breena and another barista preparing coffees and bagging pastries. She then noticed that the two women in front of her were the same two she ran into a couple of days ago. The slim brunette was dressed in a floral romper and Tory Burch sandals. Her friend, the stuck-up petite blonde, was dressed in a pair of khaki shorts and an orange tube top that showed off her buffed, tanned arms. Kelly couldn't help but hear the brunette moaning about her witch of a boss.

"Well, at least Marian gave you this entire week off. We really have to do something about your employment situation, Charlotte," said the petite blonde.

"I know, right?" Charlotte nodded. "Maybe I'll start my own agency, like Whitney."

Whitney? Were they talking about Whitney Mulhern? They had to be. Kelly started paying closer attention to their conversation.

"Better yet, marry wealthy like she's doing, and you'll never have to worry about deadlines or bitties like Marian." The blonde pulled her cell phone from her straw bag. "Oh, look, a text from the future Mrs. William Hartley." In a mocking tone, she read the message out loud. "Elanna, don't forget to confirm the time for packing the welcome bags for the guests."

"Like you could forget? Two hundred totes need to be assembled," Charlotte said. "I'll be right there with you. I can't wait until this wedding is over. What I can't believe is that she left her own bridal dinner early. Do you know where she went?"

Kelly's ears perked up. Now she was intentionally eavesdropping. If she remembered correctly from the last time they were in the shop, they mentioned the dinner was the same night Becky died. She also recalled how steamed Whitney was with Becky at the Gull Café. What time had Whitney left her own party?

"I have no idea where she went." Elanna shrugged. "Maybe she got an emergency SOS from one of her clients."

Or maybe she left to confront Becky on the beach, and things got out of hand. Even though Whitney had moved on to a new fiancé, the embarrassment of calling off an engagement when you are so high profiled must have been unpleasant. And for a person like her, someone had to pay.

Kelly leaned forward and practically popped her head between their shoulders. "Excuse me, I'm sorry to interrupt. We met the other morning when you were in here. I'm Kelly Quinn. I own a local boutique."

The two women looked at her with caution as if she was about to whip out a religious pamphlet or worse, a sales flyer to a discount store.

"Anyway, are you talking about Whitney Mulhern? I'm looking for a new PR firm. I've heard she's amazing," Kelly fibbed. From what she'd witnessed the other day, Whitney was far from amazing.

Elanna's plump lips curved upward. "Oh, she is."

"I'd love to connect with her," Kelly said. "Would you mind sharing her number so I can call her?"

"I don't know if she's taking on new clients," Charlotte said.

Kelly frowned. "That would be disappointing. But perhaps I can do a one-time consultation with her. I worked for years at Bishop's, and I have big plans for my boutique. I'd love to get back to the city and have a string of shops like Intermix." It would be a dream come true—her own fashion empire. Funny how things change. Before she inherited the boutique, her big dream had been to climb the retail ladder and one day sit in Serena Dawson's seat.

As if synchronized, both women gave sympathetic smiles. Kelly recognized the gesture from her days at Bishop's when she told people in the know who she worked for. Serena's, aka the Dragonista of Seventh Avenue, reputation was well known. And now, Charlotte and Elanna were taking pity on her.

"Oh, goodness, from the city to here? Let's give her Whit's number and see if she can help...Kelly, right?" Elanna reached into her bag.

"Yes." Kelly wanted to get up into their pore-free faces and set them straight about Lucky Cove, but she maintained control because once upon a time, she was almost one of them. When she'd fled after high school for the city, she'd forgotten what made her hometown special. While it had devastated her that her granny had died, the fact she had arranged for Kelly to come back home was a blessing. Kelly could see that now.

Elanna pulled out a business card from her Chanel cardholder and a pen from her bag. She then tapped on her phone a couple times before writing a phone number on the back of the card.

"Here you go." Elanna handed the card to Kelly. "Good luck."

"Next!" the barista called out from the counter, prompting Elanna and Charlotte to move forward to place their orders.

Curious about what was written on the other side, Kelly turned over the business card.

Elanna Everly, property auction coordinator, Peabody's Auction House.

Impressive. Peabody's was world-renowned and a premier marketplace for art and luxury goods. It's where the wealthy found their used furniture. Kelly, on the other hand, scoured flea markets and tag sales for her vintage finds.

"Excuse me." A loud, irritated voice caught Kelly's attention, and her gaze lifted toward the counter. A man, tall and tanned, sporting head-to-toe Ralph Lauren, stood glaring at Breena, who gave a forced smile. Kelly knew just beneath it was a scowl waiting to be released. But Breena had experience dealing with demanding customers, and her smile would remain intact until the customer was gone. "What part of my order didn't you understand? Should I have spoken slower?"

"I apologize. I'll get you another coffee." Breena removed the cup from the counter, but before she could move over to the coffee station, the unhappy customer lashed out again.

"If I wanted *you* to make me another coffee, I would have said so. I'd prefer someone more competent." He snapped his fingers, and the other barista looked from the coffee station. "Yes, you. *You* make my coffee."

Breena's smile slipped, and Kelly seethed at the man's rudeness. First, his tantrum was unnecessary. Sure, getting the wrong coffee order was annoying, but there were far worse things in life. It was called perspective. Obviously, something he lacked. Second, snapping his fingers at people? Expecting them to jump at his command? Third…no, there wasn't a need for a third reason to propel Kelly forward in the line. She pushed through the queue of people, apologizing as she passed to the front.

"Excuse me. There's no need to be so rude. She apologized." Kelly looked up at the dark-haired man and caught a whiff of his overpowering aftershave. It was a bit much, just like his behavior at the moment. Then again, he had an entitlement vibe about him. She guessed he was some bigshot from Wall Street or Madison Avenue. Summer people were the local businesses' bread and butter, though many pranced around town like they owned the place rather than just rented a house or a bedroom.

"This is none of your business," he said, barely looking at Kelly.

"It's okay, Kell. Not a big deal." Breena's fake smile was slipping away.

"Well, getting my order wrong is a big deal. I don't have time to waste waiting for someone to correct my order," he said.

"News flash, nobody cares about your schedule." Everything Kelly was saying went against the How to Handle a Customer 101 handbook. Okay, there really wasn't a book, but this situation was well covered in all her past sales training.

He ignored her and kept his hard stare on the other barista. "Where's my coffee?"

"Breena will make it for you," the barista said as she served her customer.

"You know what? Actually, I won't make it for you," Breena huffed. She untied her apron.

"What are you doing?" Kelly moved closer to the counter.

"Broadening my horizons."

"What? Now?"

Breena nodded. "My horoscope asked what's holding me back. Then it said I'll feel a jolt of motivation to broaden my horizons. Well, looks like he's the jolt." She pointed to the scowling man.

"Breena, he's not a jolt. He's a jerk. But not a jolt. Please don't do anything rash." Like Kelly was one to give advice about spontaneous decisions. She had a long streak of unplanned choices, and most of them led her into very precarious situations.

"I'm done serving the cranky, caffeine-depleted people of the world. I quit." Breena threw down her apron with gusto. Too bad it didn't make a sound when it landed on the counter.

"What about my coffee?" the man asked.

"Frankly, I don't give a darn about your coffee." Breena lifted her chin and then stomped out from behind the counter. She walked toward Kelly. "Come on, let's get out of here."

"You realize you just quit."

"I know." She linked arms with Kelly. "How did you like my twist on the *Gone with the Wind* line?"

Kelly looked over her shoulder. The rude customer had a scowl on his lips, and the other barista looked confused. "You just quit your job," she repeated.

"It's not like I don't have another one. Besides, I can pick up more hours since Terry is MIA."

Kelly's head whipped back around to face Breena. "What about off-season?"

Breena shrugged. "I don't know. What I do know is that I'm done serving up lattes and buttered bagels." She strode to the door, looking victorious.

Kelly looked over her shoulder again and frowned. There'd be no more free coffees.

"Hey! Look where you're going!" Breena snapped.

What on earth is going on today?

Kelly's head whipped around, and she saw her now-full-time employee shove Todd. Was he drunk again?

"My apologies. Perhaps I could buy you a coffee." He gave Breena a once-over, and even Kelly skeeved a bit.

"No thanks." Breena wrinkled her nose in disgust.

He shrugged and looked at Kelly. "Miss Quinn. Are you following me?"

"You know this creep?" Breena asked.

"Sort of. Look, Breena, why don't you go to the boutique. I'm sure Pepper will be grateful for the help."

Breena eyed Todd suspiciously from top to bottom and shrugged. "Sure. No problem." She continued out of the shop.

Todd slipped his hands into his pockets. "So, are you following me?"

"Don't flatter yourself. Besides, I was here first. Just curious, are you okay? You kinda struck out there." Kelly gestured to the door.

"Her loss, but she's not my type." Even though he'd been shot down, he flashed a mischievous grin, and his chest puffed out. "Let me buy you a coffee, and we could celebrate together."

"Celebrate what?"

"My windfall." He pulled a hand from his pocket and rubbed his thumb and forefinger together. "I'm in the money, honey. Turns out I've inherited Becky's share of Define Beauty."

"What?" *Holy Manolos.* Kelly hadn't thought about her cousin's will. Why had Becky left her part of the company to Todd?

"Her attorney called me right after we spoke earlier at the inn. Can you imagine Jessica's reaction when she finds out that I own the majority stake in the company?" His eyes lit up with amusement.

"She and Becky weren't fifty-fifty?"

He shook his head. "Nope. It makes sense since the company was Becky's idea from the start. Jessica came in after Becky had done all the preliminary work to start the business."

"Does Jessica know?"

"I have no idea."

"Guess you're going to find out." Kelly pointed toward the door, and Todd looked over his shoulder.

"Hmm…from the death glare on her face, I think she's unhappy with the new business arrangement," Todd quipped.

"You think?" Kelly braced herself for a very public and angry confrontation between the new business partners.

"You!" Jessica barreled forward at full steam with her finger stabbing the air. "No way an I going to let you get away with this."

"Get away with what?" Todd strolled to the coffee line. It seemed to Kelly he enjoyed seeing Jessica spin out of control.

"I know you must have unduly influenced Becky for her to name you as her beneficiary." Jessica lowered her hand.

"Good luck proving it. By the way, we should set up a meeting to go over a few things, seeing as I am now in charge, and you better get used to it." He stepped up when the barista called for the next person in line.

Jessica balled her fingers into tight fists and looked at Kelly while everyone in the store gawked at her. "There's no way I'm going to stand by and watch him take over the company I built with Becky. No way!" She spun around and stormed out.

"Are you going to order something?" a short, balding man asked Kelly, and she glanced over her shoulder. Right. She'd come in for a caramel coffee. She stepped into line and watched Todd get his coffee and then saunter out of the store. All the while, her brain replayed the scene she had witnessed.

Had Jessica expected to inherit the company upon Becky's death? Now she had another motive to kill Becky. What about Todd? Had he known he would inherit controlling interest in the company? A company he believed he was entitled to. Now he had another motive too.

CHAPTER TWELVE

With her large caramel coffee—Doug's kept it simple by offering only three sizes—Kelly exited the store and walked back to the boutique to get her Jeep for the drive over to Summer's house. When she arrived, she was greeted by Nancy, the housekeeper, who had been instructed to make dinner for Kelly. She'd also prepared a guest room in case Kelly wanted to spend the night.

Kelly hadn't expected such star treatment, but after the day she had, she'd take it. The housekeeper led her into the family room and then quickly disappeared, leaving Kelly with Juniper.

She made eye contact with her little cousin, who was busy on her activity mat. Juniper giggled and so did Kelly. The baby's chubby, smiling face was exactly what she needed. There was no way she could feel sad when in the presence of that little munchkin. No way.

Kelly set her tote and coffee on a side table and hurried to the mat. She got down on the floor to join Juniper. All her worries were shoved way back into the recesses of her mind. Now she was 100 percent focused on Juniper. She tickled her, and the baby squealed with happiness, and they explored all the fun things on the mat. There they played until dinnertime, which consisted of a perfectly grilled piece of salmon drizzled with a pan sauce and sauteed green beans and a glass of wine for Kelly.

"Would you like dessert?" Nancy asked as she wiped Juniper's face and then cleaned the high chair.

"No, thank you. I'm full. This was delicious."

"I'm glad you enjoyed it. I'm going to take Juniper upstairs for her bath and get her ready for bed."

"So soon?" Kelly stood as the housekeeper scooped up Juniper.

"She's only a baby. She needs her sleep. And I suspect you could use some quiet time yourself." Nancy left with Juniper.

Perhaps she was right. Kelly carried her dishes to the counter and loaded them into the dishwasher. Then she prepared a cup of tea and brought it back to the family room.

She made a beeline for the sofa and sat, kicking off her shoes. Careful not to spill, she curled up and sipped her tea.

The room had high ceilings, expensive furnishings, and artwork that cost more than the Jeep Kelly drove. She wondered if she'd ever have anything close to a home like this. Or would she forever be living in the one-bedroom apartment above the boutique?

She smiled. She'd been making some pretty great memories in her new home. Moving out would probably create a hole in her heart. After all, it had been good enough for her granny.

Her phone dinged, and she got up to retrieve it from her tote and then returned to the sofa. It was a message from Summer.

Ralphie is stable. I'll be late. Stay over if you'd like. See you soon.

There were also messages she'd missed during dinner from Liv, Gabe, Pepper, and Breena. They were all looking for updates. She replied to a group text, yes, she hated them, but they were efficient.

Ralph is stable, and I'm still at his house.

She closed her text app and opened the browser. She occupied herself with some mindless scrolling of her favorite fashion bloggers, though a distant memory distracted her. She remembered the flash of emotion that had crossed Nate's face when he reminded her she shouldn't sweat the small stuff in life. Not sure why, but his instant yet short mood swing had lingered with her, and she was curious about its cause.

She closed out of the fashion blog she was on and did a search for Detective Nate Barber. Halfway down the page was a newspaper article. She tapped on the link, and it opened. She read the article, her curiosity giving way to shock. Nate had been involved in a drug arrest gone wrong. He'd been shot and his partner killed.

No wonder his philosophy was don't sweat the small stuff. He could have died. According to the article's date, the incident happened three years ago, and he'd been working in a larger police department. She wondered when he joined the Lucky Cove police force.

After closing out of the article, she continued browsing until she came across an article about Becky's death and Define Beauty's fate. There was no mention of Todd's inheriting Becky's share of the company. Boy, she'd hate to be with Jessica when that news was posted online.

From Todd's comments earlier and his behavior at the beach house, she believed he wouldn't be as eager to sell as Jessica had been. Like Becky, he seemed to have an emotional attachment to the business. There was also the fact that Jessica wanted to sell. She sensed he would do the opposite of whatever Jessica wanted just to spite her.

Kelly closed out of the article and opened her social media to scroll some more, liking and hearting while finishing her tea. When her thumbs ached, she set the phone down and stretched her arms. It felt good to move, and as she arched her back, she heard the front door open and Summer call out.

Kelly stood and slipped her shoes back on when Summer appeared in the doorway, looking exhausted and worried. Her eyes were bloodshot and hooded while her shoulders sagged.

"How's he doing? Did he wake up?" *And tell you that I caused his heart attack?*

"He was in and out the entire time. Though, the doctors are optimistic." Summer entered the room and dropped her purse on a chair and crossed her arms. "I promise you, when he gets home there's going to be some changes to his diet, and he's going to exercise. No excuses anymore. I need my Ralphie with me for a long, long time."

"I'm glad to hear he's going to be okay. Your phone call when it happened was scary."

"It sure was. I'm going to check on Juniper, then go to bed. You're welcome to stay overnight. I had Nancy prepare the guest room."

"Thank you, but I'll go home. It's not too late. First, I'll take this into the kitchen." Kelly swiped up her empty cup from the end table.

"Oh, give it to me. You go on." Summer took the cup and walked to the doorway. "Thank you, Kelly, for coming to the hospital and staying with Juniper. It was good to know she was with family."

"Anytime."

Summer stared at Kelly for a moment before turning and continuing out of the room. Ralph's prognosis wasn't the only thing to be optimistic about. It seemed she and Summer were forging a new level in their relationship. Kelly grabbed her tote and walked out of the family room. When she reached the front door, her phone dinged. She reached into her tote and pulled out her phone. There was a text from Gabe.

They found Todd Wilson unconscious in his hotel room. He's in a coma.

She stopped midstep and absorbed what she read. A coma? How was it possible? She saw him a few hours ago, and he was fine.

She texted back.

What caused it?

She resumed walking out of the house and toward her Jeep.

Nothing official I can share.

"Well, that's never stopped him before," she murmured as she feverishly typed her next message.

Maybe he drank too much. He seemed to be doing a lot of that. Or maybe he was poisoned.

Within seconds, Gabe's reply came.

Maybe you should leave this matter to us.

"Ha! Like that's going to happen." Kelly slipped into the driver's seat. She texted back, asking to be kept updated, before starting the ignition and pulling out of the driveway.

When Kelly reached the driveway's end, she turned right onto Sea Glass Road, which would take her to Main Street.

The road was quiet for a summer weeknight. Then again, this section of town wasn't a big draw for renters. They tended to congregate closer to the beach and dunes. Sea Glass was lined with homes like Summer's and set back from the road, hidden by ornate gates. This was a section of town Kelly was sure she'd never call home.

The sky was pitch black, and only a sliver of the moon was visible. It had been a long time since she'd been out so late. Probably the last time was when she dated Mark. Before then, late nights were typical for her when she lived in the city.

A pair of high beams appearing in her rearview mirror cut short her trip down memory lane. She squinted to adjust to the bright light.

Where had the vehicle come from?

A moment later, there was only darkness. The lights were gone.

Weird.

She adjusted her hands on the steering wheel. She thought about turning on the radio but she didn't want any distractions. Her own thoughts were enough. She approached a section of the road dense with woods and wildlife, so she slowed down. Deer had a way of leaping out onto the street. And that's when the high beams appeared again.

What was going on?

Then the lights disappeared as quickly as they had appeared.

Her mind raced with thoughts of someone following her along the isolated stretch of road. Were they trying to unnerve her? If so, they were succeeding. And who exactly were *they*? Perhaps a bunch of teenagers out looking to stir up trouble? Not exactly uncommon during the summer months.

Her grip on the steering wheel tightened as she quelled the panic rising in her. Main Street wasn't much farther.

The high beams flashed once more, and she pressed her foot harder on the accelerator. With a blatant disregard for the speed limit, she made it back to the center of town in record time. And with no more strange occurrences.

She parked behind the boutique and hurried inside the building. After securing the door, she ran through to the front of the boutique.

She reached the window and peered out, looking for anything suspicious. Main Street was all quiet mostly. The restaurants were closing, so their patrons were walking back to the nearby inns. All looked good.

"Guess there's nothing to worry about," she said to no one.

Then she noticed the front door was open. Now, that was odd. Breena or Pepper wouldn't have left the door unlocked. She rushed to the door to close it and, upon closer inspection, noticed the doorjamb was damaged.

Someone had broken into the boutique.

Her heart rate kicked up as perspiration beaded on her forehead.

Was there someone in the boutique?

Or was someone upstairs in her apartment?

She listened for footsteps. There were none.

Had she walked in on a burglary?

The smart thing to do would be to call the police and get out of the building. Her tote was in the staff room, where she dropped it when she entered. But the landline handset was on the sales counter. She turned to get the telephone and tripped over something. She glanced downward and let out a bloodcurdling scream.

There was an arm on the floor.

An arm!

Finally, her scream petered out as her eyes focused on the limb.

It wasn't a human arm.

It was from a mannequin.

Oh, thank goodness.

Kelly bent over and picked up the mannequin part, chiding herself for being so silly. Of course, it wasn't from a human. She stepped forward to the mannequin, dressed in a sleeveless tank top and capri pants, to replace the part. When she got close, she noticed a sign around the figure's neck.

Beauty and the deceased. Don't end up like your cousin.

Her mouth dropped open, and her heart pounded against her chest as the words seeped in.

Don't end up like your cousin.

"What happened?"

The unexpected voice almost had Kelly jumping out of her skin. She swung around, wielding the arm as a weapon.

"Whoa!" Liv raised her hands up in surrender. "I didn't mean to scare you. I'm on my way home and saw your door open."

Kelly let out an enormous sigh and lowered her weapon, aka mannequin arm.

"Thank goodness! Coming back from my uncle's house there was a car that kept flashing its high beams and then disappearing. Then I came in and found they had forced the door open and then this note." She pointed to the mannequin.

Liv inched closer to the form. "Oh, my word. Kelly, this is a threat."

Kelly cocked her head to the side. "Thank you, Captain Obvious."

"This isn't funny."

"I know." Kelly walked to the sales counter and set the limb down before reaching for the telephone. "Why are you out so late? Don't you have to be at the bakery before dawn?"

"I'm working a half day tomorrow. I was at the Gold Sands. It was karaoke night. Gabe was there too." Liv went back to the door and poked her head out. "In fact, he was walking me home. Where'd he go?"

The Gold Sands was a bar and the hot spot for tourists in season. Kelly couldn't remember the last time she did karaoke. Oh, wait, she could. It was one of the date nights with Mark.

"Were you and Gabe out on a date?" Kelly had been picking up on subtle clues that Liv had a crush on Gabe, and she felt the same vibe from Gabe. Finally, they both realized it and went out on a date.

"No! No, no, no." Liv flushed.

"Thou protests too much." Kelly smiled.

"Hey, what's going on? Everything okay?" Gabe appeared at the door.

"No. Kelly was followed home by someone. And the boutique was broken into, and they left a threatening note." Liv pointed to the mannequin.

"I'm calling the police now." Kelly jabbed the phone's keypad. What an awful way to end a bad day. She couldn't believe she was calling 9-1-1 again. When the emergency operator answered, she explained the situation. She also informed him that there was an off-duty officer on the scene. When they were done, she disconnected the call, and another unpleasant thought slammed into her—she'd have to file an insurance claim for the door repair. The day couldn't possibly get any worse.

"Kell, what have you gotten yourself into now?" Gabe stood with his hands on his hips and a stern look in his eyes. He'd morphed into no-nonsense Officer Donovan right before her eyes.

"What about Todd? Is he still in a coma? Any update on what caused the condition?" She'd focus on Todd rather than the threatening note left for her. She was still too scared to talk about the note objectively. Maybe by tomorrow morning, after she checked, double-checked, and triple-checked the locks. Wait. The front door. It needed to be secured before she could attempt to get any shut-eye.

There was only one solution, and it would come with a scolding. She reached for the phone again. She'd have to call Pepper and ask for her husband's help.

"I told you there's nothing official I can tell you about his case."

"Fine. Then let me tell you about my theory," Kelly said.

"Another one?" Gabe asked as he dragged his fingers through his hair.

Kelly ignored the question. "I stopped into Doug's before going to see Juniper. I ran into Todd, and then Jessica came storming in. She's furious that he's inherited Becky's share of the company."

"No way!" Liv exclaimed.

Kelly nodded. "She said there was no way she'd stand by and watch him take over the company she and Becky built. She could have tried to kill him but it didn't work."

A tiny smile twitched on Gabe's lips. "You're something else, Kelly Quinn. You've just received a threat, and yet you're still trying to stick your nose into police business. My suggestion is that we focus on the matter at hand." He looked at the armless mannequin.

"This is serious, Kelly. The note is scary." Liv's hands covered her heart. "I'm scared."

Kelly hated seeing her friend worry. It made her angry and more determined to find out who was behind the break-in and creepy note.

"Liv mentioned someone followed you home. Did you get a look at the vehicle?" Gabe asked.

"I wish I had. They kept flashing their high beams and then cut the lights altogether. It could have just been teenagers," Kelly said.

"I doubt teenagers did this." Liv's hands made a sweeping motion toward the door and mannequin.

"You're probably right." Kelly leaned against the counter and crossed her arms. From previous experience, she knew that when a killer lashed out at her somehow, it meant she was getting close to revealing their identity. Over the past couple of days, had she spoken to the killer?

Was she making him or her nervous? It seemed so.

Now, if she only knew who the killer was.

CHAPTER THIRTEEN

The next morning rolled around faster than Kelly would have thought possible. Hadn't she just climbed into bed and pulled up the covers and willed herself to go to sleep? The answer had to be yes, and there had to have been something wrong with her alarm clock because it clearly was set for the wrong time.

She slit an eye open and looked out the window. Daylight streamed in through the sheer curtains. Darn. Her alarm clock wasn't wrong. It was morning. Well, later in the morning from when she went to bed. And it was time to get up.

She pulled her arm from beneath the covers and swatted at the alarm clock, making it stop its incessant beeping. With both eyes somewhat open, she searched the room for Howard.

He was nowhere to be found.

During her few hours in bed, he must have bailed because of her constant tossing and turning and inability to fall into a deep sleep.

Kelly considered staying put. Leaving the boutique closed. Indefinitely. She turned over and adjusted the pillow. It wouldn't be the first time she'd taken to her bed for solace. To hide out from the big, bad world.

Her heart squeezed at the thought. What would her granny think? Lying there like a quitter. Afraid to face the day. Well, she had good reasons to, and they flitted through her mind.

Her cousin had been murdered.

Her rekindled friendship with Ariel was doomed because of Ralph's secret.

A killer had her in their sights.

Pretty solid reasons to stay right where she was. Until she heard her granny's voice.

"There's an old saying, a woman is like a tea bag—you can't tell how strong she is until you put her in hot water."

Kelly rolled onto her back and stared up to the ceiling. She remembered her granny saying it was a quote from Eleanor Roosevelt, a woman Martha had respected. Kelly knew her granny would be disappointed by her granddaughter at the moment.

Ugh.

Kelly tossed the covers off and got out of bed. She moved through her morning routine—shower, blow-dry, makeup—with little oomph, but she got it done. Next on her morning routine was coffee—lots of it.

In the kitchen, she stifled a yawn as she measured out two scoops of coffee grounds. She considered the filter and her level of exhaustion. One more scoop it was. She closed the lid, pressed the On button, and placed her jumbo mug under the spout.

It was her favorite mug and only used on occasions like this morning—when she was dog tired. Becky had sent it last Christmas, and it was the perfect gift. The three words scrawled on the front of the mug—But First Mascara—fit Kelly so well.

A loud meow announced Howard's arrival in the kitchen as he slinked by Kelly's leg on his way to the trash can. He leaped up. From his perch, he could keep an eye on Kelly. His orange tail hung over the side of the canister, and it flicked back and forth as he stared at her. He was waiting for breakfast.

"You weren't up most of the night." Kelly pulled open the refrigerator door and took out the milk carton.

Flick. Flick. Flick.

"Okay. Okay. Okay." Kelly set the carton on the counter and retrieved his bowl from an upper cabinet. Her phone buzzed. *Again.* It had been going off since she woke—another message asking about what happened last night.

It was well after midnight when she made it up to her apartment after giving her statement to the responding officer. Somewhere between the call to report the break-in and closing, Pepper had arrived with her husband. He got to work securing the door and assured Kelly he'd have it fixed ASAP. Once everyone left, she double-checked the locks on all the doors and then climbed into bed. She'd barely had the energy to change out of her clothes and into her pj's, so she'd forgone her usual skincare routine in favor of sleep.

Given she hardly slept, she regretted her decision. She had to double-cleanse her face and break out a packet of anti-puffiness smoothing patches to apply beneath her eyes. The box of six packets had been a splurge before being fired from Bishop's. She had lost not only her job but also her employee discount. Since hundred-dollar anti-puffiness patches were no longer in her budget, she used them sparingly.

The coffee machine beeped, her cat meowed, and she slumped. It was going to be a long day.

As much as she'd come to love Howard, he could wait a few seconds for his meal. If his rounded belly was any indication, he wasn't starving.

She wrapped her fingers around her mug and took a long drink of the coffee.

Her phone buzzed again. She glanced at the message. Yep, another question about what happened last night. She ignored it and went back to savor her coffee.

The extra scoop was just what she needed.

Now she could feed the little beggar. Setting the mug down, she inhaled a fortifying breath, pushed off the counter, and pulled out his container of food. He leaped from the trash canister, victorious in getting his way. At his place mat, he waited for his meal like the king he was.

She served the kibble and then rinsed out his water bowl before filling it with fresh water.

"I think you're all set." She grabbed her mug and padded out of the kitchen and into the living room. While her face was somewhat presentable with the aid of foundation, concealer, and highlighter, she was still in her pajama shorts and a tank top. On her feet, she wore her favorite plush slippers. Even though it was the middle of July, the air-conditioning made her toes chilly.

She dropped onto the sofa and sipped her coffee while looking out the front window.

Main Street would be bustling soon. Shops and restaurants would open for the day while hers remained closed. Last night she made the executive decision to reopen only after they repaired the door. They'd take a financial hit, but both she and Pepper had been up for hours in the middle of the night, and Breena had an appointment with her daughter to attend.

She eyed a throw pillow and had the urge to lay her head down to catch some more z's, but her phone buzzed again. She grumbled. The phone wouldn't stop blowing up until she replied to everyone.

Kelly set her mug on the end table, picked up the phone, and scrolled through the incoming texts.

They all had two things in common—shock about the incident and warnings to stay out of the investigation. The simplest way to deal with this was to do a group text. Within minutes, she had a reply simply worded—she appreciated their concern—and hit the Send button.

There wouldn't be a promise to stay out of the investigation. Whoever broke into her boutique last night and left the threatening note made sure of that. Now, she was more determined to uncover the killer's identity.

Howard appeared from the kitchen and jumped up on the sofa. He nudged her arm with his head, and in the silence of the room, she heard his purring. She lowered her phone and scratched his forehead.

After finishing the coffee, Kelly got herself off the sofa and into her bedroom to dress for the day. For the first time in a long time, deciding what to wear overwhelmed her. A sign she'd been pushed to her mental limits by everything that was going on.

She stood at the garment rack and stared. About half her clothes were stored there while the rest hung in the small bedroom closet. She knew she wanted something comfortable to wear. Big help. She reached for a pair of wide-leg capri pants. Easy. Breezy. At the closet, she reached in for a horizontal-striped bateau neckline top. The blue-and-white top had three-quarter-length sleeves that would show off her bracelets and help stave off the chilly air from indoor cooling systems.

Dressed, she was ready to take on the world. Okay, that was a grand statement, but she felt a bit better and at least prepared to face the world. She swiped up her cell phone from the bed, and a new notification flashed on the screen. She opened the app and found a DM from Beauty4Everygirl.

Just heard about your cousin. So sorry. I love her makeup. Especially her lipsticks. Hope Define isn't left in the hands of JB.

The message ended with a sad emoji face.

JB had to be Jessica. Why would Beauty4Everygirl write such a comment?

Kelly tapped, navigating to Beauty4Everygirl's account.

The brief bio at the top gave her little information as to who the account owner was, though the feed made it clear Beauty4Everygirl loved makeup—a lot. Kelly kept scrolling, astonished by how many products were featured.

Kelly returned to the message and wrote back.

Thank you for reaching out. I miss my cousin very much. The details of her estate are still being worked out, and I can't comment. But I would like to talk to you about JB.

She hit the send arrow and headed out of the bedroom.

Downstairs, she found Pepper's husband, Clive, on the phone with a buddy who agreed to repair the door. There was a chance she could open the boutique by lunchtime.

It was nice to start the day off with some positive news. Kelly thanked Clive with a kiss on the cheek and proceeded into the staff room. There she found Pepper at the coffee machine, pouring a big cup. Last's night excitement had taken a toll on Pepper, and she looked tired.

"My third so far." Pepper raised the cup to her lips and sipped. "You know, there was a time when I could stay out till the wee hours of the morning, get a couple of hours of sleep, and be raring to go when the alarm went off. I think those days are officially over."

Kelly's heart squeezed with guilt. "I'm sorry I bothered you last night."

Pepper walked toward Kelly and patted her arm. "Don't be. I'm glad you called us. We're always here for you. No matter what the time is. I'd better go check on Clive. What are you up to this morning?"

Up to?

The woman is psychic.

Kelly hesitated. The errand she planned to run was one Pepper definitely would disapprove of.

"You know what? Never mind. You have that look in your eye, and I don't think I want to know what you're up to." Pepper walked past Kelly and pushed the door open and disappeared.

Kelly let out a sigh of relief and then moved to the desk where she'd stashed Terry's note the other day. It was time to turn it over to the police.

But first, she had one stop to make. She was going to give Terry one last chance to tell her side of the story.

Kelly left the boutique and got into her Jeep to drive across the town border into the quaint village where Terry lived. No longer believing anything Terry had told her, Kelly wasn't sure what to expect when she arrived at the address listed on the employment application.

* * * *

Following the GPS directions, she turned onto Baxter Drive. The bungalow-lined street was off a busy thoroughfare. Halfway down the road, she arrived at Terry's address.

So far, so good. There was actually a residence at the address.

She parked at the curb and got out. No sign of Terry's Jetta, although she caught motion in the large bay window. The sheer curtain had moved.

Someone was home.

Before getting out of her Jeep, she checked her phone for a reply from Beauty4Everygirl. There was none. And there probably would be none. Either the person only contacted Kelly to pay her condolences or just wanted to stir up drama by making the comment about Jessica. Either way, she must have moved onto something or someone else.

Kelly walked along the brick path to the front entrance, and before she knocked, the door swung open.

A woman stood protectively at the door. She appeared to be in her midfifties, wearing cropped jeans and a striped T-shirt. Her dark blond hair was swept off her face by a headband, and large silver hoops dangled from her ears. Her brows were arched high, and her eye makeup was expertly applied. Instantly, Kelly saw the resemblance and knew she was Terry's mom.

"May I help you?" Her voice was restrained as if she was expecting Kelly to whip out a vacuum cleaner or a survey form. She also looked ready to close the door.

"I'm looking for Terry Carlisle. I'm Kelly Quinn. I own the Lucky Cove Resale Boutique."

The woman's face softened as she seemed to recognize Kelly's name. Or, at least, the boutique.

"It's nice to finally meet you. I'm Lottie, Terry's mom." Her body relaxed, and she opened the door wider, giving Kelly a peek inside the tidy little house. She didn't notice anyone else moving around inside.

"I'm sorry to disturb you. Is Terry here?" Kelly asked.

"No. She left about an hour ago, saying something about having to get in early today."

"She did?" Kelly wasn't too surprised to hear another lie from Terry.

"You must be very busy. I'm going to have to stop by the boutique one of these days. You know, Terry loves her job…but I think she's working too much. And since you're here looking for her, I think you're working too hard if you can't remember her schedule." Lottie laughed.

Kelly did her best to join in, but her chuckle was halfhearted. There hadn't been much to laugh about lately. Wait. Why did Terry's mom think she was working too much? Terry had only been scheduled to work twenty hours before she ran out of the boutique and never returned.

"It's been a hectic few days, so my bad for messing up the schedule. Do you really think she's working too much?"

"Perhaps it's nothing. Never mind me, I'm probably overreacting, but after everything that has happened, I can't help but worry."

"About Terry working too much? I don't think it'll be a problem anymore." Especially since it seemed like Terry no longer worked for her.

Lottie's face clouded. "She's been acting strangely the past few days. But maybe it's the extra hours she's putting in. I'm proud of her for being a hard worker, but I'm also glad to hear you won't be giving her too many hours. I hope it won't be too much of an inconvenience for you."

"It's not going to be a problem." Kelly hadn't wanted to break the news that Terry hadn't been back to the boutique since someone she was accused of stalking was murdered. "It's understandable that you're concerned. The whole situation online had to have been tough to deal with. Especially dealing with Jessica Barron."

"Oh, I don't know any of their names." Lottie crossed her arms and rolled her eyes. "What I do know is that social media is ripe for jealousy. All my girl wanted to do was share her love and knowledge about makeup."

"She closed her accounts."

Lottie nodded. "It was ugly. Ironic, isn't it? All those beauty vloggers showed how unattractive they really were on the inside. The mean hashtags, the vile direct messages. It was too much. My baby only wanted to share makeup tutorials. It took several months before she finally came out of her shell and applied for real jobs. I was thrilled. Then you hired her. I can't tell you how happy it made me."

Lottie threw the door open wider and stepped outside. She pulled Kelly into a hug and squeezed tight. "I can't thank you enough."

"You...you don't have to thank me." Nope, thanks weren't necessary. Especially since she might be implicating Terry in Becky's murder. She still had the note Terry wrote. "I should go."

"Of course." Lottie released her hold on Kelly and stepped back into her doorway. "It was very nice to meet you."

"Same here." Kelly's tone was subdued because of her next planned stop. She turned and walked back to her Jeep. When she got in, she gave one final look at the house. Terry's mom had closed the door. It was hard to believe she was clueless about her daughter's activities for the past few days. The bigger question was—where the heck was Terry?

* * * *

Kelly entered the Lucky Cove Police Department then paused before continuing forward. She swiveled. Then shifted back around only to turn back to the door. What on earth was the matter with her? This should have been simple. She tried to find Terry and offer her a chance to explain. But it turned out, all she'd been doing was lying. As much as Kelly wanted to, she couldn't continue protecting her. So why was she considering walking out of the police department and looking for Terry, again?

Just as she reached for the door to open it, she was stopped by a question. "Kelly Quinn, right?"

Kelly looked over her shoulder at the officer seated behind the partition. With a big grin pasted on his face, his dark eyes flickered with amusement.

"Yes, I am." She turned and walked toward the communications center.

"How many bodies have you stumbled upon?" The officer chuckled. "You're quite popular here."

"I've had the unfortunate experience of finding recently deceased people far too often." It wasn't as if she intended to find murder victims. It seemed she managed to be at the wrong place at the wrong time. Or, maybe it was the right place at the right time, seeing as she had a natural knack for sleuthing. Perhaps she was supposed to stick her nose into police investigations. Who knew? It really didn't matter, because she couldn't change the past. "I'm here on official business. I would like to speak with Detective Wolman."

Officer Chuckles let out a big snort. "Official business. Good one. Have a seat, and I'll let her know you're here." He pointed to the bench and then stepped away from the desk.

Kelly followed the instructions and moved away from the communications center. She dropped to the bench and then pulled out the zipped baggie from her tote.

She shouldn't feel guilty for doing what she was doing. If Terry had wanted to share her side of the story, she'd had ample time to do so. It appeared she didn't want Kelly's help. Besides, she'd already mentioned the note to Nate. It would be better if she handed over the note to Wolman on her own.

Maybe, since she was there, she could get an update on Todd's condition?

She wondered how long the detective would make her wait.

Her cell phone rang, and for a moment, she considered letting it go to voice mail. She had to at least see who was calling. It could have been Summer with an update on her uncle. She pulled the phone out of her purse. The caller ID said it was Marvin Childers. She smiled. The retired illustrator had been an old friend of her granny's and was now a good friend of hers.

"Hey, there. How are you doing?" she asked after accepting the call.

"Good. Good. I'm in town for the day and wondering if you'd like to have lunch with me." Marvin's voice was cheerful.

Her stomach grumbled at the word "lunch," and she realized she hadn't eaten since last night at Summer's house. The salmon had been grilled to perfection, and she'd love another one. Too bad she couldn't cook as well as Summer's housekeeper.

"Yes, of course. But I can't be away for too long. It's only Pepper and me in the boutique today." Though she wasn't sure if the boutique would even be open.

"Not a problem. Gio's? My treat."

Kelly looked up at Officer Chuckles and then to the interior door that led to the police department's inner workings. "Sounds good." *If I don't get arrested for withholding evidence.*

They agreed on a time and ended the call.

She sent a quick text to Pepper about her lunch plans and offered to bring something back from the restaurant. Pepper didn't hesitate to give her order.

As she slipped her phone back into her purse, the door clicked and then opened. Wolman appeared with her usual serious expression. Her outfit of the day was monochromatic—all black. A black shirt and well-fitting blazer topped her bootcut pants.

"I was about to pay you a visit, Kelly. Thanks for saving me the trip. I understand you have something for me." Wolman reached out her hand.

Talk about getting right down to business.

Wait. Kelly hadn't mentioned she had something for Wolman when she came in. Nate must have filled his colleague in about the letter after she told him about it yesterday. Now she doubted she'd get an update on Todd. Wolman was already irritated with her.

"I do." She handed over the baggie. "The handwriting seems similar to the handwriting on the note I saw with Becky's body."

"You've had this for days, haven't you?" Wolman remained stone faced and stared Kelly down.

Kelly gulped. "Yes."

"You know I could arrest you for interfering with my investigation."

"Yes. However, in my defense, I've had a hard time believing she could be a killer. I wanted to talk to Terry." Kelly suspected Wolman wasn't interested in her defense, but she had to try.

"It's not your place to talk to a suspect." Wolman stepped forward, and the serious look on her face grew dire. *Oh, boy.* "You've crossed the line this time, Kelly."

"Are you going to arrest me?"

Wolman eased back and shook her head. "I don't have time for the paperwork. I have to find Terry Carlisle."

"Well, she's not home." That comment earned her an exasperated sigh from Wolman. *Oops.*

"How would you know?"

"I was just at her house. Her mom said she'd left an hour earlier to go to work. But she hasn't been to the boutique in days."

Wolman lifted the baggie and looked at the note. Her expression appeared neutral. She wasn't about to give anything away to Kelly. *Shoot.*

The detective lifted her gaze. "You can go now." She turned on her mid-heeled loafers, walked back to the interior door, and tapped on the keypad. When the door clicked, she opened it and entered. Kelly didn't wait for the door to close before turning and getting out of there before Wolman changed her mind about how much time she had for paperwork. That was probably the smartest thing she'd do all day.

The glass door closed behind her as a combination of relief and worry pulsed through her. Had turning over the note been the right thing to do? Could Terry really be someone who could kill? It didn't matter, did it? She had no choice but to surrender the note. Especially since Nate had told Wolman about it.

She cringed at the thought of Wolman showing up at the boutique for the note. Oh, the grief she would have gotten from Pepper. She could see the Pepper glare now.

A few steps from the entrance, she noticed the day was turning gray. Overhead, ominous clouds spread out seeming to mimic the gloominess consuming her now. She considered calling to cancel lunch but knew Marvin would be disappointed. So she pushed forward.

Walking at a slow speed, her mind replayed everything that had happened over the past few days. She wondered if she was searching for that one moment when she could have done something to prevent her cousin's death.

So much for closure.

She stopped in front of Liv's family's bakery and stared into the window. Lingering, she debated whether she should indulge in a pastry or two. Of course, the answer would be yes. How could she not? She opened the door and entered. The aromas of vanilla, sugar, and freshly baked bread mingled in the air, and her nose twitched as her mouth watered.

There was nothing fancy about the third-generation bakery: no high-end coffee machines or Wi-Fi access. The bakery harkened back to a simpler time when life wasn't so cluttered with noise from twenty-four-hour news cycles, email notification dings, and social media obsession.

Why had life gotten so complicated?

Oh, right, I'm an adult.

An adult in need of sustenance. Well, really, what she craved was comfort, and the full pastry case stretched along one wall offered a lot of comfort. And calories. Behind the case were shelves loaded with bread baskets. From traditional Italian loaves to sourdough to multigrain, there was something for everyone. There were also stacks of flat white boxes and cones of red and white twine. The bakery looked exactly as it had when Kelly was a little girl. Except for the newly updated cash register. The old-fashioned one used when the bakery first opened had been retired by Liv's mother, the manager and chief cannoli maker.

Cheerful chatter drifted from the kitchen where the Moretti women worked their magic with the simplest ingredients of flour, sugar, and yeast. Kelly inhaled another calming breath. There was no doubt in her mind she'd be fitting into only clothing with stretchy waistbands if she worked in the bakery. She spotted Aunt Mia at the counter, filling a pastry box with donuts. How she stayed so slim around all the yummy treats baffled Kelly.

About to step forward to the display case, she paused after catching sight of Whitney Mulhern seated at one of the café tables. Her shoulder-length chestnut hair fell forward as she typed on her phone with manicured nails. Set out on the table were five plates of cake slices. It looked as if she were there for a cake tasting, but her wedding was days away. It seemed kind of late in the game for selecting the wedding cake.

Kelly glanced back at the counter. Aunt Mia was still busy with her customer. They were chatting about the upcoming beach party next month, and Liv was nowhere to be found. What would it hurt if Kelly took a few minutes of Whitney's time to ask her a simple question?

Kelly crossed the black-and-white-tiled floor. When she reached the table, she cleared her throat, drawing Whitney's attention from her phone.

"Hi, Whitney. I don't know if you remember me, but we kind of met the other day at the Gull Café when I was having lunch with my cousin, Becky Quinn. I'm Kelly." She extended her hand.

Whitney looked disinterested. "I meet many people." She returned her gaze back to the phone.

Alrighty. Talk about an awkward moment. Kelly lowered her hand. Whitney would not make this easy. So she tamped down her irritation at the PR guru and followed through with her spur-of-the-moment plan. Whitney's rudeness wouldn't be a deterrent.

"I'm sure you do since you're one of the best in the PR game for up-and-coming businesses, like mine. I own the Lucky Cove Resale Boutique." Kelly pulled out a chair and sat. She opted not to wait for an invitation because none seemed forthcoming.

Whitney looked up again, her glossed lips forming an O.

Now Kelly had her attention. Good.

"Isn't it a little late for wedding cake tasting?" Kelly couldn't help but ask as her gaze drifted over all the plates. The slice with dark cherries and a thick layer of frosting had her salivating. But she'd be more than happy to eat any of them. All she needed was a fork.

"It's more than a little late, but my soon-to-be mother-in-law doesn't seem bothered by that little detail." Whitney's lips curved downward. "She waited until last night to tell me she didn't like our choice of salted caramel. Now I have to select a new one."

"Well, whichever one you go with, you can't go wrong. This is the best bakery on Long Island."

"I really don't need cake advice. What do you want? I'm on a tight schedule." She made a show of looking at her expensive, sleek watch.

"We can talk while you taste." Kelly flashed a triumphant smile. Surely, Whitney could multitask. "Since you're busy, I'll get right to the point. I'd like to know where you went when you left your bridal dinner party?"

Whitney's face flushed. "How do you know I did?"

Kelly left Whitney's question hanging in the air. She hoped by not replying right away, the PR diva would continue to talk and reveal where she went.

"I don't see how it's any of your business."

"It was the night my cousin was murdered, so I'm making it my business."

CHAPTER FOURTEEN

"You think I killed Becky? Why? Because of Liam?" Whitney gave a half snort. "I dumped him right after I found out about the two of them."

"So you're saying you harbored no ill will against Becky for dating your fiancé?"

Whitney nodded.

"Then why did you storm over to our table and then tell Becky she'd regret her decision to come to Lucky Cove for the summer?"

"Fine." Whitney let out an annoyed sigh. "I admit Liam's betrayal humiliated me. We'd announced our engagement only a week before I discovered they were dating. I guess seeing Becky pushed my buttons again. But I would never kill her. Actually, if I killed anybody, it would be Liam."

"Well, it sounds like he did you a favor by cheating. You got to see what type of man he was before you married him." Kelly's gaze flicked over the cake plates, and her stomach rumbled. No. Hunger would not distract her. She finally had Whitney talking. "Where did you go after you left your bridal dinner?"

Whitney leaned forward and lowered her voice. "I met Liam for one last fling."

Kelly's eyes bugged out. Whitney dumped him for cheating on her, and now she cheated on her soon-to-be husband with the louse? It left Kelly speechless.

"Kell, what are you doing here?" Liv appeared out of nowhere, startling Kelly. She moved like a ninja. Her hands were planted on her hips, and she had a cross look on her face.

"Ah…Whitney and I were chatting. These cakes look delicious," Kelly said, hoping to soothe Liv's apparent foul mood.

"Huh." Liv reached out and guided Kelly up from her seat. "Excuse us," she said to Whitney. She shuffled Kelly away from the table. "What are you up to? And don't tell me you were helping her choose her new cake."

"Okay. I wasn't. That woman had a motive, and I wanted to find out if she has an alibi. I couldn't help myself. She was right there." Kelly hitched a thumb over her shoulder.

"Does she have an alibi?"

"Oh, yeah. It's a doozy." Kelly glanced over at Whitney, who returned to tapping on her phone. "Why didn't you tell me you're baking her wedding cake?"

"Do you want a list of all our customers?"

"No, only the ones who are suspects in my cousin's murder."

"I really don't have all day for this." Whitney popped up from her seat. "I'll take this one." She pointed to a chocolate layered cake with chocolate ganache frosting. "It should suffice."

"Excellent choice." Liv swooped over to the table and lifted the winning plate. Her movement was so quick it felt like she didn't want Whitney to have the chance to change her mind. Kelly wondered how many other cakes the bride-to-be had sampled. "I promise you'll be very pleased."

Whitney shook her head and rolled her eyes. "It's not me you have to worry about." She grabbed her purse and passed Kelly, giving her an icy glare on her way out of the bakery.

"Did you see that?" Kelly pointed toward the door and then looked back at Liv.

"What did you say to her?" Liv walked behind the counter and set the plate down. She opened a folder and jotted down notes.

"I wanted to know what her alibi was, that's all." Kelly perused the offerings in the bakery case. She would have lunch soon, so whatever she ordered couldn't be too indulgent. "Can I get a couple pignoli cookies?"

"Sure." Liv closed the folder, snatched a piece of tissue paper from the dispenser, and grabbed a paper bag. She then slid open the case door and dropped two cookies into the bag. "Here you go. On the house."

"Aww. You don't have to do that." Kelly accepted the bag and reached in for a cookie.

"Between you and me, I'm glad you ruffled her feathers. She's a bit of a diva. I'll be happy when her wedding is over. Tell me, what's her alibi? I'm dying to know."

"I really shouldn't. You know I don't enjoy gossiping." Kelly finished her cookie and then reached in for the other one. After Ariel's accident, gossip spread like the case of chicken pox that went through her fourth-grade class. Wherever Kelly went, there were whispers and stares. What was worse was hearing how twisted some of the facts had gotten through the gossip mill. According to the rumors, she had been the driver who caused the accident. Talk about fake news. She actually was back at the party making out with a guy she'd been flirting with all semester. Admittedly, not her finest moment.

"I gave you two pignoli cookies. Spill."

Kelly swallowed her bite and then related what Whitney said only after Liv promised not to tell anyone. Liv gasped and then laughed.

"Wow. What a little minx." Liv opened the bakery case again and pulled out two more cookies. "Here you go."

Kelly lifted her empty bag and gratefully accepted her reward for gossiping. She knew she should feel guilty for doing it, but Whitney really wasn't a nice person. Besides, it was only a matter of time before Whitney's little rendezvous with Liam would be discovered and talked about by everyone.

"I should get going. I'm meeting Marvin for lunch, so I'll save these two for later."

"Okay." Liv tossed the tissue paper into the trash bin. "I hope you know what you're doing, Kell. I know Whitney can be difficult, but she knows a lot of people."

"Don't worry. I'm not going to track down Liam and confirm what she said. Oddly, I believe her." Kelly took her cookies and left the bakery.

Back on Main Street, she headed toward Gio's restaurant. It was Marvin's favorite place to eat. Before she reached Gio's, she checked her phone, and there was a new message from Beauty4Everygirl.

Let's talk in person. But not in Lucky Cove.

Darn it. She hadn't heard the message notification because she was too busy grilling Whitney.

She halted and frantically typed a message.

Sounds good. Where?

Liv's reminder, *"I hope you know what you're doing,"* echoed in her head. She hoped so too.

After she replied to the text, she continued to Gio's. The walk only took a few minutes, and she arrived right on time. Inside, the hostess escorted her to Marvin's table.

He looked dapper and relaxed in a short-sleeved button-down shirt and navy pants, a far cry from when she first met him last Christmas. Then he'd looked disheveled and unwell in a messy house with his sidekick,

Sparky. The little white dog had been the only reason back then why Marvin ventured out of his home.

Now, he was spending his summer out on Montauk in a rental cottage with an ocean view and painting again. He credited Kelly with his new lease on life.

Marvin kissed her on the cheek and then returned to his seat. "Good to see you, kiddo."

Kiddo. She loved the endearing nickname.

"Right back at you. Do you know what you're going to order?"

"I think I do. Let me double-check." He lifted his menu and browsed the selection.

Kelly chuckled. He had a short list of favorite meals, and she'd bet her Louis Vuitton six-ring case his choice would be one of those five. Meanwhile, she barely looked at her menu. She hadn't much of an appetite. The two cookies she ate at the bakery were more than enough to settle the rumble in her tummy earlier.

Marvin closed his menu and set it down. "I'm going to get the spaghetti and meatballs. What about you?"

She shrugged. "Maybe a salad. I'm not too hungry."

"I understand. Your cousin's death and now your uncle's hospitalization is a lot to deal with, but you need to eat something more than rabbit food." He smiled, and his pale blue eyes twinkled.

She eased her lips into a smile and considered the advice.

She really enjoyed the baked ravioli.

When the waitress approached, they gave their orders, and Marvin nodded with approval she'd swapped the salad for ravioli.

He unfolded his napkin and placed it on his lap. "So, how are you doing?"

Kelly leaned back. Now there was a loaded question. How was she doing? She came *this close* to being arrested again. She was probably targeted by a killer last night. She might have also caused her uncle's heart attack. No. She couldn't list all the bad things that had happened in such a short period.

"I'm hanging in there." She chose not to tell him about the break-in last night or the note left on the mannequin. Why worry him, she reasoned. She was worried enough for the both of them. "I'm waiting to hear if the boutique will be featured on *Long Island View Point.*"

"Marvelous! Their host, Jasmine Reynolds, is a pro and very nice. She interviewed me a few times." He reached for his water glass and took a sip.

"Well, it's not official yet. I'm still waiting to hear."

"I can't imagine why they wouldn't want to showcase your boutique. It's a true testament to the strength and determination of the Blake women."

Kelly's cheeks warmed at the compliment. Her granny had not only been strong and determined; she had been courageous. When her husband passed away, she had two children to raise on her own. Not one to wallow or give up, she wasted no time in turning the first floor of her home into a business and never looked back.

"Enough about me. I want to hear how your summer retreat is going."

The waitress returned with their lunch entrees. As they ate, Marvin shared how the rocky coastline where the Long Island Sound met the Atlantic Ocean inspired him every day. He said that he'd done more work in the few weeks out there than he had in five years.

Hearing about his boost of creativity blew Kelly away. It also made her happy for him, and she looked forward to attending his next art show. She was, however, disappointed he was driving back to Montauk that afternoon and wouldn't return until after Labor Day.

Marvin lifted his napkin and wiped his mouth. "You and Caroline should come out for a few days. There's a guest room in the cottage."

Kelly's phone vibrated. She made an apologetic face.

"Go on, answer. It could be important." Marvin pulled out his wallet and placed his credit card on top of the check the waitress had slipped onto the table. He'd insisted on paying for lunch and wouldn't hear of any objections from Kelly. Because of his past relationship with her granny, he treated Kelly like a granddaughter.

She lifted the phone and read the message from Beauty4Everygirl.

Meet me at Brew A Cup in an hour.

Kelly typed her reply.

~~**OK. How will I know you?**~~

Three little ellipses bounced while she waited for a response.

I'll know you. Don't be late.

~~"Is everything all right, kiddo?"~~

Kelly wondered how the anonymous texter would know her. Maybe from the few times her photo had been in the newspaper or maybe Beauty4Everygirl was a customer at the boutique.

"Yeah, everything is good. Looks like I have another meeting." She'd heard of Brew A Cup, a gourmet coffee shop not too far from Lucky Cove. It would take at least thirty minutes without traffic to get there. "I'll talk to Caroline about taking a drive to Montauk. It sounds like a lovely idea."

Kelly left the restaurant and parted with Marvin at the curb, where he'd parked his old car. Even though he had more than enough money to purchase a new one, he was frugal and said he didn't need anything fancy to get him places. After he pulled his car from its space, she hurried back to the boutique with a takeout bag. Before leaving Gio's, she'd ordered a chicken parmesan sandwich for Pepper.

When she arrived at the boutique, she wanted to kick herself for not taking longer. She'd hoped to use the walk to come up with a reason to dash back out to meet Beauty4Everygirl. Telling Pepper the truth—that she agreed to meet a stranger to talk about Jessica after receiving a threat last night—would be a huge mistake. There would be the speech, the expression of concern, and then the *glare*.

Pepper caught sight of Kelly, thwarting her plan to continue walking until she had a plausible story.

It looked like she didn't have a choice. But then she noticed that the front door had been repaired, and the boutique was open for business. Finally, something good had happened.

She entered the boutique, handed Pepper the carryout bag, and told her to take a break while she came up with an excuse to head back out.

"Thanks." Pepper smiled. Chicken parmesan was her favorite sandwich. "Did you have a pleasant lunch with Marvin?"

"I did. It was nice to see him again. I know he's only been gone since June, but I've missed him."

"He's a sweet man," Pepper said.

Pepper had encouraged Kelly's relationship with Marvin. For years she'd known he had feelings for Martha. She even knew they'd eloped on a seniors only trip to Las Vegas. However, the marriage hadn't been legal, so Marvin hadn't become Kelly's step-grandfather.

"He invited Caroline and me out to his rental for a weekend. It's been a long time since I've been out to Montauk." The last time she drove out to the very end of Long Island was for a coworker's wedding. She'd indulged in staying at the famous Guernsey Inn. It had burned a hole in her credit card, but she enjoyed the weekend and got great photos for her Instagram.

"What a wonderful idea!" Pepper patted Kelly's arm. "Getting away for a few days would be good for you."

Kelly shrugged. "Maybe."

"You know what I think?" Pepper arched a perfectly sculpted brow.

Kelly shook her head. "But you're going to tell me."

"You need a little self-care. What's happening is very traumatic. You're so busy chasing someone who doesn't want to talk to you and trying to figure out who killed Becky, you're not dealing with the fact that you found your cousin's murdered body."

Kelly opened her mouth to speak, but Pepper shushed her.

"I'm not finished."

Kelly pressed her lips together.

"Last night, a clear warning was sent to you. I hope you listen to it." Pepper gave a hopeful smile as she let go of Kelly's arm and headed to the staff room. "Oh, I almost forgot. Camille called a few minutes ago. She wanted to remind you that she has a bunch more clothes for consignment."

"Oh, I know how many clothes she has." Kelly walked around the sales counter. She rapped her fingers on the glass top. Maybe she could use Camille as her cover story for dashing back out for a bit. She glanced in the direction of the staff room. She just had to make sure she didn't outright lie to Pepper.

She chewed on her lower lip. She didn't like playing fast and loose with the truth. Especially with her dear friend. But she really didn't have a choice. Besides, Pepper would forgive her.

She always had.

* * * *

Kelly arrived for her coffee date with Beauty4Everygirl with a few minutes to spare. Luckily, Pepper really hadn't known everything; otherwise, she would have found some way to put a stop to this meeting. She pulled her Jeep into a parking space across the street and scanned Brew A Cup's outdoor café. All the tables were occupied, with a few having only one person seated sipping coffee.

Which one of them was Beauty4Everygirl?

Since the anonymous texter had set up the meeting, Kelly expected the person would already be there waiting. She shut off the ignition and grabbed her tote. Ready to end all this cloak-and-dagger stuff, she exited the Jeep.

Both sides of the street were busy with pedestrians leisurely strolling, shopping, or dining outdoors. Like Lucky Cove, this quaint village swelled in population during the summer months.

She continued searching the coffee shop's patrons, hoping to recognize someone. The person she was meeting with could be inside the air-conditioned shop watching her.

A chill skittered along her spine at that creepy thought.

She set her tote's straps on her shoulder and stepped off the curb to cross the four-lane road.

When there was a break in traffic, she walked forward. After barely crossing one lane, her tote slid from her shoulder. When she attempted to wrestle it back up, all the while keeping her gaze on the coffee shop, she slipped, and her ankle twisted, knocking her off balance. Her tote fell from her arm and onto the pavement.

Shoot!

She did a quick look to make sure there was no oncoming traffic. Good. She'd scoop up her tote fast and run across the road. Bent over, she grabbed her bag, which had opened and its contents had spilled out. Of course this would not be easy. She'd corralled her makeup bag and sunglass case into her tote when the sound of an engine prompted her to look up.

Her eyes widened, and her heart slammed against her chest.

A dark sedan raced toward her.

Where had it come from?

A woman shouted for her to move. Or maybe that was Kelly's inner voice screaming.

She wasn't sure. All she knew was that the vehicle was heading straight toward her, and she froze in place.

Kelly's life flashed before her eyes. Snippets of carefree beach days, fashion school graduation, lunchtime sample sale shopping, her granny's smile, Howard's soft fur. No way this could be the end for her. Summoning all her strength and will to live, she squeezed her eyes shut and propelled to the side. Her feet peeled away from the road. She landed hard on the pavement just out of the path of the oncoming vehicle.

The car whizzed by, and within seconds people gathered around her. She heard a man's voice now, asking if she was okay.

"I think I am." Even though she was lightheaded from her rapid heartbeat, everything seemed to be intact. However, the stranger had gotten too close to her. She felt his heavy breathing on her face. He needed a lesson in boundaries. A slobbering lick startled her, and she pried open her eyes.

She was eye to eye with a horse. Okay, it wasn't a horse. Just a big, hairy dog. It licked her again. "Yuck." She wiped her mouth with the back of her hand.

"Sorry about that." The deep, husky voice was familiar to Kelly. "Wally is friendly. Sometimes too friendly."

Kelly's gaze moved from the dog to its handler. The doctor from the beach! "Dr. Linden?" she asked, not sure if her memory served her correctly.

"Yes." A moment later, recollection flashed in his brown eyes. "Kelly Quinn." He pulled his mammoth of a canine back. What were the odds that twice he would appear when she needed help? He'd been kind enough to stay with Becky until she was transported from the beach to the coroner's office; now he was there when she almost got hit by a car.

"Are you hurt? Do you need an ambulance?" he asked.

Kelly did a quick inventory of her limbs. They seemed to work fine. But doing a body slam on the road was going to leave her sore. Then she did a quick assessment of the doctor. Tall and slender, his dark hair was styled in a messy tapered cut, and his dark-framed glasses gave him an appealing nerdy vibe.

"I don't think so, Dr. Linden. Nothing feels broken, and I didn't hit my head." She looked around at the crowd that had started to form. "I really should get up."

"Only if you're sure you're not injured. And it's Arnold." He extended his hand and smiled, and Kelly swooned. *Bad, Kelly, bad.* She shouldn't be swooning, she was almost killed by a speeding car. She accepted his assistance to stand and quickly let go of his hand before she swooned again.

"I'm sure I'm not hurt." She eyed the dog. He must have weighed over a hundred pounds, yet he looked lovable and cuddly. His eyes were alert, and he looked as if he had a smile on his face. "What is he?"

"A Leonberger. This guy weighs in at one fifty."

"Wow! And I think my cat is a lot to handle." She patted Wally on the head, her gaze drifting along the street. "Where did that car come from? One minute the road was clear, and the next I was..." Her words trailed off as her near miss replayed in her mind.

"Hey, are you sure you're okay?" Arnold asked.

"Yeah, I'm good. Just a little shaken. I wish I got a look at the driver."

"Or the license plate. Come on, let's get you back on the sidewalk where it's safe." Arnold, along with Wally, guided Kelly back to the curb, and the small crowd dispersed since there was nothing left to see. "Do you want to call the police?"

Kelly shook her head. The last thing she wanted was another police report. "There's really nothing to tell them. Thank you for helping me... again." Kelly couldn't imagine what the handsome doctor thought of her. In less than a week, he'd come to her aid when she was in trouble, which seemed to happen quite a bit. The guy should run, run away fast with his dog.

"Glad I was here...with Wally." He stepped back, tugging on his dog's leash. "If you need anything, don't hesitate to contact me. Take care of yourself."

"Will do."

Arnold and Wally walked toward the sidewalk, leaving Kelly to look around, wondering if Beauty4Everygirl was still waiting for her or if she was the driver of the speeding car.

Her stomach knotted at a disturbing thought.

Had she been set up?

CHAPTER FIFTEEN

Kelly dusted herself off and continued to Brew A Cup, though she glanced over her shoulder a couple of times before entering the café to see where Arnold went. He and Wally had disappeared down a side street. Did they live in town? Or were they vacationing? She guessed she'd never know, and that was okay. She wasn't looking for a new relationship, and he was probably married.

By the time she reached the door, it seemed everyone had forgotten about her incident with a speeding car. Grateful for short attention spans, she made her way to the counter and ordered a large dark magic with milk. According to the sign, it was bold, deep, and intense. Too bad she couldn't make it a double.

The café's interior was decorated in bright pops of color and comfortable chairs. She easily imagined spending the day there writing her articles for Budget Chic. Definitely a far better way to spend the afternoon than almost getting run down by a car.

She paid the barista and carried her cup to a table. Seated, she took a long sip. Perhaps caffeine wasn't the best option for soothing her jittery nerves. *Shocker! Kelly Quinn has made yet another bad decision.* The previous one was agreeing to meet a stranger from the internet. How would she explain what happened to Pepper, Liv, Gabe, Caroline? She took another drink and smiled. The coffee lived up to its hype. And it was very smooth. Another sip helped fortify her plan on how to deal with telling her friends and family about what happened—she wouldn't. Right now, there wasn't any reason to worry them any more than they already were. She'd wait until she had more information. Like a lead on who had been driving the car.

She pulled out a notepad and pen from her tote. It was time to figure out who had been behind her brush with death. Too bad she hadn't gotten a look at the driver. Her brain had been too busy flashing her life before her eyes.

With the notepad open, she listed the people connected to Becky and present in Lucky Cove at the time of her murder.

Whitney. Todd. Jessica. Terry.

She added Beauty4Everygirl even though she hadn't a clue who she was or if she'd been in town when Becky was murdered.

Next to each name, she wrote whatever popped into her head.

Whitney had an alibi for the time of the murder. A horrible reason, but nonetheless, she was otherwise engaged that night. Kelly made a face at the thought. How could she cheat on her soon-to-be husband?

Todd had two motives. He felt cheated out of the company he believed he'd helped create, and it turned out he was Becky's heir. Had he known about the will and killed Becky for the inheritance? It was one way to get what he believed he was owed. Though he was in a coma now—poisoned. Who poisoned him?

Jessica had a motive. She wanted to sell Define Beauty, but Becky hadn't agreed.

Terry seemed like she had more of a motive to kill Jessica, and it didn't appear like she could have made a mistake in killing Becky.

Until almost being run down, Kelly wouldn't even have considered Beauty4Everygirl a suspect. What would her motive have been?

Kelly reached for her cup again and sipped as everything she wrote bounced around in her head. Which one of them gave Becky the note to meet at midnight? Todd and Jessica were at the house that night. Who knew how long the message had been in the cardigan's pocket?

Her cell phone rang, and she swiped it on quickly to take Frankie's call.

"Hey, how's your dad?" She pushed her notepad aside and rested her elbows on the table.

"He's ready to have visitors." Frankie's voice sounded relieved, and she understood. Yesterday had been scary for the entire family. While Frankie and his dad hadn't always seen eye to eye on many things, like Frankie not going into the family business, he loved his father. Maybe this scare could bring them closer together.

"Great. I'm on my way." She closed her notepad and ended the call.

Before leaving the café, she checked Beauty4Everygirl's social media account. This time, she paid closer attention to the posts. There were a lot, but they'd all been added within the past few days. She concentrated on the captions, and they were all short. Five words or less with no hashtags.

Holy Manolos. The account is fake. And I fell for it.

Now she had no doubt about Beauty4Everygirl's intention for their meeting.

Kelly drained the last of her coffee as she tried to figure out what was going on. Well, one thing was for sure, it didn't take a genius to figure this mystery out. The unknown texter was most likely the driver. But why would this stranger want Kelly dead?

* * * *

On the drive to the hospital, Kelly called Pepper to update her on her next stop, careful not to mention she hadn't been to Camille's house yet. Yes, the conversation had been tricky, but she steered the chat toward Ralph and his recovery. Pepper had been happy to hear he was making progress and told Kelly not to rush back. There were customers, but nothing she couldn't handle.

After disconnecting the call, Kelly made a mental note to place an ad for another salesperson. She had to do it quickly before the next issue of the *Lucky Cove Weekly* went out.

She arrived at the hospital and found a parking space. Inside, she stopped by the main desk for Ralph's room number and took the elevator up to the second floor. She walked along the corridor, past patients' rooms that had all sorts of sounds trickling out—machines beeping, hushed voices, and some laughter. That made Kelly feel good. A reminder that no matter how bleak the moment seemed, there was hope.

Following the room numbers, she was getting closer to Ralph's room. There it was.

She arrived at the doorway only to be confronted by Summer and Frankie. They blocked her entry and forced her back out into the hall.

Oh, boy.

"What's going on? Is it Uncle Ralph?"

"He's fine." Summer's arms were crossed, and she had what appeared to be a scowl on her face. Though, with all her injectables, it was hard to tell. "Camille told me you were at Ralph's office right before he had his heart attack. Why didn't you tell me?"

"I…I didn't think it was important at the time," Kelly said as a sudden headache exploded across her forehead.

"He was yelling when you were there, and then he had a heart attack. It sounds like it was important." Frankie's usually easygoing nature had vanished. Poof. Just like that.

"It doesn't matter now. He's going to be okay." Kelly's brand-spanking-new headache intensified. She couldn't tell them her uncle's secret, even though she wanted to get it out in the open.

"No thanks to you." Summer spun around and returned inside her husband's room. So much for building the foundation for their new relationship. It seemed to be business as usual.

"Kell, come on, you gotta tell me what's going on," Frankie urged.

Kelly had a good mind to tell her cousin the truth about the argument. Luckily, though, her phone rang, and after fumbling to pull it out of her tote, she saw it was her sister calling.

"Sorry." She raised the phone to her ear and gave a regretful look to Frankie. "I have to take this. Really, I do. It's Caroline." She'd never been so grateful to speak with her sister.

He sighed and returned to the room.

"Thank goodness you called." Kelly walked a few feet and stopped, leaning against a wall. She was out of earshot of her cousin and his stepmother.

"Why? Has something else happened?" Concern had wiggled its way into Caroline's normally even-keeled tone.

"No. Well, maybe. But I'm okay. Well, maybe, I'm not. Okay, I'm not hurt or in danger. Well, at least now." She was babbling and making no sense. "Why did you call?" *Yes, much better, Kell.*

"Just tell me. Should I be worried?" Direct and straight to the point was how Caroline rolled. Grounded with her eye on the prize, as their grandfather used to say, she hadn't had time to dillydally, as her granny used to say. While Kelly traipsed off to the mall on Saturday afternoons, Caroline prepared for Debate Club and studied for her college prep courses.

"No. No need to worry."

There was a moment of silence on the line. Kelly figured her sister was deciding whether to believe what she had said.

"We need to discuss the funeral arrangements for Becky." Caroline's tone had become somber. "I told Uncle Joe we'd take care of a few of the basics so when he and Aunt Arlene arrive, they won't have so much on their plate."

Kelly glanced to the floor. Why hadn't she thought of that? Because she was doing something important too—finding Becky's killer. Her aunt and uncle decided to hold the services in Lucky Cove along with the burial. Generations of Quinns and Blakes were laid to rest in a nearby cemetery.

"Can you come over to my office?" Caroline asked.

Kelly looked over her shoulder, back at her uncle's room. She really didn't want to go in there and face another round of questions from Summer and Frankie.

"Sure. I can't stay too long. Pepper is working by herself today. I'll be there soon." Kelly ended the call and left the hospital without seeing her uncle. Entering his room would have been a mistake considering the moods Summer and Frankie were in. Walking toward the exit, she congratulated herself on making her second smart decision of the day, though she worried both revolved around her leaving somewhere. Passing through the automatic doors, she decided not to dwell on the specifics, just appreciate the fact she wouldn't leak her uncle's secret in front of his wife and son.

* * * *

Driving out to East Hampton, Kelly hit traffic and arrived at her sister's office later than she expected. She found a parking space at the curb and hurried to the building's main entrance. Before the start of summer, Caroline's law firm moved locations and was now in a nondescript two-story building. The move had been necessary because the practice added staff after promoting Caroline to partner.

Entering the building, she glanced at the four interior doors and found the one for Caroline's firm. She pivoted and then paused a moment to admire the lettering on the door. Her heart swelled. *Harper, Johnson, and Quinn.* She was beyond proud of her sister's accomplishment at such a young age.

She opened the door and entered the firm's reception area. Her gaze traveled around the large room, and she marveled at the sleek, modern furniture, the abundance of sun streaming in, and the glossy wood flooring. *Way to go, Caroline.*

The receptionist looked up and greeted Kelly. The coral sheath dress she wore accentuated her curvy body and her tan. She lowered her glasses and smiled.

"Your sister is expecting you. Go right in." She pointed to the hallway.

Kelly thanked her and proceeded along the hall. Tasteful art hung on the cream-colored walls, and all but one door was shut. Kelly peeked in. She'd found Caroline's office.

She knocked on the wooden door as she entered.

"Hope I'm not interrupting." Kelly walked to a chair in front of her sister's desk and dropped onto it. She exhaled a heavy breath. She'd had a heck of a day so far, and it felt good to just sit.

Caroline looked up from her laptop. She gave Kelly a small smile that didn't quite reach her eyes. Another reminder that their visit wouldn't be a pleasant one.

"Not at all." Caroline pushed the laptop away and then leaned back. She tucked a lock of hair behind her ear, revealing a simple pearl stud earring. Professionally, she preferred to keep her jewelry simple and her clothing sophisticated yet feminine. The navy sweater she wore had a ditsy garden print with short puff sleeves. "What's wrong?"

Her sister had an uncanny sixth sense when it came to her and always knew when something was up.

"Just a busy day." Kelly hoped she sounded as easy and breezy as she intended.

Caroline held Kelly's gaze for a moment and then reached for her agenda and opened it. It looked as if Kelly pulled off the fake carefree tone.

"Same here. Let's start. So far, I've made reservations for everyone at the Blue Harbor Inn."

"I can't believe we're doing this." Kelly slumped. "How is any of this real? I keep waiting to wake up from this nightmare."

"Me too. Though, you had the unpleasant task of finding Becky. I can't imagine how that felt."

"Awful. Absolutely awful." Kelly shifted in her seat. "So much has happened since then."

"Like what?"

"Todd Wilson is in a coma."

"His name is familiar. What happened?"

"He and Becky were friends." Kelly gave a brief recap of the relationship. "Then the other day, he told me that Becky left him her share of the company. We were at Doug's, and Jessica showed up. Boy, was she furious. And she's convinced he made Becky change the will."

"It sounds like Jessica had thought she'd control the company."

"Exactly. I'm curious if Becky had changed her will. There's a chance her beneficiary had always been Todd, and Jessica didn't know. Then, after Jessica finds out, Todd ends up in a coma." Kelly drummed her fingers on the chair's arm.

Caroline closed her agenda. "Have you forgotten that your curiosity got you into trouble before? And last night, someone left you a threat, remember?"

"I haven't forgotten. I'm careful, and I won't do anything dangerous."

Luckily, I leap from oncoming cars in a single bound.

"Yeah, I've heard that before." Caroline stood and walked around to the front of her desk. Disapproval showed on her face. "You may not believe me, but I know how your mind works. You feel responsible for Becky's death somehow. Don't you?"

Kelly blinked. She hated that her sister was so perceptive when it came to her.

"I'm the one who encouraged her to come to Lucky Cove for the summer. I said it would be fun for us all to get back together. Then she ends up dead." Kelly looked away.

"What happened wasn't your fault. You couldn't have known someone would murder Becky. Despite all your talents, you can't predict the future."

Kelly looked back at her sister and gave a small smile. "All my talents?"

Caroline rolled her eyes and grinned. "Don't go getting a big head." She pushed off the desk and returned to her seat.

The moment of levity felt good, and it helped Kelly push through the conversation about funeral arrangements without breaking down.

* * * *

An hour later, Kelly left the law firm feeling both accomplished and sad. Planning her cousin's funeral hadn't been something she ever wanted to do. She slipped into her Jeep and pulled out of the parking space with her summer playlist filling the silence. From her favorite song, "Boys of Summer," to the Beach Boys' top hits, she let the music lift her mood. Even so, her shoulder hurt. She'd landed on it when she lunged out of the path of the oncoming car. She needed either hot or cold therapy, she couldn't remember which, and also an over-the-counter painkiller. Pronto.

But first, she had to run the errand she told Pepper she'd do, and that was to visit Camille. She tried her best not to think about what had happened earlier during her drive back to Lucky Cove. Instead, she let the music distract her, and before she knew it, she'd arrived at Camille's house.

Immediately, Camille swept her inside and presented a garment rack crammed with clothes. She stood beside the clothing with a proud look on her face.

"You've been working hard. I'm impressed."

Camille's cheeks reddened, and she tipped her head. "Thank you. I sorted it into three categories. Donate, toss and sell. These are for the boutique. I still have sweaters and jeans to go through."

"This is great. It really is." Kelly grabbed an armful of dresses from the rack. "No wonder you're in such a good mood." She hoped it would rub off.

Camille grabbed a group of blouses and followed Kelly outside. "To be honest, I didn't realize how much lighter I would feel getting rid of all this clothing."

"I'm not surprised. We don't realize how all the stuff we own affects us."

"Well, I'm ready to do a deep clean and sort on everything in my house." Camille laughed. "Oh, I heard some other good news. Ralph will be discharged soon. Even though he's difficult to work for, I'm happy he's doing well."

Kelly's stomach clenched. She couldn't keep evading Summer and Frankie's questions about what happened the day her uncle had his heart attack. *Darn Ralph*. Maybe his brush with death would help him be honest about his affair with Ariel's mother all those years ago.

She opened the Jeep's cargo door and set the clothes inside. Camille laid her armful of clothes in there when a delivery truck pulled into the driveway. The driver approached with a large box.

Kelly recognized the logo on the box—it was from a clothing subscription service. She locked her gaze on Camille, and the woman squirmed.

"It's the last one. I promise." Camille hurried inside with the box. They loaded up the rest of the clothing for the next twenty minutes until the garment rack was empty.

Kelly closed the cargo door. She wanted to believe Camille, but she didn't have time to worry about it. If Camille continued buying excessive amounts of clothes, it was entirely her decision. Kelly could only hope she'd consign what she no longer wanted.

* * * *

Kelly returned to the boutique and found business had picked up. The crush of customers lifted her mood. She quickly deposited Camille's clothes in the staff room and then hurried to the sales floor to help Pepper.

A tourist from Pennsylvania dropped an armful of clothes on the counter. It pleased Kelly to see that all the short-sleeved tops she selected came from Camille's overstuffed closets. Ringing up the sale, Kelly chatted with her newest convert to resale shopping. The petite redhead said she'd never thought of shopping in a consignment shop, especially not on vacation, but the window display drew her in. As she swiped her credit card, she joked as she looked at the filled shopping bag, "And the rest is history."

Kelly thanked her for her business and dropped in a business card with her website's address. It'd been slow going, but Kelly was adding more inventory to her website and shipping items.

Another customer approached with a more modest purchase. After ringing up the sale, Kelly took a breather for a few minutes while the other customers browsed.

The jingling of the bell over the door alerted her to another potential customer. Time to look alive. She took a quick gulp of water from the bottle she'd stashed under the counter and squared her shoulders before stepping back out onto the sales floor.

The person who had entered wasn't a customer. Nope, instead, she was trouble.

CHAPTER SIXTEEN

"I heard you had an incident here last night. A break-in?" Ella Marshall's stride was purposeful and confident as she approached Kelly. The *Lucky Cove Weekly* reporter wore a boatneck shell over matching pants finished with a pair of huggie gold-tone earrings, a sleek tote, and nude mules. A smart, classic look for the professional woman. "Would you like to make a comment for the *Weekly*?"

Kelly slipped a glance at her customers, who appeared not to have heard Ella's question. She'd rather comment about how business had been up since May. Or how shopping habits had been changing steadily. She'd love to talk about how resale shoppers had higher expectations and were more selective about the clothing they purchased. It meant resellers, like herself, needed to shift from decades-old practices and embrace out-of-the-box thinking when it came to sourcing merchandise and marketing. She returned her gaze to Ella.

"I'm sorry you wasted a trip over here. There's not much to comment on. Someone broke in, but nothing was taken, and there was no vandalism." Except for the dismantled mannequin. And the threatening note.

"Really?" Ella tilted her head. "Doesn't it seem odd someone would break in and take nothing?"

Kelly shrugged. "Perhaps they got scared off. Maybe I'd arrived back just as they entered. I guess we won't know for sure until the person or persons are caught."

Ella stepped forward. "Come on, Kelly, I know how you got involved in Tawny's case. Are you nosing around your cousin's case? Could last night's break-in be connected to that?"

Last spring, Kelly had found the body of fitness guru Tawny Lee. Because of circumstances beyond her control, she'd gotten caught up in the investigation. Her ex-boss had been the prime suspect. Kelly knew two things at the time—Serena Dawson wasn't a killer, and she wanted Serena gone from Lucky Cove ASAP.

Along the way to clearing her ex-boss of the murder, Kelly might have illegally entered Ella's house and gotten caught with Liv in tow. It took some pleading and a promise of an exclusive interview about the murder investigation in exchange for Ella not reporting Kelly's trespassing.

"No comment."

Ella grinned. "Your no comment tells me a whole lot." She dug into her purse and pulled out a notepad. She flipped to a clean sheet. "What do you know about Todd Wilson?"

"No comment."

"Oh, come on, Kelly. I have a job to do." Ella lowered her voice. "I'm very sorry for your loss. I can't imagine what you're going through, but your cousin's death is news. I need something for my editor. Anything."

Unlike other media outlets, Ella hadn't sensationalized Tawny's murder or the people involved. Perhaps Kelly could trust her to do the same in regard to Becky.

"Okay. Here's the truth: I don't know much about Todd. Until a few days ago, I hadn't met him."

"Word is that he inherited Becky's portion of the company. True?"
Kelly nodded.

"Now he's in a coma. Do you know what happened to him?"

"No idea."

"Hmmm…Jessica Barron is a person of interest in your cousin's murder. Do you think she could have tried to kill Todd?"

"I don't know. Anything is possible."

"Your new employee, Terry Carlisle, is also a person of interest. Did you know she had a connection to your cousin and her business partner when you hired her?"

"No, I didn't. I'm sorry, Ella. Clearly, I don't know anything that can help your story."

"Yet someone broke in here last night and didn't steal or vandalize anything. I think you know something. You can tell me. I'll quote you as an anonymous source. Who knows, maybe it could lead to something?"

"I don't know." Kelly noticed a customer struggling with a bounty of clothes in her arms. "I really need to get back to work."

"Give me something. Anything. I won't name you." Ella gave Kelly a pleading look.

"Fine. I just hope it doesn't screw up the investigation. Someone saw Todd with a woman at his hotel room two nights before he ended up in a coma. No idea who the woman was."

"You saw her?"

"No. Someone who had been at the inn told me. That's all I have. Maybe you're right. Maybe someone else saw her and knows who she is." Her stomach somersaulted, making her second-guess her decision to share that tidbit with Ella. She feared somehow making it public that there had been a woman with Todd before his poisoning could backfire. "I really have to work."

"Sure. Thanks." Ella turned and left the boutique.

"What did she want?" Pepper swept out to the sales counter from the smaller room where the bathing suits and cover-ups were displayed. Once the dining room, the space had been underutilized for far too long by Kelly's granny and now her.

At the start of the summer, Kelly had sat down and worked on the boutique's five-year projections. She had a line of credit but was still paying off the new roof. It was tempting to dip into the credit for more projects, but she wanted to remain fiscally cautious. One thing on her wish list was to open up the smaller room and merge it seamlessly with the main selling area of the boutique. She eyed the fireplace. Its wall was the one she wanted to have knocked down. The estimated cost of the project made her insides quiver. Tearing down a load-bearing wall along with a fireplace wouldn't be cheap. But the result would give her a boutique with open sight lines and the ability to easily funnel customers toward specific merchandise zones.

"Huh? Oh, she wanted a comment about the break-in."

Pepper's head swiveled toward the door. "Did she?"

"I said there wasn't much to comment about. Nothing was stolen or broken, other than the door." Kelly checked the shopping bags to see if she needed to add any to the stack. It looked like they hadn't used many. The last few customers she rang up had opted to purchase the reusable shopper totes she had made for the boutique. It was a great way to help her beloved planet Earth, get a little free advertising, and make a tidy profit.

"Looks like the dreary weather is working in our favor." Pepper looked back at Kelly and reached for her tube of hand cream on a lower shelf.

"It does, doesn't it?" Kelly rested a hand on the counter. The forecast for the rest of the week was definitely not beach weather. There was a storm rolling in, and the prediction was that it would hit the area hard. So, she'd take as many customers as she could get before they packed their bags and headed home. "A bunch of Camille's stuff sold."

"Wonderful!" Pepper squirted out a dollop of cream and massaged her hands. "You know, I'd also like to hear more about what you've been up to. Why did someone break in last night and leave that kind of note for you?"

Kelly had thought they'd moved on from that topic. Looks like they hadn't.

Pepper stared at Kelly over the rim of her glasses. It was intense and made Kelly feel like a child again.

"You do realize our lovely town has a competent police department. It so happens, my son is an officer. This makes me wonder why you insist on putting yourself in harm's way."

"For your information, I haven't put myself in harm's way." Except for the incident outside of Brew A Cup. Kelly picked up the hand cream and helped herself to a dollop. "I've only been talking to the people who were in Becky's life. It's not my fault if one of them is a murderer."

"Don't get smart with me." Pepper snatched the tube out of Kelly's hands. "I know what I'm about to say will go in one ear and out the other, because it always does, but I'm going to say it anyway. You need to leave the investigating to the police."

"That's it?" Usually, Pepper's lecture had more oomph. What happened?

"I've come to accept you don't listen very well." Pepper returned her hand cream back in its spot and walked away from the counter to the changing rooms, where a line of customers waited.

Kelly leaned against the counter, thinking about Pepper's comment. It was true; she didn't listen well. Never had. But maybe a woman who'd known her since she was a baby realized she had a talent for this sleuthing thing and didn't wanted to come out and say it.

"Where can I try these on?" A shopper approached the counter with two dresses in her hand.

Kelly straightened and then led the customer to the changing rooms.

The rest of the day continued with a steady stream of customers for both buying and consigning. Pepper had left when Kelly was bagging the last customer's purchases. When Kelly turned over the Open sign to Closed, she was wiped out. Her plan for the rest of the day was to head upstairs, make a quick salad, and binge on whatever reality show was playing. *Hashtag goals,* she mused.

The whole scenario sounded delightful, and she was eager to dash up the stairs to her apartment. But first, there were the end-of-the-day tasks she needed to do before sinking into her sofa. In the staff room, she deposited the cash bag in the safe. Either she or Pepper would make a trip to the bank in the morning. Next, she tidied her desk and closed her laptop computer. With her duties complete, now she could officially clock out.

* * * *

The next morning, over a quick cup of coffee and a slice of toast, Kelly tried to talk herself out of proceeding with a plan she had formulated overnight. As much as she tried, she wasn't successful in changing her mind. Now, countless people in her life could have talked her out of doing what she was thinking of doing. And each one of them was a phone call away, which was the reason she shoved her phone into her tote. Then she hurried downstairs and grabbed a maxi dress from the rack and hung it inside a garment bag. In order for her plan to work, she needed the prop.

When Breena arrived, Kelly left the boutique in her capable hands and off she went to hopefully gather some intelligence to help solve her cousin's murder.

Not too much later, Kelly entered the Lucky Cove Inn and scanned the lobby for anyone she knew. Like Renata. Getting past her would be tricky. Seeing that the coast was clear, Kelly kept her head down and remained on the lobby's perimeter as she made her way to the staircase with the garment bag over her shoulder. If caught, her story would be she was delivering a dress to a guest, but it looked like she got the information wrong. She'd claim it was an honest mistake. She hastily climbed the stairs to the second floor, and when she reached the hall, she did a quick look at the numbers and headed left.

She wasn't sure if the police still considered Todd's room a crime scene or if it had already been processed and released. If the latter, then would his belongings still be in the room? Or had everything been taken to the police department? There was only one way to find out. As she approached Todd's room, she saw a housekeeping cart, exactly what she'd been hoping for, nearby but no housekeeper. Then she heard a child whining.

As she got closer to the cart, she also got closer to the whining. She peered around the cart and saw the housekeeper bent down cleaning up a milk spill with a little boy next to her having a meltdown. Not sure how long the housekeeper would be distracted, she looked at the door she was standing in front of to see how far she was from Todd's room and discovered she was already there. And the door was slightly ajar.

Perfect. Now she wouldn't have to try to convince the housekeeper to open the door. When she conceived her plan, how she'd gain entry to the room was murky. She guessed she'd hope for the housekeeper to be an acquaintance, one of the perks of living in a small town, and help her break the rules.

Another quick look at the preoccupied housekeeper and then Kelly dashed into the room.

Okay, she was in. Now what?

She walked past the bathroom and closet, dropping the garment bag on the bed. The room's neutral color palette was soothing and pleasing to the eye, from the bed's crisp white linens to muted shades of taupe. Kelly reminded herself she wasn't there to critique the décor. She was there to find how Todd was connected to Becky's death. Maybe even find out why he was in a coma.

On the nightstand was a notepad. She stepped over to inspect it. Flipping through the pages, she found nothing. Though, the slight ivory coloring of the paper looked similar to the note she found with Becky's body. Coincidence? Perhaps. Then again, she'd only gotten a glimpse of the note.

She backed away from the nightstand and walked to the closet, pulling open the doors: nothing but hangers, an ironing board, and an iron. Todd's luggage was gone. She closed the closet doors and looked inside the bathroom. Its brass fixtures and walk-in rain shower were pretty luxurious.

She sighed. Other than the notepad, she found nothing connecting Todd to Becky's murder. However, the note might have come from another room in the inn or a different pad. Still, it seemed unlikely.

"Can I help you, miss?"

Kelly practically jumped at the unexpected voice. She pulled her head out of the bathroom and looked at the doorway. The housekeeper was standing there.

Keep calm. Stick to my story.

"Oh, no…maybe." It took a moment for Kelly to recognize the redhead standing in the doorway. "Mrs. Jensen?"

"Kelly…Kelly Quinn? It's been ages." Mrs. Jensen's cornflower-blue eyes lit up. "It's so good to see you. I heard you came back to take over Martha's shop."

"I have. How are Calista and Violet?" Kelly had gone to school with Mrs. Jensen's two daughters. She heard they'd both moved across country after college.

"They're both doing great out in Oregon. Wish they'd come to their senses like you did and move back to Lucky Cove." Mrs. Jensen's light heartiness gave way as her gaze surveyed the room. "What are you doing in here?"

"Oh, I'm delivering a dress to Mary Jones." Kelly inwardly groaned at her poor choice of a fake name. Why hadn't she just said Jane Doe and left no doubt she was fibbing? "This is her room, right?"

"No, dear, it's not. The guest who was staying in this room is now in the hospital. One of my coworkers found him unconscious. Terrible, really terrible."

"Gosh, I hope he's okay." Kelly hated lying and keeping up a ruse with Mrs. Jensen. "It must have been awful for your coworker."

"It scared the daylights out of her. Him lying there." Mrs. Jensen pointed at the bed.

"Was there any indication of what happened? How he ended up unconscious?"

Mrs. Jensen shook her head. "We don't like to gossip about our guests."

"Of course. I understand. I probably should go down to the front desk and find out which room Ms. Jones is actually in. It looks like there was a miscommunication." Kelly scooped up the garment bag and went to walk out of the room; she paused when Mrs. Jensen touched her arm.

"I don't know what happened to that man, but I do know there weren't any pill bottles or anything like that found in his room," Mrs. Jensen whispered and then let go of Kelly to close the door.

Kelly nodded her thanks for the information and then kept walking to the elevator.

When she reached the elevator, she picked up her pace to get to the staircase, but she wasn't fast enough. The elevator door swished open, and out stepped Wolman, putting her directly in Kelly's path. Behind her was Gabe.

Kelly cringed.

This is not good.

"Kelly, what are you doing here?" Wolman asked as she rested her hand on her hip, brushing back her blazer and flashing her badge.

Gabe kept silent but shook his head.

"I…I was making a delivery." Kelly lifted the garment bag from her shoulder. She willed herself to stick with her story and not trip up by saying something like, *I just searched Todd's room, and my sources tell me there weren't any pill bottles in there when he was found.* She'd been handcuffed once by order of Wolman; she didn't want to repeat that experience. "But it looks like I got the info mixed up."

Wolman's lips formed a small, wry smile. "When did your boutique start a delivery service?"

"We're always adding new services to meet the demands of our customers. I have to get going back to the boutique and straighten this mess out." Kelly draped the garment bag over her arm.

"Okay, then." Because Wolman had a perpetual scowl, it was hard to tell whether she believed Kelly. Then again, if the detective doubted Kelly's story, she would have said so. She wasn't a shrinking violet, shy about expressing an opinion. Especially one about Kelly.

Gabe, on the other hand, looked as if he wasn't buying what Kelly was selling. He blocked her getaway as the detective walked down the hall.

"Don't you have to go with her?" Kelly asked.

"What are you really doing here?" His eyes narrowed and bore into her as if he were searching her soul. He'd been doing that since they were kids. Yeah, the guy was always meant to be a cop. What he failed to learn was that he didn't send Kelly quaking in her pumps.

"I'd like to know what you two are doing here? Didn't your department already process Todd's room?"

"How would you know that?"

"Let's see. Todd told me what his room number was a couple of days ago, and as I've walked along this floor, I didn't see any police tape. Ergo, it appears his room has been released from the police."

"Ergo?"

"That's what I said. Now, if you'll excuse me." She walked past him but paused long enough to say, "I think the paper found with Becky's body came from the notepad in Todd's room. Just saying." She scooted to the stairs before Gabe had time to respond. Hurrying down the stairs, she almost tripped, so she slowed down. Breaking her neck wouldn't help her find Becky's killer. Nor would it bode well for explaining to Pepper why she was at the inn.

She made it to the lobby in one piece and darted out of the inn onto Main Street. Her pulse raced as adrenaline pumped through her body. Getting caught by the housekeeper and then coming face-to-face with Wolman was a close call. Too close. And she had to ask herself had it been worth the risk? Honestly, probably not.

Outside, she power-walked to her Jeep then dropped the garment bag on the back seat and scooted into the driver's seat. For a few moments, she stared out the windshield, drumming her fingers on the steering wheel as she considered what to do next.

The first thing that came to her mind was to return to the boutique, but a sudden urge to visit Jessica surfaced. Why? She wasn't sure.

Maybe it was simply to check on her, though Jessica was more than capable of taking care of herself. Starting the ignition, she accepted that her need to see Jessica was primarily because she wanted to learn more about the latest twist with Becky's will. She hoped Jessica had calmed down since her run-in with Todd. However, there was the chance she'd become more enraged if she was told by her legal team there was nothing she could do about Todd taking control of the company.

As she backed out of her parking space, an idea popped into her head. She'd make a pit stop at Liv's family's bakery to get a box of cookies for her visit. It would be hard for Jessica to turn her away with a tasty assortment of Italian cookies in her hands.

Kelly arrived at the beach house and carried the pastry box up the stairs to the deck. Her gaze wandered to the breaking waves on the beach. She smiled at a fleeting childhood memory of being chased by those swells. Caroline, Becky, and Frankie were close by, laughing, as always.

Her heart squeezed. Now that section of beach would always hold a sad memory, because it was where the laughter had died only nights ago.

A loud voice drew her attention from the beach and toward the open slider door. It was Jessica. She sounded angry—she probably hadn't calmed down since her run-in with Todd. Kelly stepped closer to the house and looked inside.

"You're not listening. I'm in charge. Not Todd." Jessica, barefoot and dressed in a floral romper, paced the length of the living room while talking on her cell phone. "He's not even conscious. Once my lawyers get through with him, he won't have a penny to his name. Trust me, one way or another, he won't be around anymore."

Kelly froze in place when she heard Jessica's menacing pledge. What had Jessica meant when she said, *"One way or another, he won't be around anymore"*? Had she been behind Todd's poisoning?

Jessica turned and finally saw Kelly standing at the door. "I have to go." She disconnected the call and stopped pacing. Her face was free of any makeup except for a swipe of clear lip gloss. "You're eavesdropping on me?"

"I...I...the door is open, and your voice wasn't exactly low." Not waiting for an invitation to come in, she stepped over the slider's track and entered the house. "I brought you cookies from the best bakery in town."

"You're a lot like Becky. She loved her cookies and treats too." Jessica set her phone on an end table and accepted the pastry box. "What really brings you by?"

"I wanted to check on you. See if you're doing okay." Kelly followed Jessica into the kitchen.

"I think you really came here to find out more about Becky's will. And probably to see if I had anything to do with Todd's coma." Jessica opened the box and took out an Italian butter cookie.

It appeared Jessica wasn't in the mood for small talk. So, Kelly obliged. She could cut to the chase better than anyone.

"Is it a coincidence that your partner was murdered, and then the person who inherited her share of the company is now in a coma? It seems you now get to run the company as you see fit." Kelly dropped onto a stool at the peninsula and set her tote on the countertop.

Jessica bit into the cookie and chewed. After she swallowed, she reached for a napkin. "All I see is an unfortunate string of events."

Nice spin.

"You're not here just to find out about Becky's will. You're here to find out once and for all if I killed her. Let me be clear—I didn't. I didn't need to kill her to sell Define Beauty. In the past few weeks, she started to see the benefits of selling. Chantelle had even sweetened the offer by letting her stay on as the creative director. It was a nice deal."

"What would you have gotten out of it?"

"A nice check and then some freedom to do anything I wanted. There are a million opportunities for someone like me." Jessica leaned forward, resting her palms on the counter's edge. "Look, I'll say it again. I didn't kill your cousin. Terry was obsessed with her. It wouldn't be the first time obsession led to murder."

"I don't think reaching out a few times via direct messaging could be considered being obsessed. I actually think she had more of a reason to kill you than Becky."

Jessica drew back, apparently shocked by the statement.

"You harassed her online," Kelly said.

"I did no such thing. I simply stood up for myself. It's not my fault she's weak. Believe me, social media isn't the place to be if you have confidence issues. And you definitely don't want to put yourself out there as an influencer if you can't handle the haters and trolls. They're out there just waiting to pounce on their next prey."

"Like you did?"

Jessica shook her head. "You have it backward."

"Okay, let's say that I do. What about Todd? Why would Terry want to hurt him?"

"I don't know. For all we know, Todd tried to harm himself. Maybe he killed Becky and couldn't live with his guilt anymore."

Kelly couldn't discount Jessica's theory. It seemed solid. He and Becky could have argued, and he pushed her by accident. Then guilt ate away at him and he couldn't live with it any longer.

"I understand why you're doing what you're doing. Becky was family. I just wish there were a way to convince you that I'm not the guilty party." Jessica reached for another cookie. "These are really good."

"Ah-ha." Normally, Kelly would have already been contemplating eating a third cookie by now. Yet her hands remained folded on the counter. Something had killed her appetite. Was it the fact that she started to believe Jessica? When was believing in someone's innocence a bad thing?

She knew the answer—when it was someone you didn't trust.

Kelly wasn't buying Jessica's claim that she had to stand up for herself with Terry. Of the two, Jessica seemed more likely to be the aggressor. There was also the fact, according to Jessica, that Becky had been considering selling the company. Which meant Jessica had no motive to kill Becky.

Kelly's mind rewound to the conversation she had with her cousin the night of her murder. Becky never said she wouldn't sell the company. She said selling was a huge decision. If only Kelly could get some intel from inside the company. There had to be someone else her cousin confided in.

"Do you have any more questions?" Jessica closed the pastry box and pushed it out of reach.

"What can you tell me about Whitney Mulhern and Liam Stewart?" Even though Whitney had an alibi, and so did Liam if the hookup story was true, Kelly still had suspicions about them.

"Talk about a mistake. Becky met him and fell in love instantly. Not too long after their first date, she found out he was engaged to Whitney. Becky broke up with him without hesitation. But it wasn't enough to satisfy Whitney."

"What happened?"

"Whitney confronted Becky a few days later and accused her of knowing Liam was engaged. She dumped Liam and then went on to make it her mission to sabotage Define Beauty any chance she got. Being in public relations, she has a lot of contacts."

"Did Whitney ever threaten to physically harm Becky?"

Jessica shook her head. "I'm not aware of any of those kinds of threats. They're really not Whitney's style. I can tell you the company has had a tremendous struggle because of Becky's relationship with Liam. You know what they say about payback. And Whitney is an expert in it."

"Do you happen to know anyone who uses the handle Beauty4Everygirl?"

Jessica looked thoughtful for a moment and then shook her head. "No. Why?"

Before Kelly could answer, the doorbell chimed.

"Guess it's my day for unexpected visitors." Jessica walked out of the kitchen and crossed the open living space to the front door.

Kelly ignored the dig but realized she'd overstayed her welcome. When she heard Jessica returning, she swiveled on the stool, and that's when she caught sight of Detective Wolman. She swiveled back around, scrunching her face because she was going to get the third degree about why she was there.

"I see you have company. I hope I'm not interrupting." Wolman approached the peninsula, and she stood only a few feet from Kelly.

"No, not at all." Kelly shifted so her gaze met the detective's.

"What are you doing here, Kelly?" Wolman asked.

"I came by to check on Jessica. See how she's holding up." Kelly intentionally left out being curious about the will, which she hadn't discussed yet with Jessica. She was already on Wolman's bad side. Why make things worse?

Wolman's jaw set, and her lips formed a thin line. It didn't look like she believed Kelly's answer for a minute.

"We'll talk later. Right now, I'd like for you"—Wolman looked at Jessica—"to come back to the police department with me."

"Why?" Jessica crossed her arms.

"For a follow-up interview."

"Are you arresting me?"

"No. I am not."

"Then I don't have to go with you."

Kelly watched the exchange and, if asked, would put her money on Wolman winning the standoff. But Jessica had a valid point. If she wasn't under arrest, she wasn't required to go with the detective.

"Answering my questions would clear up a few things in the investigation, and I would appreciate your help."

Kelly's mouth gaped when she realized what was going on. Wolman suspected Jessica. But her spidey senses went off. Something didn't make sense.

"Detective, it's clear you have your suspicions about Jessica, just like you have about other people who were in Becky's life. What's also clear is that Becky was meeting someone down at the beach. Why would Jessica write a note to meet Becky at the beach when they lived together?" Kelly asked.

Wolman's mouth set in a hard line. "Miss Quinn, I'll remind you again to stay out of my investigation."

"All she did was ask a question, and I'd like to hear your answer." Jessica tilted her head and waited.

"I'm not going to discuss an ongoing case in front of a civilian. You and I can talk about this at my office." Wolman gave Kelly one last look before she walked toward the door, and it left nothing to Kelly's imagination. Once again, she'd ticked off the detective.

"Fine. But I'm taking my own car and calling my lawyer on the way." Jessica huffed and spun around. She followed the detective. "Just lock up!" she instructed Kelly over her shoulder before she grabbed her purse from a console table in the entry hall.

Kelly stood and stepped forward but stopped. There was no point chasing after them. Wolman wouldn't listen to anything she had to say. Instead, she grabbed her tote and walked out onto the deck.

At the railing, she stood staring out at the angry water. The crashing waves intensified, landing on shore with a wallop. The sparse light from the gloomy day had begun to fade. A gust of wind whipped her hair across her face. The storm that had been brewing all day was going to be a doozy when it finally hit Lucky Cove.

The hairs on the back of her neck prickled, and her spidey senses went off again, alerting her to someone's presence behind her.

And she was right.

"Kelly, we need to talk."

CHAPTER SEVENTEEN

The break in the silence startled Kelly, and she swung around. She couldn't believe who was standing at the top of the stairs. What was she doing there?

"I'm sorry I snuck up on you." Terry barely looked like herself. Her caramel-colored waves were messy and not in a chic bedhead kind of way. Her skin was sallow, and dark circles rimmed her fatigued eyes. Even her denim skirt and a black T-shirt missed the fashion mark. Both were oversized and not in a stylish way. "I saw Jessica leave with the detective."

"Are you following me?" Kelly eased her hand into the interior pocket of her tote, where she kept her phone. Her fingers felt for the device. Where was it?

"I'm keeping an eye on Jessica." Terry stepped farther onto the deck. She had a black nylon backpack slung over her shoulder, and she held on tightly to its strap.

Kelly arched an eyebrow. She interpreted Terry's statement as stalking. And now she was alone with said stalker. And a potential murderer. She took a step to the side. Her goal was to get closer to the slider and inside the house to escape through the front door.

"I also wanted to talk to you. Alone."

"You should have called me back. We could have met at the boutique." Where there were people. Lots of people.

"Why does everyone keep telling me what to do?" Terry snapped, balling her free hand into a fist. "My mother, my therapist, now you!"

Kelly shrank back, pulling her hand out of her tote.

"I'm sorry." Terry inhaled a breath. Kelly hoped it was a cleansing one. "It feels like no one listens to me. Instead, people order me around to do things they think are best for me."

Kelly realized she had to be careful with what she said next and how she said it.

"We're here now. What did you want to talk to me about?" Kelly braced herself for the possibility of a confession.

"I need for you to understand what happened and what role Jessica played in it."

"Why?"

"Because it will prove to you she's not who she says she is, and she probably killed your cousin."

Despite her inner voice, the one shouting, *Run, Kelly, run*, her interest was piqued. She wanted to hear what Terry had to say.

Terry moved toward the seating area on the deck. Kelly thought she was going to sit, but Terry remained standing beside a chair.

"Jessica harassed me online after Lansing Cosmetics paid for a trip to Morocco for me and another influencer."

Kelly tipped her head to the side. "Morocco?" Years ago, a coworker at Bishop's who had a beauty blog hardly got any perks from brands she talked about in her posts. Every now and again, she got lucky and received a few makeup palettes and mascaras. So Kelly couldn't help but be skeptical about Terry's claim of such an expensive trip.

"It's true," Terry insisted. "I wasn't always this messed up. Before my crash and burn, I was popular in my niche. Anyway, I found out Jessica had been on the short list of influencers to go on the junket. She started taking jabs at me in her videos. At first, they were backhanded compliments, and then they got nastier."

"All because she didn't get to go on the trip?" While Kelly doubted Terry's claim of being so popular online that she'd been given a fabulous trip, she didn't doubt another influencer could be jealous. She saw it all the time in fashion and even when she worked at Bishop's.

"You have no idea how envious a lot of those women are. Someone filed a complaint against me for not correctly labeling an advertisement in one of my videos."

"You could have gotten into a lot of trouble because of the complaint." Kelly knew enough about the online world to know there were stringent regulations in place regarding disclosures for paid advertisements. Accounts risked being fined and shut down if they failed to comply.

Terry scoffed. "I'm sure it disappointed Jessica when I didn't get into trouble. So, she went with plan B. She out and out lied about me. And her followers believed what she said. They started trolling me. You should have seen the awful things they left in my comments. I...I couldn't eat or sleep. It literally ruined my life and career. My deals fell through, which meant I wasn't earning any money."

Terry stepped away from the chair and paced, wringing her hands together. "After my very public meltdown... Gosh, it wasn't what I'd planned for my goodbye." She pulled her hands apart, and they dropped to her sides, her shoulders slumping and her eyes quickly going somber. "I was off the internet for months during therapy. When I went back on, I did some cybersleuthing."

"What for?"

Terry's chin lifted, and a small glimmer of satisfaction sparked in her eyes. "To find out the truth about Jessica. And I did. I found out she had done the same thing to three other beauty bloggers. Somehow, their paths crossed with Jessica, and suddenly they were being trolled and losing sponsorships. Then she latched onto Becky."

Latched on? Kelly didn't like the sound of that.

"Why didn't you go to the police?"

"Because no crime had been committed. At best, maybe she could have been charged with cyberbullying. You have to remember, at the time, I was only a few months into therapy, and I'm not sure anyone would have taken me seriously. What I had was speculation, and it prompted me to continue digging. Her name kept popping up on boards and chats. Those messages had one thing in common."

"What was that?"

"To stay clear of Jessica Barron. It's why I reached out to Becky. I wanted to warn her about her new partner. I realized they were already in business together, but maybe it wasn't too late for Becky to back out. Jessica's not the person she pretends to be."

"That's a pretty bold statement. What do you have to prove it?"

Terry sat on the chair, dropping her backpack to the deck floor. She crossed her legs and leaned forward, resting her arms on her thigh. "Through my research, I learned her bio is all fake. For starters, it says she was raised in suburban Philadelphia."

Kelly, feeling a bit more relaxed and less threatened, moved to a chair opposite Terry and sat. "She wasn't?"

"No. She was raised in Philadelphia in the foster care system. Her education? Lies. Her work history? More lies. She never worked for L'Oréal

Paris or Christian Dior. The only truth I could find was her birthday. May twenty-sixth."

Keeping her expression neutral as not to agitate Terry, Kelly processed what she'd just heard. Was Jessica really the monster Terry was making her out to be? Had Becky been targeted by a skilled manipulator? Or was Terry still unhinged and looking for a scapegoat? Her head hurt from so many questions she had no answers for.

"How do you explain the note that was found with Becky's body?"

Terry's forehead creased as her jaw slacked, leaving her mouth open. It took her a moment to regroup before asking, "What note are you talking about?"

"The one that told Becky to meet you on the beach at midnight. I saw it. The handwriting looked like yours."

"No. Not possible." Terry shook her head vigorously to the point where Kelly became concerned about another outburst. "I didn't write her a note, so how can it be my handwriting? You have to believe me. I didn't kill your cousin. I swear."

Kelly cast a skeptical gaze at Terry. She knew what she saw; yet, she wasn't a handwriting expert, so she could have been mistaken.

"You need to go to the police and tell them everything you told me about Jessica. It's important they know."

Terry threw her arms up in the air as she leaped from the chair. "I can't do that! Jessica has very cleverly made me look like a crazy person no one would believe. You don't even believe me."

"Not true, Terry. I want to believe you. I really, really do. You saw Jessica leave with the detective. Sure, Wolman said it was for a follow-up interview, but we both know Jessica had a motive to murder Becky. You need to tell them what you know to help build a case against her."

Terry's expression wavered, and for a moment, it looked like she agreed with what Kelly had said. But then her eyes narrowed and drew back. "Wow. You want me to walk into the police department after Jessica has spun a web of lies about me. I thought I could trust you. Looks like I can't trust anyone." She turned and ran into the house.

Not again.

Kelly sprang up and chased Terry through the house. But she wasn't fast enough. By the time she reached the opened door, Terry had disappeared. She grasped the knob while muttering a few words her granny wouldn't have approved of.

Her ringing phone interrupted the string of not-so-G-rated words she continued to say as she stared out at the quiet road, hoping to see a sign of

Terry. But then what if she did? Chase after her again? Instead, she reached into the tote and finally found her phone beneath her continental wallet. She really needed to use the interior pocket for either the phone or the wallet.

The caller ID gave her a heads-up that it was Gabe on the other end.

"Hey, you won't believe what happened." Kelly spun around and walked back through the house to close and lock the slider door.

"I'm not sure I want to know. But I think you'll want to know this."

Her ears perked up. Was there finally some good news?

"Don't leave me hanging. Come on, tell me." She returned to the front door and pulled it closed behind her as she stepped outside. It was time to go. And, hopefully, she'd never see the house again.

"Lab tests came back. Someone poisoned Todd."

"I knew it." Kelly stopped midstep. "Didn't I say he could have been poisoned?"

"Yes, you did."

"What was he poisoned with? Any leads who did it?"

"Even if I knew the answers to those questions, I couldn't tell you. Look, I probably shouldn't have told you this much. I have to get going."

"I appreciate the call and the info." She approached her Jeep and opened the driver's side. "Talk to you later."

Inside her vehicle, she started the ignition and then pulled out of the driveway. The drive back to the boutique allowed her to sort through all the information she had, only to leave her with more questions.

The first question she had was whether Terry had been telling the truth about Jessica's cyberbullying and lies about her background. Or was Terry the one lying to shift suspicion onto Jessica? Had Wolman taken the wrong person in for further questioning? Kelly slowed as she approached a red light at an intersection. Besides Jessica, there were Whitney and Todd. Both had motives. Yet Whitney had an alibi, while Todd's was still unknown. When the light changed, Kelly proceeded through the intersection. She was a few minutes out from the boutique. The question of whether Todd had been bitter enough to murder Becky nagged at Kelly. They had been such close friends. She guessed he could have snapped. Her mind wound its way back to Terry. She appeared to have been telling the truth at the beach house. It also seemed to Kelly that Terry hadn't had a motive to kill Becky. Her beef had been with Jessica.

Speaking of Jessica, her motive was a whopper. She wanted to sell the company and cash in a huge check. She now faced the possibility of not being able to sell and having to answer to Todd since he inherited the company's controlling interest.

None of Kelly's other suspects had a motive to want Todd dead. Only Jessica.

Her phone rang, jarring her from her thoughts. She accepted the call as she pulled into the parking lot behind her boutique.

"Hi, Kelly. It's Leanne from *Long Island View Point.*"

"Oh, hi—"

"I'm so sorry," Leanne interrupted, "we won't be featuring your boutique."

"But—"

"I promise we'll keep you in mind for future segments—"

"I thought—"

"Things change all the time in television. Talk soon. Have a great day!" And with that cheery sign-off, the line went silent.

Have a great day? Seriously?

As Kelly navigated her Jeep into her reserved spot, she absorbed what Leanne had said. The producer's assistant hadn't taken a breath, so Kelly had barely had a chance to say a word or ask why all of a sudden she was out. It was clear; Leanne hadn't called to have a conversation. Only to deliver bad news. It sounded like she was a pro at the task.

Kelly yanked her tote up and exited her vehicle. Walking to the back door, her shoulders sagged, and her steps were heavy. Only a few days ago, it had sounded like being on the show had been a sure thing.

What on earth happened?

When she entered the staff room, the answer hit her. Whitney Mulhern.

I should have known. Frankie warned me about her.

"From what I hear about Whitney, she knows everyone, and if you end up on her naughty list, you can kiss your career goodbye."

Kelly groaned. It looked like she was on Whitney's naughty list.

Liv warned me too.

"I know Whitney can be difficult, but she knows a lot of people."

Yep. She probably knew people at *Long Island View Point*, and that's why Kelly was cut from the segment.

The overwhelming urge to have a pity party nearly had her collapsing onto the chair at her desk. She'd just lost an enormous opportunity to promote her business because of a vindictive Bridezilla. The nerve of that woman. Playing with people's lives. All Kelly had done was ask her a few questions. Was she going to hold a grudge against Kelly forever? Kelly had a hankering to track Whitney down and give her a piece of her mind.

"Yeah, keep pushing her buttons and see how fast she destroys everything," Kelly muttered as she pulled the chair out and sat, dropping her tote on the desktop.

She dug into her bag and took out her notebook where she'd jotted down notes earlier at Brew A Cup. She opened to the page where she listed her suspects and drew a line through Whitney's name.

She closed the notebook and set it to the side. She had real work to do. Top on the list was bookkeeping. She reached for her laptop computer, pulling it closer to her. With the laptop opened, she tapped on the keyboard and opened her financial spreadsheet. The numbers weren't as anemic as they had been when she took over, and it was all because of a lot of hard work and creative thinking to promote the business. Appearing on *Long Island View Point* would have been another avenue to showcase what the boutique offered.

The temptation to feel sorry for herself resurfaced, and it was almost too strong to resist. Luckily, an idea came to her, preempting a pity party. Earlier she'd had a thought that Becky had to have had someone at work she trusted. That person might be able to give Kelly some information about the potential sale to Chantelle or about Jessica. Or, maybe both.

She reached into her tote and pulled out her phone to send Liv a text.

I'm going into the city tomorrow morning to Becky's office. I know it's last minute, but do you want to join me?

Not waiting for Liv's reply, she closed her computer, stood, and headed out of the staff room. Before Kelly reached the sales counter, where she found Breena ringing up a purchase, Liv replied.

Someone has to keep an eye on you. What time are you picking me up?

CHAPTER EIGHTEEN

The next morning Kelly picked Liv up on the way to the train station bright and early, and they joined the horde of daily commuters who were either caffeine depleted or in a tech trance with their phones. Kelly had flashbacks to the days when she traveled from her tiny apartment to Midtown, where she worked, via the subway. At first, when she moved back to Lucky Cove, she missed the daily grind. Now, she couldn't imagine ever doing it again.

For the trek into the city, Kelly chose a pair of blush-colored tailored trousers and a matching blazer worn over a simple white tank. It was easy yet stylish for her trip into Manhattan. Liv went less for fashion and more for comfort in white skinny jeans and a black tunic. Both sported shades and oversized bags.

"I love the city," Liv said, stepping out of the Uber and onto the cement sidewalk. "The nonstop action. On the go all the time."

"It's not all glamourous. Trust me. I lived in an overpriced walk-up short on amenities. And my neighborhood wasn't trendy."

"Oh, I know. I'd never want to live here. Lucky Cove is my home."

"Come on," Kelly said. What Liv hadn't loved was what happened to Kelly the day before. Right as the train was pulling into Penn Station, she shared how she almost became roadkill in front of Brew A Cup. The confession earned her a hug from Liv, followed by a lecture covering several points. First, she should have said something earlier. Second, she should have gone to the emergency room to be examined. Third, investigating is far too dangerous, and they should take the next train back to Long Island.

Kelly disagreed with all three points and insisted they stick with the plan.

"What exactly is the plan?" Liv asked as they exited the train onto the platform.

Kelly hadn't completely worked it out because her mind had been churning with so many other thoughts—like searching Todd's room at the inn. After Liv's reaction to what happened at Brew A Cup, she opted to keep that to herself. She pretended she hadn't heard the question as they made their way to the street. There, they got into their ride and headed downtown.

Kelly completed the transaction with her driver and then stepped out of the minivan onto the sidewalk. The moment her Christian Louboutins hit the sidewalk, she felt like she'd returned home. Patent leather four-inch stilettos in classic beige. Those ridiculously expensive shoes were a gift last spring and perfect for visiting the offices of Define Beauty.

A teen on a skateboard whizzed by, kicking up a rare breeze on the avenue. Once the kid was by, Kelly launched forward to the towering office building. A pang of homesickness struck her. Gosh, she hadn't realized how much she missed the hustle and bustle of the city.

Even so, the hustle had been exhausting—long hours, achy feet, and unreasonable deadlines. It seemed like much hadn't changed in the year since she left the city, because owning a business was a whole new level of hustle. Though now she wore more comfortable shoes. Well, usually. She glanced to her Louboutin-clad feet.

At the heavy glass door, she reached for the handle and pulled. Inside, frigid air and a busy lobby with people coming and going greeted her. Her heels clicked across the marble floor to the bank of elevators. There she scanned the list of companies and found that Define Beauty was on the nineteenth floor. She waved Liv along and pressed the Up button.

"You haven't answered my question. What is the plan?" Liv asked as she followed Kelly. "Do you even have one? Do you think they'll talk to us?"

Kelly pulled out an envelope from her purse. "They'll have to when they sign the card." When she'd met with her sister, they'd discussed the idea of having Becky's employees sign a sympathy card for Becky's parents. Last night, she went to Courtney's Treasures and bought the card. Now it looked like they would have a cover for asking questions about Becky's relationship with Jessica and about the possible sale to Chantelle.

"Doesn't this feel...wrong?" The elevator door slid open, and a group of professionals exited, heading for the main entrance. When the car emptied out, Liv entered.

"Not as wrong as someone murdering my cousin." Kelly followed Liv into the elevator. She pressed the button for the nineteenth floor. "What I'm really doing is allowing her employees the opportunity to talk about her."

"I see. You're helping them through the grieving process."

The elevator stopped at the fourth floor, and two women entered the small space. Both carried coffee to-go cups. The tall brunette went to push a button but lowered her hand when she saw the nineteenth floor had been pressed. She returned to the side of the blonde with a severe bob.

"I can't believe she sent such a callous memo out to everyone," petite blonde said in a hushed tone but loud enough for Kelly to hear.

"It's like she's dancing on Becky's grave," tall brunette said.

"Ewww. That's a horrible image," the blonde replied.

"It's an expression my nana used. I can't believe the day after Becky's funeral, we're having a company meeting. I know we have to discuss what's next for Define, but the day after?"

"Jessica's never been a sentimental person."

The elevator hitched and then came to a stop, its door sliding open. The two women exited with Kelly and Liv behind them. At the glass door etched with the company's name and logo, the blonde pulled it open and entered the reception area. Both employees waved to the receptionist as they continued down the aisle of the open-concept office space until they parted for opposing cubicles.

"It doesn't look like Jessica is wasting any time taking over," Liv whispered.

"No, it doesn't." Kelly started toward the receptionist's curved desk. "Hi, I'm Kelly Quinn. Becky's cousin."

The receptionist frowned. "I'm so sorry for your loss."

"Thank you. This is my friend, Liv Moretti." Kelly turned and gestured for Liv to join her. "We came in from Lucky Cove with this sympathy card. It would mean a lot to me and Becky's parents if we could get some of her friends to sign it."

"Oh…well…I don't see a problem with it, but I'm not in charge. Let me call Jessica." The receptionist reached for the telephone.

Kelly thought quickly. She hadn't wanted the receptionist to let Jessica know she was there. Then again, she hadn't gotten an update about Jessica's status since leaving the beach house with Wolman. For all she knew, Jessica could have been booked, fingerprinted, and set for an arraignment. She needed to text Gabe.

"Kelly!" A familiar voice called to her.

She looked toward the aisle and saw an old friend approaching. Lincoln Paxton had worked at Bishop's department store in the cosmetics buying office. He'd left a year before Kelly got her pink slip.

"Lincoln? You work here?" Kelly held out her arms and gave him a hug. "I had no idea."

"Yeah, for about eight months." Linc let go of Kelly. "So sorry about Becky. Heck of a shock."

Linc stood several inches taller than Kelly, and his black hair was parted on the side and slicked back. He was infamous for how much styling gel he used. He shook off the good-natured ribbing with a reminder that he never looked bad in a photo.

"Linc, you remember me talking about my best friend from Lucky Cove? Well, here she is. Liv Moretti. Liv, this is Lincoln Paxton. We worked together at Bishop's."

He extended his hand and shook Liv's. "We both survived the Dragonista of Seventh Avenue." He leaned forward. "Now it looks like I'm working for another monster."

"It's nice to meet you." Liv took back her hand.

"You're talking about Jessica?" Kelly asked.

Linc nodded. "What brings you by today? Jessica isn't here."

"No, she's still in Lucky Cove. I have a sympathy card I'd like for Becky's friends to sign for her parents." Kelly waved the card.

"I was about to call Jessica to see if it's okay," the receptionist said.

"Of course it's okay. Come on, I'll walk you around and introduce you to everyone." Linc led Kelly and Liv down the aisle. The cubicles were typical office fare, nothing fancy, nothing unique. What gave the office space a pop of personality were the large campaign posters hung at various junctures. Kelly recognized them from magazine ads.

He stopped and pointed. "Becky's office." He shivered. "Just got a chill thinking she won't be back. Ever."

Kelly swallowed the lump in her throat. Maybe this wasn't such a good idea. "Would you mind if I drop my bag in there?"

"Oh, sure. Go ahead." Linc glanced at his watch. "You know, I have to check my emails for an important reply. I'll meet you back here in a few minutes, okay?"

"Great." Kelly walked to the office door and pushed it open while Linc turned and disappeared into a cubicle. She looked to Liv. "Come on."

Inside the office, Kelly dropped her purse on the sofa. There were a bank of windows behind the glass-top desk. Along one wall was a bookcase decorated with thick fashion books and accessories collected from Becky's travels. On the other wall was a giant dry-erase board. There were lists, and one of the lists, written in red marker, was labeled New products: Pros and Cons.

It looked like Define Beauty was exploring moving into skincare products. Define Skincare. There was a long list of pros. But a short list of cons. Expensive. Saturated market. Chantelle.

"You doing okay?" Liv set her bag down on one of the chairs in front of the desk.

Kelly shrugged. She wasn't sure how she was doing. "This office looks and feels like her. So does this." She pointed to the board.

"Your cousin loved lists." Linc returned and moved toward the room's small conference table.

"It's a good way to sort out thoughts and stay organized," Liv said.

"How far along was the skincare project?" Kelly asked.

"Not far." Linc stepped forward and shoved his hands into his pants pockets. "We weren't even to the product development phase. Although, Becky had a few ideas to launch with. Like a capsule collection for the face and body."

"Why is Chantelle on this list?" Kelly pointed.

"They own a huge segment of the market. It's one thing to sell lipsticks and blushes. Skincare is a whole other level. Development, testing, marketing," Linc said. "They own Sienna Grey, our main competitor."

"Then why did they want to buy Define Beauty?" Liv asked.

Linc shrugged. "Maybe merge Define into Sienna Grey? Maybe reposition Define Beauty to another demographic? Maybe make it exclusive to one retailer?"

"How did Becky feel about the sale?" Kelly asked.

"Torn. She loved this company, but she also saw the benefits of selling to a company like Chantelle. It wasn't as cut and dry as it was for Jessica." Linc pulled his hands out of his pockets and crossed them over his chest. He eyed Kelly, nodding as if he'd realized something. "You think she killed Becky? That's why you're here!"

"No…I have this card." Kelly held up the card and envelope.

Linc's lips thinned, and he propped his hands on his hips. "Oh, no, you don't. You're not going to stand there and lie to me. I've heard about your snooping in murder cases out on the island. You're here to snoop. Looking for gossip."

Kelly lowered the card and envelope. Since he was offering. "You got any?"

He gave an exaggerated nod. "About a week ago, before Becky left for Lucky Cove, I overheard a telephone conversation."

"You eavesdropped on your boss?" Kelly gave a sly smile.

"It was an unfortunate timing issue, and before I could turn away to leave, she finished her call." Linc dropped his hands and walked to the desk, eyeing the telephone. "She must have just dialed the number because I heard her introduce herself and ask for Emerson Andrews."

"Who's he?" Liv asked.

"At the time, I had no idea. Then, later in the day, when I came in here for a meeting, Becky seemed distracted. We were right here." He pointed to the conference table. "She left the fourth-quarter projections out when she headed off to another meeting." He glanced down at the desk. "Of course, I popped up to grab them, and that's when I saw the business card."

"Emerson Andrews's business card?" Kelly stepped away from the board and hurried to the desk. "Is it still here?"

Linc shook his head. "No. I looked after we got the news."

Kelly frowned. "Well, did it have a business name? Occupation?"

Linc leaned forward and, in a low voice, said, "Private investigator."

"What?" Both Kelly and Liv said at the same time.

"My bet is she hired him because of Jessica. Some rumors had started circulating over the spring when a handful of beauty bloggers turned down our offer of ambassadorships." He gave Kelly a pointed look. "When was the last time you heard of a blogger turning down an ambassador deal?"

"Did they say why?" Kelly asked.

"Bogus excuses, but we kind of figured it had something to do with Jessica. She did more than ruffle a few feathers when she was blogging," Linc said.

"But you don't know for sure Becky hired this PI to investigate Jessica?" Liv dropped down to a chair at the table.

"No." Linc glanced at his flashy watch. "Duty calls. I have a conference call with our manufacturer. You good to go around and get the card signed?"

"Yeah, yeah, go on. I'll swing by your cubicle before we leave." Kelly turned to Liv but then swiveled back to stop Linc from leaving. "Wait, one more question. Does the handle Beauty4Everygirl mean anything to you?"

He thought for a moment and then shook his head. "No. Sorry. Why?"

"Just someone who reached out to me about Jessica. Thanks." Kelly shifted her attention back to Liv after Linc left the office. "You only hire a PI if you're suspicious about someone. I wonder if Becky could have broken their partnership agreement?"

"That would mean if the sale went through, then Jessica would be out her share of the money," Liv said.

"What Jessica hadn't counted on was that Becky left her portion of the company to Todd. Come on, we have to get back to Lucky Cove and tell Wolman about the PI." Kelly spun around and headed out of the office. The temptation to pay a visit to the PI herself was a strong one to resist, but she expected he wouldn't tell her much. But he'd have to spill the beans to the police. And maybe this was a small way to get back into the good graces of Wolman.

Before leaving Define Beauty, Kelly passed around the sympathy card and Liv provided the tissues. By the time they were in the elevator going down to the lobby, Kelly's eyes were swollen and red. Becky had been beloved among her staff. When they were outside, Kelly could tell that Liv was trying to perk up her mood by buying her a pretzel from a sidewalk cart. Even eating the warm, salty carb hadn't been enough to make Kelly feel better. No, she'd feel a whole lot better when the person who killed her cousin was behind bars. And it was looking more and more like it was the one person Becky had trusted the most—her business partner.

* * * *

Ominous clouds greeted Kelly and Liv when they arrived back in Lucky Cove. The storm's front finally had swept in and promised to batter the coastal town along with its neighbors. After dropping Liv off at her apartment, Kelly drove back to the boutique. She darted from the Jeep to inside to avoid getting soaked. Unlocking the back door, she heard her phone ring, but she didn't answer in time, and it went to voice mail.

She wasn't too wet, thankfully. And neither were her shoes. She slipped them off and set them under her desk and then slipped on a pair of ballet flats. After she took care of her footwear, she checked the message on her phone.

"Hey, Kelly. It's Julie. Sorry, it's taken so long to get back to you. It's crazy here. Anyway, the woman with Smith is Lorena Taft. She's an executive at Chantelle Cosmetics. BTW, Smith is also an executive at Chantelle. Gotta go. Call later. We need to get together for drinks or something."

Kelly lowered the phone. Jessica was dating a guy who worked at the company trying to buy out Define Beauty. Had the two of them improperly influenced Becky? Had they grown impatient for Becky to finally agree to sell and killed her to speed up the process?

It looked like Terry had been telling the truth.

Now Kelly had to find her. *Again.*

She walked out of the staff room for the sales floor, where she found Breena bagging Mrs. Marr's purchases. The retired schoolteacher was in the boutique at least once a week to shop, consign, and shop some more. She was Kelly's ideal customer.

"Hi, Kelly. Glad you're back." Breena handed Mrs. Marr her shopping bag.

"I was very saddened to hear the news about your cousin." Mrs. Marr gave a sympathetic smile. "I read the article in the *Weekly*. She sounded like a brilliant, ambitious young woman, starting her own cosmetics company."

"She was." Kelly's gaze dropped for a moment, and then she composed herself. "You better get home before the storm really hits."

"No worries. We've seen worse storms than what's coming. You girls have a good day." Mrs. Marr turned and ambled out of the boutique.

"She's so sweet." Breena gathered the hangers from the clothes Mrs. Marr had just purchased and dropped them into a basket. "So, how was the city?"

"It was nice to see where Becky worked, but it was hard talking to her employees. Everybody loved her." Kelly rested her palms on the counter.

"Why don't you go upstairs and relax? We're only open for a few more hours, and I'm closing. Given the storm is coming in, I don't think we'll get a lot of customers."

Kelly glanced at the windows. Rain pelted against them, and the wind had kicked up.

She appreciated Breena's offer, but she wasn't in the mood to relax. Her body hummed with energy, though it wasn't the productive kind. No, it felt more frenetic. She felt she had to keep busy. She drifted to the window. Maybe she could change the display. There was an adorable striped sundress that would catch the eyes of pedestrians as they passed by. Before she turned to find the dress, she saw Smith walking out of the bed-and-breakfast across the street carrying a duffel bag.

He's leaving Lucky Cove?

He couldn't leave before she had the chance to talk to him. She darted to the door and opened it, stepping out into the rain. She slipped off her blazer and covered her head as she hurried across the street, mindful of her near brush with death the day before when she stepped off the curb. Fortunately, she made it to the other side of Main Street and called out to Smith.

He looked in her direction while he swung the duffel onto the passenger seat of a Mercedes Roadster. The car suited Smith—pretentious.

"What is it now, Kelly?"

"You're leaving town? Why?" Kelly's questions went unanswered by Smith. He didn't look the least bit interested in what she was saying. "Have you talked to Jessica? She could be in trouble. She was taken in by the police for an interview yesterday."

Smith closed the car door. "Look, to be completely honest, it's getting too complicated for me."

Kelly's forehead creased. "Complicated?"

"I was looking for a merger, not a murder. Now, if you don't mind, I'm getting soaked." He walked around the front of the car.

"So you two weren't really dating?"

"I had a job to do. It's a shame the deal is dead, because it could have been awesome." He got into the driver's side.

She knew it the first time she saw them together. They were in a fake relationship. It seemed there was a lot fake about Jessica.

The Mercedes pulled away from the curb, but another vehicle quickly replaced it, with the passenger window rolled down.

"You're soaked. Get in."

CHAPTER NINETEEN

Kelly hadn't realized the blazer over her head was soaked, and so was most of her. Gratefully, she pulled open the passenger door of Nate's vehicle and slipped into the seat.

"You're a lifesaver," she murmured as she settled. The air-conditioning sent a chill through her body. Nate must have noticed because he turned down the cooling system.

"What were you doing out there without an umbrella?"

Kelly folded the blazer up and dropped it on the floor.

"I saw Smith leaving the B&B, and I wanted to talk to him. Turns out he's Jessica's make-believe boyfriend."

"Which leads me to my next question. How do you manage to be exactly where Wolman is? Is it a sixth sense or something?"

Kelly gave him a sidelong look. She wished she could blame her bad luck on some unpredictable supernatural power. But she couldn't. It was just dumb luck.

"I guess it's serendipity."

Nate let out a hearty laugh. "I'm not sure Marcy views it that way."

"Well, if it means anything, I think she was right to reinterview Jessica."

"Why do you say that?"

"I went into the city this morning, to Becky's office, to have her employees sign a card for my aunt and uncle. Turns out an old friend works there, and he told me Becky hired a private investigator a few weeks ago. He thinks it had to do with Jessica."

"There could have been other reasons."

"True. But, let's face it. She doesn't seem to be an honest person. Terry said she lied about mostly everything in her bio."

"When did you speak to Terry?"

Oops. Kelly thought quickly. She was in enough hot water, so she needed to do a little backpedaling.

"It doesn't matter. And no, I don't know where she is." She rubbed her hands together. Her body still shivered.

"How about we get you a cup of coffee to help warm you up."

She considered the invitation. Coffee would be nice. Coffee with Nate would be nicer. Whoa. The last thing she wanted to do was run her ballet flats right into another relationship. She was still smarting from her breakup with Mark.

"Maybe next time? I really think I need a hot shower and some dry clothes." Kelly stopped shivering and relaxed into the leather seat, even though she'd be there for only another minute or so.

"Sure. I'll drop you back at the boutique." He gripped the steering wheel and pulled the vehicle from the curb, making a U-turn when there was a break in the traffic.

"Is that legal?" she asked with a giggle. *Oh, boy. I'm giggling. Play it cool, Kell.*

"What, you gonna call a cop?" His retort was playful. Oh, boy. They were bantering. She and Mark hadn't bantered much.

"Maybe. Or, who knows? Wolman might walk out of that bookshop." Kelly pointed to Lucky Cove Books.

Nate let out a heartier laugh as he pulled his sedan into a space in front of Danny's Seafood. He cut the ignition, leaned on his arm on the steering wheel, and looked at Kelly.

"How about you tell me what was going on back there? Why were you talking to that Smith Henshaw?"

"So you can tell Wolman?"

"I'm a police officer. I had to share any information I received with my colleague. After all, it's her case."

Despite her best efforts, she smiled. "You've made your point. I asked Smith why he was leaving since it seemed his girlfriend is in trouble."

Nate lowered his hand. "You mean his fake girlfriend."

"I wonder if Becky knew it was all a lie? What's happening with Jessica?" On the train ride back to Lucky Cove, she'd texted Gabe asking about Jessica, but he hadn't replied.

"She's been arrested."

The news hadn't surprised Kelly. Which was kind of sad. Her cousin trusted Jessica enough to let her into her life and make her a part of Define Beauty. And then Becky suffered the ultimate betrayal. Kelly's shoulders slumped as a mix of relief, anger, and regret coursed through her body. "I can't help but think how things could have turned out differently if Becky and Jessica hadn't met."

"Hey, hey." Nate reached for Kelly's hand and squeezed. "You can't go down that road. You can't change the past."

The warmth of his touch sent a zing through Kelly. Gosh, it had been so long since she'd felt a zing. No. No zings. A romance wasn't in the cards for her. At least, not now.

"I know you're right. I really do. Though my heart feels differently." She rested her other hand on top of Nate's, and they stared at each other for what seemed to be forever. The whole world stood still, and the sounds from the road and heavy downpour disappeared. It was only her and Nate. Their heads inched closer together, and she was on the verge of breaking her no-relationship rule.

I'm going to kiss him.

Her eyes fluttered closed. Her lips were so close to his when rapping on the passenger side window broke the moment. The sounds of passing cars and the heavy rain battering the car's roof returned.

Kelly pulled back and glanced at the window.

Frankie!

A part of her was relieved he'd shown up. Another part was furious with him.

He tapped on the window again.

Nate lowered the window from his control panel, and Frankie leaned in, grasping the door frame with his hands.

"You and me, we need to talk."

Kelly gulped. Her cousin's tone was severe, much like it had been at the hospital when he and Summer asked her about her visit with Uncle Ralph right before his heart attack. Since he hadn't gotten the answers he was looking for then, it seemed like he was planning on getting them now.

"Everything all right?" Nate asked.

"Yeah, only some family stuff." Frankie opened the door for Kelly. "Come on, I'm getting drenched."

"Thanks for the lift," Kelly said to Nate. "Could you pass along a message to Wolman for me?"

"It's probably best if you keep your distance for a while. So, sure. What is it?"

Kelly started to speak, but emotion balled up in her throat, cutting off her words. She swallowed it and tried again. "Thank you for finding the person responsible for Becky's death."

He nodded. "I'll pass it along."

"Thank you. Don't forget my rain check on coffee." Why was she pursuing a coffee date when she knew where it would probably lead? Right straight to a broken heart, like always.

"I'll call." Nate grinned.

Kelly's cheeks warmed. Great. She was blushing like a teenager. She grabbed her wet blazer and exited the vehicle. Frankie closed the door, and the two of them hurried to the boutique. She opened the front door, and they hurried inside.

"I need to change out of these clothes." Kelly shook off the rain—well, at least the droplets that weren't soaked into her clothing. "Come on upstairs. I'll make tea."

Frankie closed the front door and waved at Breena. "Your dad battening down the hatches at the marina?"

"He should be. I think this storm is going to pack a punch," Breena said. At the counter, she was busy marking down T-shirts that hadn't sold. "You both are soaked."

"We're going upstairs to dry off. Text if you need help." Kelly led Frankie through the boutique in silence. She popped into the staff room to get her purse and then dug out her key holder.

With the staircase door unlocked, they went up to the second floor. More silence. This wasn't good. She and Frankie were never at a loss for words. They could gab for hours. Before reaching the landing, she looked over her shoulder. Yep, the serious look was still there.

When she reached her apartment door, she slid the key into the lock and turned it. The anticipation of talking about what happened before her uncle's heart attack bubbled inside her.

In the apartment, Howard met them and meowed loudly. She gave him a quick pat on the head, and then she gestured to the living room and told Frankie she'd be a moment. He removed his rain jacket and hung it on the coat tree. As he walked into the living room, she hurried to her bedroom.

After toweling dry, she put on a pair of joggers and a V-neck T-shirt. Back out in the living room, she found the two guys on the sofa. Frankie stroked the cat's back, and Howard ate up the attention.

"I'm going to put the kettle on." She waited for a reply. Even a grunt. All she got was a sharp nod. Kelly turned and walked to the kitchen. Her granny believed tea was the cure-all. She wasn't too sure about the claim, but preparing the tea gave her something to do.

She set the kettle on the stove, and when she turned, she found Frankie filling the doorway with his arms crossed.

"What is going on? Are you going to say something? Or are you just going to stare at me with that look on your face?"

"You know Ariel is my sister, don't you?"

Kelly's mouth opened then closed. That wasn't what she thought he was going to say. Maybe it was. It didn't matter. How would she explain knowing the secret?

"Wow. Kelly Quinn, speechless. Guess there's a first time for everything." Any other day, he would have chuckled while saying that, but not then. There was nothing funny about finding out your father had a daughter he never mentioned. Frankie entered the kitchen and took out two mugs from an upper cabinet. "You were talking to my dad about it before he had his heart attack, weren't you?"

Kelly nodded.

"How long have you known?"

"Does it matter now?" Kelly slid the tea canister along the counter, plucked out two tea bags, and dropped each into a mug. She'd worried that when the truth came out, she'd feel worse than when she was keeping the secret. She'd been right. There was no feeling of relief—just more worries and regret.

"I guess not. However, how you found out is important. At least to me, since my father failed to tell me." Frankie leaned against the counter and crossed his arms again.

"Believe me, your dad hadn't meant to tell me. He blurted it out after I pushed to know why he seemed so intent on making my life miserable. There had to be more than just Granny leaving me this business and the building in her will." In retrospect, she probably should have left it alone and dealt with her uncle's ire.

"I don't understand."

The kettle whistled, and Kelly turned off the burner. Filling the mugs, she explained. "He blames me for the accident that left Ariel paralyzed. When he said that, I pushed harder. Maybe too hard. I'm not sure. Then out of nowhere, he revealed she's his daughter. It shocked both of us."

"Wait until Ariel finds out." Frankie opened the refrigerator and took out the milk carton. He prepared his tea. "I got my family tree match yesterday."

Kelly swallowed. She couldn't even imagine how her friend would feel once she learned the truth and that Kelly had known for months but never said a word. Gosh, how she hated being caught in the middle. It was a no-win situation for her and a life-changing revelation for Ariel.

"She's on vacation with her family, so she's probably been too busy to check her account." Kelly added milk to her mug, removed the tea bag, and returned the milk carton to the refrigerator. "I begged him to tell Ariel and you. And Summer."

"He's never listened very well." Frankie unfolded his arms and reached for his mug. "Got any cookies?"

With a bounce in her step, Kelly smiled and moved from the stove to the corner of the counter by the refrigerator. "Yes, I do. Milanos." She pulled out a half-filled bag from the cookie jar.

He gave a shrug. "They'll do."

Kelly gaped. "I may not be a French-trained baker like you, but these cookies are delicious." She carried her mug and the bag of cookies out of the kitchen to the dining table, which had come with the apartment. The large, dark-stained table with ornate legs wasn't Kelly's style, but it was within her budget—free.

Months ago, she moved the coordinating hutch to her storage unit. In its place stood a wide two-drawer sideboard with a chestnut top and a distressed finish that gave it an heirloom-from-an-old-French-country-farmhouse vibe. At some point, she'd have enough money to buy a new table. Until then, the one she had was good enough.

"I wanted to tell you and Ariel, but it's not my secret to tell." She opened the package and took out a cookie.

"I get it." Frankie took a long drink and then set his mug down. He leaned back and dragged his fingers through his hair. "What I can't wrap my head around is how long my dad and Ariel's mom lived with the deception."

"You're not angry?" She bit into her cookie and chewed. Kelly wasn't sure how she'd react if she was in his position.

"Oh, believe me, I am. But what can I do? Stay angry forever? How would that help any of us?" He reached for the bag and pulled out a cookie.

"It wouldn't. I hope Ariel feels the same way when she finds out." Kelly took another drink of her tea, and for several minutes they sat in silence, finishing their tea and snack.

Frankie leaned forward and helped himself to another cookie. "On a different note, it looked like I interrupted something when I tapped on the car window. Is there something you want to tell me?"

"No."

"Then why are you blushing?"

"Am not." She felt her cheeks warm.

"Are so. Come on." Frankie nudged her elbow. "He said he's going to call you."

Kelly dipped her head to hide the color on her face. "For coffee. Only coffee."

"Okay. Okay. You're not ready to talk about it yet."

"There's nothing to talk about." At least not at that moment. Her heart wasn't ready for another go at love. Maybe Nate wasn't looking for love either. Maybe a few dates with no expectations were exactly what they both wanted. Maybe she wasn't meant to settle down just yet. It could be the reason why she swooned a little over Dr. Arnold.

"There's plenty to talk about. But I get it. You don't want to discuss your private life right now. How about we change topics? Any update on the break-in and the threat?"

"No. My guess is it was Jessica trying to scare me off. And when that failed, she tried to run me down." Kelly stood and padded to the living room window. Howard had moved from the sofa to the windowsill and looked out onto Main Street. He'd spend hours there watching everything that went on outside. Especially when there was a storm battering Lucky Cove. Tree limbs whipping fiercely in the powerful gusts of wind kept him mesmerized.

"What?"

Oops. "It sounds worse than it was."

"How exactly was it?"

Kelly explained how she received DMs from Beauty4Everygirl and went to meet the person at Brew A Cup only to find it had been a setup.

"Kell, what on earth possessed you to do something like that? Wait, never mind answering. I already know the answer. You're sure you weren't hurt?"

"Positive. Only a little sore. I didn't see the driver, but it had to be Jessica." She sat on the sofa and crossed her legs.

"Man, this is a bad storm." Frankie joined Kelly and Howard at the window. "You're convinced she murdered Becky?"

"The police are too, seeing as they arrested her. Everything I've learned so far points to her. I found out Becky hired a private investigator a few weeks ago, and I think it was because she was having doubts about Jessica."

Frankie looked over his shoulder. "What kind of doubts?"

"A former coworker of mine now works at Define Beauty, and he told me several beauty bloggers declined ambassadorships. Why would they do that? Maybe it's because Jessica is a partner in the company and what Terry said about her was true? Nobody in the influencer world wanted to work with her. I'm not sure, but it does seem that Jessica is a habitual liar and a skilled manipulator. I'm not sure what legal action Becky could have taken to get Jessica out of the company."

"Jessica stood to potentially lose a lot of money."

"It seems that way. I hope we find out why Jessica did it. But I'm not sure it'll help much." Kelly dropped her head back against the cushion and wondered if she'd be chasing closure for the rest of her life.

Frankie joined Kelly on the sofa and swung his arm around her. "I think knowing the truth helps a whole lot."

Kelly gave her cousin a pointed look. He spoke from personal experience. Her cell phone chimed, alerting her that she had a new text message. She untangled herself from Frankie's hold and dashed to her tote. She pulled out her phone.

"It's from Ariel." She pressed the phone against her chest. "What do I do?"

"Read the message," Frankie said.

"Right. Okay." Her stomach somersaulted as she prepared for an unpleasant message. She pulled the phone away from her chest with shaky hands and read the text.

Hey, just checking in. We're having a blast. Wish you were here.

"Phew. It looks like she doesn't know. Yet." Kelly typed a reply and then set the phone down on the table. Before heading back to the sofa, she looked inside the Milanos bag. There were only two left. She took them out and bit into one, saving the other for Frankie. When she sat back on the sofa, she handed the other cookie to Frankie.

"You know, I'm getting hungry." Frankie bit into the cookie and swallowed. "How about Chinese for dinner? We could do takeout."

"Sounds good. I do have a few things left to do downstairs, and I want to send Breena home. The storm is intensifying. Do you mind picking up dinner?" Kelly finished her cookie.

"Sure, no problem. The usual?" He stood, pulling his cell phone from his back pocket.

The usual for Kelly was beef with broccoli and an egg roll. There always had to be an egg roll. She nodded and then pulled herself up from the sofa. What she really wanted to do was snuggle there with Howard and read the new issue of *Vogue*. Was that too much for a gal to ask for?

"Okay. Be back soon with food." Frankie tapped on his phone. As he raised it to his ear, he walked to the door and left the apartment.

Kelly hurried into the kitchen. She took out the plates and utensils, so all they had to do when he returned with the food was to eat. Once she set the table, she went downstairs to the boutique.

Jogging down the stairs, she had a decadent thought—a soak in the tub with a glass of wine after dinner. It sounded luxurious, and it was something she hadn't done in a long time. She was way overdue for a self-care day. By the time she reached the sales counter, it was settled. After she ate dinner, she'd quickly send Frankie home, and she'd fill the tub.

When she reached the first floor, she went into the staff room and grabbed her laptop. She carried it out to the sales floor where Breena was vacuuming. When she caught Breena's attention, she gestured for her to turn off the vacuum.

"What's up?" Breena asked.

"Go on and head home before it gets too bad out there."

"Okay. If you're sure. I want to stop by the marina to see if they need help." The Lucky Cove Fishing Boat Marina had been in the Collins family for three generations. One of the benefits to her family owning the marina was that Breena got to take her friends out for leisurely cruises. It was a perk Kelly enjoyed.

"I'm sure. See you tomorrow." Kelly opened her laptop and scanned her emails.

"You probably should close up. I don't think there will be any more customers." Breena went to the door. She flipped over the Open sign to Closed and then locked the door. She grabbed the vacuum and pulled it behind her as she headed for the staff room. "Oh, I sent a marketing plan to you. We can review it tomorrow."

Kelly said goodbye to Breena as she passed by and looked for the marketing email. Her gaze traveled along the long list of emails from vendors to newsletter subscriptions to spam.

In the middle of all those communications, she spotted one from Breena.

The subject line read—Marketing Q4 Goals.

Having Breena now working full-time meant she'd have more time to devote to marketing and promotion for the boutique. Since it was her area of study at college, she used the boutique as a guinea pig for her ideas. Kelly was cool with that as long as it didn't cost her any extra money. She made a mental note to read that email later and see what recommendations Breena had.

Even though she was happy to have Breena for more hours during the week, she felt terrible about Terry. She'd been as much a victim of Jessica as Becky had been. Maybe she should call Terry and see if she could work a few hours. There was enough in the budget to cover ten hours a week for extra help. Kelly blew out a breath. She was probably asking for trouble, but she wasn't as confident as everyone else that Terry was crazy. She had a different view. Terry had been through a lot emotionally and wasn't fully healed yet. With everyone doubting and labeling her, the chances of her ever fully recovering from the online attack would be slim. It was settled. Kelly grabbed the phone and called. She was prepared to leave a message, so when Terry answered her call, she was pleasantly surprised.

"Hey, thanks for taking my call. I think we should talk again." Kelly clicked on a new tab and did a search for Terry. Before she'd officially hire her back, Kelly wanted to have a serious talk with her that she needed information for, so her search began. A few links came up, and she clicked on the first one.

"About what?" Terry's voice sounded wary. "I'm not going to the police."

"I understand. Though you should know Jessica has been arrested for Becky's murder and what she did to you may help the case against her. It's something to think about."

"Finally, she's going to get what she deserves."

Kelly couldn't have agreed more. "Terry, I'd like to discuss the possibility of you coming back to work for a few hours a week."

"Oh...okay. I'm actually not too far from the boutique. How about I come over?"

"Great. See you soon." Kelly disconnected the call and returned to her email inbox to read Breena's email. Curious about the plans for the next quarter, she opened the email. She read through the bullet points, nodding in agreement with each idea. When she reached the bottom, there was a link to an astrology website plus an encouraging note to read hers.

Against Kelly's better judgment, she clicked on the link. What harm could it do to check her horoscope? Her day was more than half over, and she could see how accurate the mumbo jumbo would be.

The link led her to a website, and she scrolled down the page to find her astrological sign. She stopped midscroll at the Pisces sign.

Above the Pisces's daily horoscope was a drawing, and it looked familiar. Her head tilted to the side as she studied the image. Where had she seen it?

The gold necklace!

The necklace she saw beside Becky's body had the same design.

"Huh. Becky's birthday was in December, which meant she wasn't a Pisces. The necklace wasn't hers. Oh. My. Gosh. Her killer was a Pisces?"

CHAPTER TWENTY

Kelly considered what to do next with this new information. Before she could decide, there was a knock on the door. Terry must have really been close by to get there so fast. Before stepping out from behind the counter, she clicked off the horoscope page and went to let Terry inside.

When she unlocked the door, it surprised her to find Renata standing there with an umbrella shielding her from the heavy downpour. Kelly quickly pulled her friend inside and then closed the door.

"I'm sorry. I didn't realize how late it was." Renata lowered her umbrella. "I got caught up with a disagreeable guest."

"The cookies didn't work?" Kelly returned to the counter.

"No. Which is surprising." Renata followed her. "Thanks for holding the dress for me. Though, honestly, with this weather, I think the dinner party will be canceled." The day before, she had stopped in and tried on one of the many dresses Camille had consigned. It fit Renata like a dream and was within her budget. She paid for it, but she asked if she could pick it up after she got off work, which turned into today because she'd been running late yesterday and had to go to a Little League game.

"I wouldn't be surprised if it were. Hopefully they'll reschedule, because you look great in the dress—great. Let me get it." Kelly hustled to the staff room to fetch the dress. When she returned, she found Renata staring at the computer screen, which was still open to the page Kelly had clicked on about Terry.

"This is her," Renata said, pointing to the screen. "I'm sorry. I didn't mean to be nosy."

"Don't worry about it. Who do you think she is?" Kelly approached, handing off the dress.

"The woman who was with Todd the other night. The one I told you about, and you then told the reporter."

Busted. Kelly figured the only way Renata knew she'd given the tidbit to Ella was because no one else knew.

"Are you sure?" Kelly hadn't been aware that Terry and Todd knew each other. Though, both being in the beauty industry and online, it could have been possible.

"Absolutely. In my line of work, I never forget a face." Renata glanced at the dress, covered in a dry cleaner's plastic bag to protect it. "Thanks again for holding this for me. I better get going."

"Get home safely," Kelly called out as Renata left the boutique.

Kelly shifted her gaze from the door back to the computer. Why would Terry have been meeting Todd? An unsettling thought niggled its way into her head, and she shuddered. Before she overthought, she grabbed the phone and called Breena.

One the second ring, Breena answered. "Hey, what's up? Don't tell me you're still down in the boutique working? This storm is going to be major." She sounded breathless, and it rushed her words. When foul weather happened, it was all hands on deck to secure the boats at the marina. "I'm helping shore things up here at the marina."

"I won't keep you. I have a quick question. What sign is Terry?"

"Finally, you're getting into horoscopes."

Kelly heard the enthusiasm in her employee's voice, and she needed to tamp it down because horoscopes were a bunch of hooey. "No, not really. What's her sign?"

"You don't remember? I read her horoscope to her the other day and you were there. She's a Pisces. Why?"

Kelly palmed her forehead. Breena was right. She'd been there when that awful foreshadowing horoscope was read. "What's the sign for a May twenty-sixth birthday?"

"Gemini. What's going on, Kelly?"

A loud thud from Breena's end of the call startled Kelly, and she jumped. "What was that?"

"My lame brother. Seriously, seeing him work, you'd never think he was raised at a marina. I have to go. Need anything else?"

"No. Thanks." Kelly ended the call, setting the phone down. She found the horoscope site again and stared at the Pisces symbol. She swallowed hard.

"Terry, not Jessica, killed Becky." Kelly closed out of the website and turned off her computer. "She also tried to kill Todd. But why?"

She had to call Gabe because he'd take her call, unlike Wolman. He'd make sure her message got to the detective. As she reached for the phone, she heard a creak.

It sounded like a floorboard.

There wasn't anyone else in the boutique.

Or was there?

Before she could grip the phone, there was another creak.

"I'm here now, Kelly. Let's talk."

Kelly looked over her shoulder and found Terry standing in the doorway from the back hall. She must have entered through the staff room's back door. A weird vibe bounced off Terry, and all the little hairs on the back of Kelly's neck prickled.

"I didn't hear you come in." Kelly hoped Terry hadn't heard her theorizing out loud. She glanced at the phone. It was one quick pickup from being the lifeline she sensed she needed.

Terry lunged forward, surprising Kelly, and grabbed the phone from the counter. She threw it on the floor and stomped on it.

Any doubts Kelly had about Terry being the killer vanished. She was 100 percent certain she was alone with a murderer.

CHAPTER TWENTY-ONE

Kelly met Terry's gaze directly. Finally, she was face-to-face with Becky's murderer. Fury pounded through her body. She willed herself to remain calm, not escalate the situation. But it was damn hard.

"How about you start with why you killed my cousin. What did she ever do to you? What happened on the beach? Go ahead, tell me everything."

Terry blinked. The boldness she'd displayed a moment ago when breaking the phone evaporated, and in its place was what looked like regret.

"I swear, I never wanted to hurt Becky. Never."

"Yet you did! Tell me why. Tell me, was Todd involved? You owe me an explanation." That was the only thing she wanted from Terry. Once she had it, she hoped to never see the woman again. Well, maybe at the sentencing hearing.

"I met Todd a while ago online, and then we finally met in person at a beauty convention. We found that we had something in common—we both hated Jessica. Until we met in person, I didn't know how close he was to Becky. I thought he'd be able to help me meet with her. Maybe she'd feel differently about meeting with a crazy, washed-up beauty influencer if she knew he knew me." Terry pressed her lips together as her gaze drifted to a display of bead bracelets on the counter. Kelly had discovered they were a great impulse buy and kept the chrome T-bar display stocked all the time.

"What happened?"

"When I found out he was here in Lucky Cove, I went to see him at the inn. I asked him to slip Becky a note. He agreed."

"He went to see her that night at the beach house to do you a favor?" Kelly's blood boiled. Her fingers curled into a tight fist. How many more people had Terry dragged into her web of lies? Was anything she said true?

Terry's gaze moved back to Kelly, and it had taken on a sinister glow. Kelly should have taken it as a warning sign, but she was too enraged to worry about her own safety. She wanted the truth. But she had to make sure she made it out of there alive to tell the police.

"Becky wasn't listening to his warning about Jessica. He thought she might listen to me."

"How did he end up poisoned? You did it, didn't you? Why? Tying up loose ends?"

"The only reason I had to do it was because of you!" Terry jabbed a finger in the air.

"Me? Are you serious?"

"After you asked him about the note, he put two and two together. He figured out that I killed Becky since I was the one who met her on the beach."

Kelly's stomach soured at hearing Terry's confession.

"I tried to explain that I hadn't meant to hurt Becky. That was the last thing I wanted to do, but he wouldn't listen to me. He was the only person who knew I wrote the note. That I met with Becky. He said he was going to the police. Can you believe that! After everything she did to him, he still loved her."

"You couldn't let him go to the police, could you?"

"Oh, Kelly, you have to believe me. I'm not a cold-blooded killer. I'm truly sorry for what I've done. If only Becky hadn't dismissed me that night on the beach."

"You're blaming her now?"

"All I wanted her to do was to listen to me. But she wouldn't. I…I got so angry with her. I lost my temper, and she pushed me out of the way. I don't know what happened, what came over me. I grabbed her, and we scuffled…and I shoved her…she fell, hitting her head on the log." Terry's chin trembled, and tears streamed down her face.

"What are you going to do now, Terry?" The sourness in Kelly's stomach churned, and a wave of nausea hit her. She wanted to believe Terry never set out to kill, but she'd murdered one person and put another in a coma.

"I really don't have a choice. I tried to warn you."

"You broke in and left the threatening note?"

Terry nodded.

"You're Beauty4Everygirl, aren't you?"

Terry nodded again. "I wasn't going to hit you with the car. I thought you'd back off and let Jessica take the rap. She really was the perfect suspect. I'm sorry it has to end this way."

Kelly gulped. She had to think fast. *Wait! Frankie.* He'd be back any minute with their dinner. He was the distraction she needed. *Okay. New plan.* Drag out this insane conversation with Terry until Frankie arrived.

"What are you going to do after you get rid of me?"

Terry shrugged. "I'm not sure. Maybe I'll open a boutique. I really enjoyed working here."

"You're going to let Jessica go to prison for crimes she didn't commit."

"Consider it payback for what she's done to so many others. Meanwhile, I'll be starting over."

"What kind of life will you have knowing that an innocent woman is paying for crimes you committed?" Kelly really didn't care about what Terry faced next in her life. Trying to sound compassionate and concerned about the murderer left a bitter taste in her mouth. But she had no choice. She needed to keep Terry talking.

"I'm touched that you care, but you don't need to worry. I'll be okay. Every night when I lay my head down on my pillow, I will rest easily knowing Jessica Barron is rotting away in a cell. Guess I'm not as weak as she thought I was."

Kelly's heart rate kicked up to a speed she was sure would cause her to pass out. But she couldn't. She had to stay alert to fight for her life. The one good thing was that Terry didn't appear to have a weapon.

"I really didn't want things to end like this." Terry's voice was emotionless and chilling.

"No. Of course you didn't. You can fix this." Where was Frankie? Did he drive into the city's Chinatown to pick up dinner?

Terry shook her head. "I doubt it. Just so you know, I really appreciated the job, and I liked working for you. It's why I thought leaving the note around the mannequin's neck would be enough to scare you off. It should have scared you off."

"What do you plan to do with me?" There wasn't any trepidation in Kelly's voice. She needed to know what Terry intended to do so she could come up with her own defense. She shoved down all the hurt and sorrow and anger consuming her to stay clear, to stay focused. To make sure Terry wouldn't be able to hurt another person.

Before Terry could answer, the front door swung open, and Frankie bounded in with their takeout order in his hands. A strong gust of wind followed.

"Boy, you won't believe how busy the restaurant is," he said, struggling to close the door.

Terry looked over her shoulder, and the momentary distraction was what Kelly needed. A surge of adrenaline shot through her body, and she leaped forward with her arms stretched out and tackled a surprised Terry to the floor.

"Goodness! What's wrong with you, Kell?" Frankie's eyes bugged out. "Sure, she's not the best employee, but don't you think you're overreacting?"

Kelly straddled Terry, pinning her down. "Call the police!"

"What for? I missed something, didn't I?" He dashed to the counter and set the bag of food down. "What happened?"

"She killed Becky and poisoned Todd. Now, call the police." Kelly kept her eyes on Terry. There was no way she was going to let her get away. But by the looks of Terry, who was sobbing uncontrollably, she would not be running away.

"Let me take her, and you call the police." Frankie grabbed one of Terry's arms and pulled her up once Kelly was standing. "I got her."

Kelly blew out a relieved breath as she regained her composure. "Thanks."

"Glad I got here when I did." Frankie had a tight grip on Terry's arm.

"I'm...really...sorry," Terry murmured between sobs. "I'm...not...a horrible person. Really, I'm not."

Kelly shook her head and gestured for Frankie's cell phone. With it in hand, she walked to the counter because she couldn't deal with Terry's regret at the moment. Or even look at the person who killed her cousin.

Within minutes of Kelly's call to 9-1-1, two police vehicles pulled up in front of the boutique, and uniformed officers entered with skeptical looks on their faces. Maybe blurting out "I've caught a killer" when she spoke to the emergency dispatcher was a bit dramatic. Still, considering the circumstance, it was understandable.

Kelly filled them in on what happened, and the taller of the two officers took Terry into custody. She was still sobbing when the officer handcuffed her and led her out to one of the waiting patrol cars. The other officer took Kelly's and Frankie's statements. Next on the scene was Gabe, who had been off duty but noticed the activity outside the boutique. Behind him came Detective Wolman. It seemed she was always on duty.

Kelly and Frankie recounted what happened to Wolman, and she took notes. The detective stepped away for a moment, and that's when Liv appeared at the door.

"Oh, my goodness! Are you okay?" Liv closed her umbrella and darted toward Kelly at warp speed, shoving Gabe out of the way with her arms stretched out, ready to pull Kelly into a hug. And boy, was it a doozy of a hug. "It was Terry? And you were here all alone with her?"

After Kelly's call to 9-1-1, she called Liv so her best friend wouldn't have to hear the news through the Main Street gossip chain.

"Too. Tight. To. Breathe." Kelly's ribs were being squeezed, and she was getting lightheaded.

Gabe approached, setting a hand on Liv's shoulder. "She's okay despite herself."

"Hey," Kelly managed to say. "Still. Not. Breathing."

Liv released her hold on Kelly but kept her fingers wrapped around her shoulders. "What on earth happened? Did she break in? Oh, my goodness. It was her the other night, wasn't it?"

"Actually, Kelly invited her over today," Gabe said.

Kelly shot him a look. "Not helping."

"Why on earth would you invite her over? She was a suspect. Well, now we know she's a murderer, right?"

"Yes, she confessed everything to me." Kelly broke free of Liv's grasp to sit on the stool beside the sales counter. "The last thing I want is to feel sorry for her, but you should have heard her. She's truly troubled."

"I'd say so. You're lucky you didn't get hurt." Liv moved toward Kelly. She wasn't done mothering her best friend.

"I'm lucky Frankie showed up when he did." Kelly leveled a grateful look at her cousin, and he gave his best *aw shucks* face. "You're going to milk this for all it's worth, aren't you?"

Frankie nodded, grinning.

"Kelly, are you sure you don't want to go to the hospital?" Wolman had reentered the boutique, droplets dripping from her black rain hat.

"I'm sure." Kelly expected she'd be sore—again—but she hadn't been injured when she tackled Terry. "Is there anything else you need from Frankie or me?"

"Not at this time. We're going to take her in now." Wolman pivoted but then turned back to face Kelly. "I'm glad you weren't hurt. But I do fear your luck will run out someday if you insist on sticking your nose where it doesn't belong."

"Is that your way of saying thank you?" Kelly asked, earning her a nudge from Liv and a scowl from Wolman. Maybe her luck had just run out.

"We'll be in touch." Wolman held her gaze on Kelly a moment longer and then turned to leave the boutique.

"It's like poking a bear. You shouldn't do it," Liv whispered.

"I think you're growing on her," Frankie said.

"I doubt that," Gabe added.

"It doesn't matter. What she said is true, Kell. One day you may not be so lucky as today. Come on, let's go upstairs, and I'll make tea." Liv headed to the staircase.

"Frankie got Chinese food. There should be enough for all of us." Kelly's appetite had disappeared, but she didn't want to be alone.

"I'll lock up for you." Gabe walked to the door.

"Thanks." Kelly followed Frankie and Liv up the stairs. After dinner, she intended to soak in the tub, but instead of using a wineglass, she was just going to take the bottle into the bathroom.

CHAPTER TWENTY-TWO

The next morning, Kelly woke from another night of restless sleep. There were too many times to count how the scene between her and Terry replayed in her sleepy subconscious. Each time her mind revisited the scene, she woke with a start, which finally caused Howard to leap out of bed and search for a more peaceful sleeping spot. So it wasn't a surprise when Kelly made it to the kitchen to drink not one but two strong cups of coffee to jump-start her day. Howard appeared rested and playful, batting around his catnip toy.

She tidied the kitchen and returned the milk carton to the refrigerator. On the middle shelf were the containers of Chinese food from last night. After her altercation with Terry and giving her statement to the police, she hadn't had much of an appetite. It turned out, Frankie, Gabe, and Liv hadn't been hungry either. They barely ate, leaving plenty of leftovers.

Maybe she'd have an appetite later in the day. Then again, she was on her way to the hospital to visit her uncle. Depending on how that went, who knew if she'd be hungry. Worry about Frankie's discovery of his half sister gnawed at her. Would Frankie confront his father about it today? Would Ralph twist it around and blame her? How? She had no idea but wouldn't put it past him to try.

A meow stirred Kelly from her thoughts, and she looked down as Howard slinked his body against her leg. Was he offering his support? Or was he looking for food? It was hard to tell. She guessed the latter and quickly filled his bowl and refreshed his water. Then she grabbed her purse and headed out the door.

She hadn't been in the mood to fuss with getting dressed after she'd toweled off from her shower. At the closet, she'd pulled out a gray polo shirtdress and white sneakers. It was summery and casual. Perfect for her visit to see her uncle. Next, she swept her hair up into a loose ponytail. On her way out of her apartment, she grabbed a pair of Gucci sunglasses she'd purchased from a luxury consignment website.

Hurrying down the stairs, she checked her watch. Despite her slow start, she was right on time. Outside, she got into her Jeep and drove to the hospital.

Her opinion of hospitals hadn't changed. She hated them. Thankfully, it looked like this would be the last time she would have to be there. On her drive over, she'd gotten a text from Summer with the news Ralph would go home today. She walked along the corridor toward her uncle's room.

"Stop fussing. I can do this myself." Uncle Ralph's voice boomed out of his room. Yep. It indeed sounded like he was ready to be released.

Kelly reached the doorway.

"You can't overexert yourself," Summer pleaded from the foot of the bed. Her back was to Kelly, but her usually squared and lifted shoulders, thanks to years of doing Pilates, seemed to sag.

"Listen to her." Frankie stood at the window with his arms crossed and a neutral expression on his face.

Kelly fixed a smile on her lips and entered the room. She would be cheery and perky even though inside, she was a grieving, worried mess. The grief was for Becky. From experience, she knew it would hurt less with each passing day. The worry was about the situation between Frankie and his father. She caught his eye, and he gave a subtle nod. Not sure what it meant, she returned the nod, hoping the subject wouldn't be discussed there. Then again, what better place just in case her uncle had another heart attack? *Bad, Kelly.* She couldn't think like that. No more heart attacks. No more deep, dark secrets within the family.

"Glad you're here." Summer pivoted, and like with the unusual slump of her shoulders, she had a frown on her face. "Maybe you can talk some sense into your uncle."

I doubt that.

"I'm not some invalid. I can pack my bag." Ralph stuffed a pair of sweatpants into his leather overnight bag. He looked much better than the last time Kelly had seen him. Now there was color back in his face, his eyes were alert, and he was grumbling. Her uncle had returned. "Though, by the sour look on my son's face, you'd think I was still lying in this darn bed."

Kelly shot her cousin another look. It was apparent he wasn't happy. Frankie had always worn his heart on his sleeve.

"I'm glad you're better and that you're going home today. There's just a lot on my mind." Frankie pulled back from the window and walked toward Kelly. Passing by her on his way out of the room, he whispered, "Everything's cool. It's not the time."

Kelly breathed a sigh of relief.

"Let's get out of here." Ralph zipped his bag.

"You have to wait to be discharged." Summer moved around the bed to her husband's side. "And you'll have to leave in a wheelchair."

"What? I'm perfectly capable of walking."

"Don't get upset." Summer patted her husband's arm. "Remember what the doctor said."

That was Kelly's cue to leave. Her uncle and Summer were about to have a spirited conversation, and it was better that she wasn't present for it. She exited the room so fast that she bumped into Nate when she exited the room.

He grabbed her elbow, steadying her. A slow smile slid onto his face, and his eyes lit up. "I didn't expect to see you here this morning."

After she said goodbye to Liv, Gabe, and Frankie last night, she called Nate and filled him in on Terry's confession. He offered to come by; even though she wanted to be alone, it comforted her to hear his voice. There had been so many emotions running through her that she felt it was best to snuggle with only Howard for the night. Now, looking up into Nate's eyes, she wondered if she'd made a mistake. Leaning on his shoulder would have been far more pleasant than the twisty position Howard forced her into on the sofa so he could be comfortable.

"Oh…well…I…" Why was she fumbling her words?

Nate squinted, and it appeared he had the same question. He let go of her, and instantly her brain fog cleared up.

"My uncle is being released this morning." Phew. She got out a complete, coherent sentence.

"Good. Glad to hear he's recovered." Nate shoved his hands into his pants pockets. He was dressed in loden-green slacks and a collared beige shirt, and she couldn't tell if he was on duty. "I'm here to follow up on Todd."

"You're on duty." Bummer. But she wasn't sure why she was disappointed. It wasn't like they were dating. "How's he doing? Any improvement?"

"Unfortunately, he's still in a coma." Nate's expression sobered. "There's no telling how long he'll remain in that state."

"Sorry to hear." She couldn't imagine what his family was going through, living in limbo, not knowing whether he'd ever wake up. Then again, would she mind the limbo if it meant Becky would still be alive?

She'd never know. What did she know was that she needed to stop dwelling on how things could have ended. What was done was done.

"Hey, I like your dress." The corner of his mouth lifted in a crooked smile.

Warmth spread on Kelly's cheeks, and she bashfully lowered her head. Her dress wasn't anything special, so she knew he was trying to make her feel better, and it was working. She lifted her head and smiled.

"Your smile is even prettier."

Gosh darn it. He was making her feel all the feels. She wouldn't lie. She enjoyed it.

"I have a thought." He closed the small space between them. "Instead of coffee, how about we have dinner?"

Caught up in his gaze, she answered immediately. "Yes. I'd lo—" Whoa. She didn't want to use the L word. "I'd like to have dinner with you." *Good save.* She used the other L word. Much better choice.

"I'll call you." He glanced at his watch. "I should get back to work."

"Okay." Her heart fluttered with happiness like a silly teenager. "Have a good day."

He nodded and then turned to walk down the corridor. She leaned against the wall and watched him. The view wasn't bad at all.

A nurse passed by Kelly, drawing her attention from one of Nate's finest assets. The nurse entered her uncle's room.

Kelly turned and craned her neck to check on what was going on. It looked like the nurse was providing instructions to Uncle Ralph, who wanted no part of whatever was being said. His voice was loud as he insisted he could walk. It was definitely time to leave. She stepped back and headed toward the elevator.

The elevator door slid open, and a group of doctors in deep conversation exited, prompting Kelly to step to the side until they were all out. In the center of the group she spotted Dr. Arnold. So, he and Wally weren't weekenders. He looked in her direction and gave a timid smile as he continued past with his colleagues. Before he entered a room off the corridor, he glanced back, and Kelly gave a little wave before stepping into the elevator. She pressed the lobby button. As the door slid closed, the thrill of seeing Dr. Arnold again disappeared. She remembered her very quick "yes" to dinner with Nate. Besides, Dr. Arnold would always be the man who was there on the beach when she found Becky and helped her when she was almost hit by a car. Now, that was a mood killer. The ride down to the lobby was quick, and she made her way to the exit.

Fresh, salty air greeted her. It was a welcome relief from the medicinal air inside.

On her way to her Jeep, she heard a text notification. She pulled her phone from her purse as she opened the vehicle's door. She read Frankie's text.

HEADS UP. ARIEL KNOWS.

Panic clutched her, and she couldn't breathe as the parking lot spun around. Okay, that wasn't really happening, but still, she grabbed hold of the door just to make sure she'd stay standing. When the sensation passed, she thought quickly.

Ariel knew Frankie was her brother. It was only a matter of time before she figured out Ralph was her biological father. Though, she guessed the report pretty much laid out all the details of their connection. There was a slim chance Ariel wouldn't find out that Kelly knew about the secret.

Kelly's phone vibrated.

There was an incoming call from Ariel.

Slipping into the driver's seat, she sucked in a deep breath and exhaled. She was hoping for a quick infusion of zen, but it wasn't happening.

She tapped on the phone with a shaky finger.

"Hi, Ariel. What's up?"

What's up? How lame was that?

"I'm coming home. You won't believe what I found out." Ariel's words were garbled, as if she was trying to talk and cry at the same time. "My parents have been lying to me for my entire life. Everything is a mess."

Kelly chewed on her lower lip, and she pressed her head against the seat's headrest. She mulled over what to say. She didn't want to slip up and let Ariel know she knew. Yet she couldn't say anything. Ariel was her friend.

"I'm sure it's not all that bad." Kelly's face scrunched. *Not all that bad?* The girl just found out her father wasn't really her father. And that she had a brother. And that Kelly was her cousin. Now that indeed was the bright side to this whole mess, right?

"Frankie is my brother. Half brother. It was the most awkward conversation I've ever had with my parents. I don't even know them anymore!"

"Ariel, don't do anything rash. This will all work out. Somehow." Kelly was in no place to offer advice given her track record of running away from her problems. And when she found out about Ariel's parentage, what did she do? Nothing. She should have given her friend a heads-up that her life was about to be turned upside down.

"How can you say that?" Ariel paused, sniffled, and then sighed. "How come you don't sound surprised by this? I discovered that my father isn't my biological father. I found out I'm related to you. Wait...you knew? Tell me you didn't know. If you did, you would have told me. Right?"

"We'll talk when you get home."

"Oh, my, goodness. You did know, and you didn't tell me. How could you not tell me?" Ariel cried.

"You have to understand, it wasn't my secret to tell."

"I can't believe you! I thought we were friends!"

Before Kelly could say they were friends, the line went silent. Ariel was gone.

"So not the way I wanted it to go." Kelly tossed her phone on the passenger seat and then started the ignition. Backing out of her space, her heart ached for her friend and the amount of pain she was in now. If only her uncle had taken her advice and told Ariel himself, it would have been easier than finding out through a DNA analysis. Kelly navigated her Jeep toward the lot's exit. Would Ariel ever be able to forgive her a second time?

* * * *

"You watch, she'll leave with everything," Pepper whispered to Kelly. Her appraisal of Lilith Dunning was based on over twenty years of experience selling to the retired librarian. Upon entering the boutique, she always reminded Kelly and Pepper that she'd been a loyal customer for two decades.

"I love this blouse. The color is so pretty." Lilith held a blush-colored blouse up in front of her and stared at her reflection in the mirror. She was an attractive woman in her midsixties with striking silver hair. "Do you think it looks good on me?"

Kelly's thoughts were still on the disastrous conversation she had with Ariel. If she had to use an emoji to sum up how she felt when the call ended, she'd have to use at least four—crying, worried, sad, and scared.

A nudge from Pepper snapped Kelly out of her thoughts, and she looked at their customer. So far, Lilith had racked up a pile of clothes to try on. Most of the items were from Camille, including the blouse Lilith was deciding on now.

Kelly cleared her throat and focused. She had a business to run. If her personal life was going to be a mess, she had better make sure her business was a success.

"It does, and I think you'll especially love it with those silky jogger pants you put in the changing room."

"You think? Isn't this top too dressy for joggers?" Lilith lowered the blouse from her chest.

"Not if you make the joggers dressy. Add a strappy heel or sandal with some jewelry. You'll look effortlessly fabulous and be extremely comfortable."

"Oooh, I have the perfect pair of heels." Lilith's smile broadened, and her pale green eyes shimmered. Kelly loved seeing the look on her customers' faces when they realized there was no need to spend a fortune on clothing to look great.

"Great. Do you want to try on what you have picked out so far? While you do, I can pull a few more items that I think you'd like."

Lilith nodded. "You know what I like."

Lilith walked past Kelly toward the changing rooms. They were small with full-length mirrors, stools, and hooks. While not fancy, they were private, thanks to the generous curtains Kelly had hung.

"While you take care of Lilith, I'm going into the accessories department. I want to finish putting out the new wedges we got." Pepper pivoted and walked out of the room.

Kelly moved to the long rustic table where she displayed T-shirts and short-sleeved pullovers. There was a pastel floral–pattern top Kelly had in mind for Lilith. As she lifted the top from the table, the bell over the front door jingled and Jessica entered.

Kelly's grip on the soft T-shirt tightened at the sight of Jessica, whose smile faltered. Whatever look was on Kelly's face, it must have been emitting a not-happy-to-see-you vibe.

Jessica closed the door and then stepped forward.

"I didn't expect you'd come back here."

Kelly knew she'd see Jessica at Becky's funeral, which was scheduled to happen in two days. Then there would be family and friends, more than enough people to keep Kelly away from her cousin's conniving business partner.

"I wanted to come by and tell you that I'm very sorry for everything that has happened." Jessica closed the gap between them. "If I could go back and change what I've done, what happened, I would. I feel personally responsible for Becky's death and for what happened to Todd." Tears welled in her eyes. "This is the first time I've lost someone I cared about. Please know I loved your cousin. Her death has changed me."

Kelly wasn't interested in Jessica's rebirth or whatever she was calling it. Words meant nothing. Actions were what mattered. And so far, Jessica's actions had been horrible.

"Everything Terry said about you, it was true?" Kelly carried the top to the sales counter. She didn't want to be in the presence of Jessica, much less be next to her.

"I'm not proud of it, and I have no excuse for my behavior. I made some bad decisions, and I regret them." Jessica wiped away a tear. "All I ever wanted was…something like this." She gestured to the surroundings.

"A boutique?"

"Maybe. I guess what I've wanted is something to be proud of. You have that. Becky had it with Define Beauty, and Terry had it with her beauty account."

"From what I heard, you were just as successful as Terry. If not more."

Jessica nodded. "Back then, I didn't know we all could succeed. Turns out, we didn't need to be competing against each other. What's that saying about candles lighting other candles?"

"When a candle lights another candle, it loses nothing."

"Exactly. I didn't realize that by helping someone else, I wouldn't lose anything."

"Now that you know better, what are you going to do?"

"You're very direct, Kelly Quinn. I like it." Jessica pressed her lips together. "I'm going to honor Becky's wishes and not sell Define Beauty. This way, it'll be here when Todd comes out of his coma. Then together, we can decide the company's future."

Okay, Kelly hadn't seen that twist coming. Still, a part of her decided to take a wait-and-see attitude. Zebras didn't change their stripes, and people like Jessica were a lot like zebras—change wasn't a part of their DNA.

"I don't know what to say."

"You don't have to say anything. I should let you get back to work."

When Jessica turned, Kelly had an unexpected urge to hug her. She dashed out from behind the counter and pulled Jessica into an embrace. Now it was her turn to get teary eyed.

"Thank you for stopping by today." Kelly pulled back and wiped away her tears. Jessica simply nodded and then left the boutique.

A few minutes later, after Kelly dried her tears, the door opened again, and the bell jingled. Camille bustled in, carrying a bin.

"I have good news," Camille said, approaching the counter.

"Well, let me have it. Good news is very much welcomed."

"It's official. I'm unsubscribed from all those style subscriptions."

Kelly swooped in for another hug. She guessed she was in that kind of mood suddenly. But this hug was pure happiness.

"How exciting!" Kelly leaned back and looked Camille in the eye. "Are you nervous about not getting those packages anymore?"

Camille inhaled a deep breath before answering. "I thought I would be, but I'm not. I have you and this shop. My wardrobe is going to be amazing."

"It most certainly is. Oh, by the way, your clothes are selling." Kelly walked to the counter and lifted the cover off the bin. "Graphic T-shirts! They sell like hotcakes."

"Good to hear. I'd better get going back to the office. I heard Ralph was released. I expect he'll be micromanaging from his home." Camille turned toward the door.

"Good luck, you're going to need it." Kelly and Camille laughed. "I'll call you next week to arrange a time to pick up your fall clothes."

"Sounds good." Camille waved before leaving the boutique.

Kelly returned to the clothes in the bin. Graphic T-shirts did sell out fast because they were expensive. The ones from Camille looked barely worn. As Breena would say, cha-ching.

Once Camille's new consigned items were added to the inventory, Kelly checked her phone for messages. Actually, she looked for one specifically from Ariel. So far, her voice mails and texts had been ignored. This didn't bode well for their friendship. She had to find a way to make it right with Ariel. A ping got her hopes up, but it wasn't a text from Ariel; it was from Liv.

Liv's text was short, sweet, and exactly what Kelly needed. They were going to have a girls' night in with takeout from Gio's.

She replied with her dinner choice and prayed she'd have an appetite by the time Liv showed up. The day had been such a roller coaster, she hadn't had much of an appetite, and when she did, she couldn't fathom eating anything. But the thought of Gio's spaghetti and meatballs had her stomach rumbling. Right on the dot at closing time, she locked the front door and headed upstairs to set the table and feed Howard before Liv showed up.

Howard was vocal the moment she entered the apartment. Clearly, he wasn't having issues with his appetite. She hurried into the kitchen and filled his bowl. While he chowed down, she grabbed the plates and utensils. When the dining table was set, she dashed into her bedroom and changed into a cute terrycloth shorts set she'd ordered online a few weeks ago. The top was long sleeved and perfect for warding off the chill from the air conditioner.

She'd slipped on her flip-flops just before another text notified her that Liv was downstairs. Time for dinner. She wasted no time in heading down to the back door to let Liv in. The heavenly aroma from the bag had Kelly salivating.

Back up in the apartment, they dished out their meals and poured wine. Kelly broke off a piece of garlic bread and popped it into her mouth. After she swallowed, she told Liv about Jessica's unexpected visit.

"She caused a lot of trouble." Liv drizzled dressing over her salad. "How do you feel about what she said?"

Kelly swirled spaghetti onto her fork. "She apologized for it, and she seemed sincere."

Liv shrugged. "Guess only time will tell. Like whether Todd wakes up. I can't imagine what his family is going through."

Kelly swallowed her mouthful of spaghetti. "You know, I really don't want to talk about them."

"I understand." Liv reached for the garlic bread. An impish smile came to her lips. "How about we talk about Detective Nate Barber."

Kelly's gaze drifted upward for a moment. Of course Liv wanted to talk about Nate. "What about him?"

"Come on, he asked you to dinner. A date! I'm so excited for you. He seems like a good guy."

Mark had seemed like a good guy too. And look how that turned out. "We'll see. It's only a meal. *One* meal." Kelly broke apart a meatball and took a bite. She opted to stay mum about Dr. Arnold because there really wasn't much to say except...he'd been flitting in and out of her thoughts all day.

Liv gave a dismissive wave. "We'll see."

They finished dinner with a serving of tiramisu. Once the dishes were cleared, they took their glasses and wine bottle to the living room. Liv searched for a movie. Kelly requested one that was lighthearted, and Liv agreed.

"*Notting Hill,*" Liv declared as she clicked the remote.

"Perfect choice," Kelly agreed as she shuffled over to the sofa to join her friend. Before the movie started, she refilled her glass.

"Hey, what lipstick are you wearing? There's been no transfer to your glass all night." Liv studied the lipstick smudge marks on her glass.

Kelly smiled. "It's Define Beauty's Thrive lipstick. Rosewood shade."

"The color is magnificent on you."

"It's my new favorite lipstick."

Liv raised her glass. "A toast? To Becky. Beloved cousin, beautiful soul."

Kelly raised her glass and clinked Liv's.

"To Becky."

ABOUT THE AUTHOR

Debra Sennefelder is an avid reader who reads across a range of genres, but mystery fiction is her obsession. Her interest in people and relationships is channeled into her novels against a backdrop of crime and mystery. When she's not reading, she enjoys cooking and baking and as a former food blogger, she is constantly taking photographs of her food. *Yeah, she's that person*. Born and raised in New York City, where she majored in her hobby of fashion buying, she now lives and writes in Connecticut with her family. She's worked in retail and publishing before becoming a full-time author. Her writing companion is her adorable and slightly spoiled Shih-Tzu, Connie.

You can learn more about Debra at www.DebraSennefelder.com

ie United States
Taylor Publisher Services

Printed in t
by Baker &

ABOUT THE AUTHOR

Debra Sennefelder is an avid reader who reads across a range of genres, but mystery fiction is her obsession. Her interest in people and relationships is channeled into her novels against a backdrop of crime and mystery. When she's not reading, she enjoys cooking and baking and as a former food blogger, she is constantly taking photographs of her food. *Yeah, she's that person.* Born and raised in New York City, where she majored in her hobby of fashion buying, she now lives and writes in Connecticut with her family. She's worked in retail and publishing before becoming a full-time author. Her writing companion is her adorable and slightly spoiled Shih-Tzu, Connie.

You can learn more about Debra at www.DebraSennefelder.com

Printed in the United States
by Baker & Taylor Publisher Services